AWAKE CHIMERA

51-GRAY

AWAKE
CHIMERA

*To Farah,
Thanks for your
support! Enjoy!
Justine*

M. J. Graykin

This is a work of fiction. Names, characters, places and incidents either are the product of the author's imagination or are used fictitiously, and any resemblance to any actual persons, living or dead, events, or locales is entirely coincidental.

This book was printed in the United States of America.

To order additional copies of this book, contact:
Xlibris Corporation
1-888-7-XLIBRIS
www.Xlibris.com
Orders@Xlibris.com

CONTENTS

I humbly dedicate this work to the First Peoples of all lands who have suffered the arrogant cruelty of conquering invaders. May your day of justice come before it is too late--for all of us.

CHAPTER 1

Ah, the smell of engine fumes, oil, and rotting foliage! Nothing like Farport in the spring!

Lieutenant Morris leaned against one of the supports to the control tower, watching the ships at the docks. People hustled about, swearing and shouting; forklifts and loaders transferred cargo from one hold to another, the thick water sloshed against the docks and the mushy shore as ships maneuvered in and around the docks and the channel. The air was full of the lilting music of grunting, shrieking machinery and foul language.

Normally, Morris avoided the docks unless duty sent him there. It was not his favorite place. In fact, Farport, itself, was not his favorite place. It was far, far down the list. But as an officer in service to the United Peoples, he went where he was assigned and he made the best of it. Morris was pretty good at making the best of a bad situation. It was what got him this far from rather humble beginnings. And kept him in good humor in spite of having to sweat it out in the swamp amid the pirates, merchants, and assorted lost souls of this territorial outpost.

Then he spotted what he had been waiting for, what had drawn him out here to the noise and smell of the docks. It was a sleek, good-looking ship, small but sophisticated. The *Chimera*—an odd name, no doubt something in the language of the creature who owned it. Morris waited patiently for that creature to emerge. He'd never seen a Byahail before, and this was probably the strangest specimen of Byahail one could ever hope to see. He was curious, as no doubt an awful lot of others were, too. The creature would attract a goodly crowd during its stopover.

There it was, coming out of the cabin. Several dock hands

sauntered over to toss ropes onto the posts and make the ship fast. The creature inspected their work, nodding, moving gracefully and efficiently, giving the impression it knew what it was doing as well as any experienced captain. It seemed to be ignoring the stares it was getting, stepping down onto the dock, with of all things, a ginseng smoke dangling from its lips. It took a draw off the smoke and then tossed the butt casually into the water. Looking around, it then headed straight for Morris, no doubt noting his uniform. Morris tried not to stare at . . . him? Her? It? From what he'd heard about the Byahail, the distinction was pointless. They were all of the above. This one was about six feet tall, and looked pretty much like the pictures he seen. It had a great, leonine mane of something between fur and feathers which hung down over its shoulders. The face looked definitely non-human, with its black, beady eyes and cleft upper lip, the nose almost muzzle-like. But it walked upright, arms at the sides and ending in hands which, although somewhat bony and claw-like, were recognizable hands with four fingers and an opposing thumb. Distinctly non-human was the long, stout, reptilian tail which curled and twitched restlessly behind it as it walked. I'd like to meet your tailor, Morris thought, noting the modifications in the standard freighter captain's suit that it wore, accommodating the non-standard shape.

Morris straightened up, trying to look as official as possible.

"Can I help you?" he asked briskly.

"Am looking for Chief of Security," the Byahail said with a thick, odd accent. "Have questions about procedure."

Its mane looked like a city woman's fancy hairdo and the uniform swelled out in the chest with what appeared to be rather ample breasts. It spoke in a comparatively high register, reinforcing an overall vague impression of femininity, as unfeminine as it was otherwise. Unlike the average freighter captain, which she—what the heck, it was as good a pronoun as any—wouldn't have been anyway, there was no personal decoration on her suit. No patches, no ribbons, no colorful stencils or rude devices. Plain and no-nonsense. Her boots were formidable to say the least. Knee-high, studded with metal spikes and reinforced in the heel and toe. It was clear she needed to carry no weapons. She wore them on her feet. Morris tried to look casual and efficient and not to gape too much as he answered her question.

"That would be Castellan Prilock. He is the governor of this port."

"Castellan does not have officer for security?" the beast inquired curiously.

"Yes, Captain, but he prefers to handle matters of port security himself whenever possible." The fact was, Prilock didn't trust anyone else, and probably with good reason. Farport had been the despair of the U.P., with administrative corruption so rampant and the criminal element so deeply entrenched that all hope of cleaning up the place had been abandoned long ago. Then somebody up in Malowi had had the bright idea of solving two problems at once; this, and the solution for something else they had no idea what to do about. So they made Prilock castellan of Farport and told him to have at it. The place would never be the same.

"Where, then, can be finding Castellan Prilock?" the Byahail asked.

"Let's see," Morris murmured, looking past her, scanning the docks to see where folks looked the most nervous and upset. "Ah, yes. I believe you'll find him on pier 4, inspecting that Northman freighter."

The beast inclined her head courteously, bowing slightly with a sharp click of her boot heels. Then she strode purposefully off. Morris watched her go. A formidable creature. Morris wished he could watch how she dealt with Prilock, but his lunch hour was almost over. He'd best hustle back to his post. At least he had a bit of a story to share with the others; he'd talked to the Byahail face to face.

The tall, broad-shouldered officer with the sternly chiseled face and the iron-grey hair was obviously the Castellan. He radiated merciless authority. He finished grilling the Northman captain, and then, leaving frustration and undisguised fury in his wake,

strode off the ship oblivious to the glares of its crew. He scanned
his databoard, intent on getting on to the next victim of his
uncompromising scrutiny, walking briskly up the pier. The Byahail
captain strode up to him. "Castellan Prilock?" she inquired in her
stilted accents.

"Yes," he acknowledged with a nod, brisk as if Byahail pulled
into his port every day, "What can I do for you?"

"Am Captain Shaka Mahdi, owning freighter *Chimera*,
registration UPFT 511-59. Am wishing to inquire what is proper
procedure. Have cargo of contraband for legitimate trade."

The Castellan frowned. It wasn't uncommon for freighters to
come through the port with questionable goods. What was
contraband in one nation was legal merchandise in another. Farport
was a neutral settlement, technically under U.P. control but not
subject to the restrictions of any particular nation. So contraband
wasn't necessarily illegal. But anybody carrying the stuff was
supposed list it clearly on the ship's manifest. "I saw no note of
contraband in any of the freighter manifests I reviewed this
morning," he said, scowling at his databoard. "Is this an
unscheduled docking?"

"No, am docking on schedule. Pick up shipment at last port.
Not on manifest."

Well, at least the fault wasn't on his end. He would have been
furious if the port traffic crew had authorized an unscheduled
docking without notifying him first. He addressed the freighter
captain sternly. "Your ship's manifest should have been updated
immediately upon taking aboard restricted substances. You should
not have waited until docking at your next port."

The Byahail looked annoyed but apologetic, apparently more
irritated at her own mistake than at the rule itself. "Am not aware
of this. Many rules am still learning. Must pay fine for penalty?"

The Castellan eyed her appraisingly. The rules concerning contraband cargo were difficult to enforce, and he had grudgingly
resigned himself to the fact that unregistered contraband went
through the port every day and there wasn't a thing he could do to

stop it. The Byahail could have done what just about any other small-time freighter captain would have done: Just gone through and said nothing about it. The chances were excellent she would never have been caught. Either she was admirably honest, or she was hiding something else hoping to deflect suspicion through misdirection. His experiences with most traders led him to expect the latter. And he had no reason to think the Byahail was any different.

"Since you have been so prompt in reporting to me," the Castellan said, watching her closely, "I think we can consider the violation a mere oversight and waive the fine. That is, so long as all your paperwork is in order. May I have your permission to see it and to inspect your cargo?"

She snapped together the heels of her boots and gave a quick, curt bow. "Whenever is convenient." If she was hiding something she was being damned slick about it. The Castellan's suspicions were further pricked.

"Now would be convenient," he said. It didn't seem to disquiet her in the slightest.

"Ship is docked in Bay 23-D," she said, turning to go and waiting for him politely.

The *Chimera* was a sophisticated, single-pilot model, not new but well cared-for, and Shaka Mahdi was obviously quite proud of it. "Work hard, many years, qualify for credit. Is fine ship, yes?"

"Yes, indeed," he murmured, wondering how she could afford the payments. He scanned her paperwork. Everything seemed to be scrupulously in order. He nodded with approval. "Yes, I think we can see our way clear to waive the penalty for violation of procedure. I'll see to it that your manifest is properly updated."

"Are most kind," she said, again with the clicking of heels and slight bow.

"Hmm," he said neutrally. "May I see your cargo hold now?"

"Is here," she said gesturing, and she slid the hatch open for him. He bent down and descended into the hold, examining the labels on the boxes. "Sirian opium brandy," he murmured. "And lots of it. You could get a small fortune for this on the black market."

"Not sell to black market," the Byahail replied sharply. "Have buyer in Northlands. Is legitimate sale."

"Yes, so your papers said." He looked around There were a number of other items, some of which he took the time to inspect, but nothing seemed out of order.

"Everything is proper, yes?"

He nodded. "Yes, so far." He paused. "What are these?"

"Ginseng smokes," she said. "Is for personal consumption. Not part of cargo." She cocked her head questioningly. "Is not necessary to list personal consumption on manifest, yes?"

"That's correct," he said. "You could get a pretty good price for those in some places, too."

There was a touch of anger in her voice this time. "Not sell illegal! Shaka is honest!"

He eyed her. "Of course."

"What is rule about consumption of contraband on ship while in dock?" she asked coldly.

He looked around himself as he answered. "You can light up a ginseng anywhere you want. They aren't restricted in Farport, except where there is a fire hazard. All forms of fortified alcohol are prohibited on shore, but if you want to have a glass of brandy in the privacy of your ship it's fine with me. Just as long as you conduct yourself in a manner that does not present a hazard to other personnel or property."

"Good," she said, and took a ginseng out of the box. She lit it, inhaling the smoke deeply and with obvious pleasure.

Prilock went over to a door on one side of the hold. "Special cargo?"

"Is for hazardous or fragile cargo. Empty now."

"Mind if I look?"

Her mouth tightened. "Is empty," she said again. "Look."

He did, and it was.

"Shaka is honest," she said again, and took another angry pull on the ginseng smoke.

The Castellan nodded and left the cargo hold, returning to

the cabin. The Byahail followed. Everything seemed just too much in order. His every instinct told him he was missing something. Nobody was this honest. "Do you have any other cargo holds?"

Shaka Mahdi's piercing black eyes narrowed. "No. Is only cargo hold. Have only personal storage in living quarters."

"Mind if I take a look around?"

At last he seemed to have hit a nerve. "Why?" she asked furiously. "Am doing everything Castellan asks! Everything is in order, yes? Why are suspecting?"

"I am merely doing my job," he replied.

"No! Not merely doing job! Humans!" she said with disgust. "Are so full of cheating are thinking everyone else cheat, too! Am not cheating! Shaka is honest! Have honor! Not like humans!"

"I am not human," Prilock said icily.

She was taken back. "Not human?"

"No. But your observation about humans being full of cheating is an accurate one. Mind if I search your ship?"

Shaka took another deep pull on the ginseng, eyeing Prilock curiously. "Search ship. Will see. Shaka is honest. Not like humans."

She followed him down the corridor from the cabin to the quarters in back, watching as he inspected the walls for a hidden compartment. "Are not human?" she asked. "What, if not human?"

"They don't really have a name for my species, seeing as I'm the only one there is that anyone knows about." He took out a hand scanner and checked the seams. "I can assume any shape I wish. I appear human because it's easier to deal with other humans that way." He glanced over at her. "Believe me, it would not have been my first choice."

Shaka nodded. "Understand. Am Byahail. Not like humans. Is difficult, because not male, not female. Humans make bad jokes. Do not respect. Most humans think Byahail look female. So am not arguing. Is easier. Sometimes helps."

"Oh? Why?"

She shrugged. "Male humans not pick fights so much. But," she sighed, "make other problems. Is always problem with humans."

"No doubt," Prilock said with genuine sympathy. "I am uncomfortably familiar with the average human's obsession with sex."

"Are disgusting creatures!" Shaka said vehemently. "Full of cheating! Full of mocking! And filthy thoughts!"

"You'll get no argument from me." He paused at a door. "Personal quarters?"

She reached out and opened the door. "Go. Search. Will see." He stepped inside. Her quarters were simple and austere, very neat. Little decoration. She immediately went to a closet and opened it. "In here. Personal consumption. Sirian opium brandy and ginseng smokes."

"You drink that stuff?"

"Sometimes, when am in dock. When no harm." She added hastily, "Am only drinking in ship. No trouble to Castellan."

He frowned. "According to your schedule, you do a regular eight week run out to the Eastlands, to Heng So and then to Simpan, then back again. From here, you'll be making the six week run to the Northlands. You carry no passengers and you have no crew. And yet when you get into dock you sit in your ship and drink by yourself?"

Her expression was hard. "No crew, so not having to pay. Route to far East ports is good money. Also make good money selling contraband in Northlands. Pay back credit for ship in good time." She tapped the ashes off the ginseng. "And is peaceful in swamp. Is no humans mocking. No humans saying stupid things, filthy things and trying cheat, or to get Shaka to fight or do pleasure for them. Humans!" she spat. "Is better to be alone!"

Well, that explained a great deal about how she could afford the payments for the ship. A freighter could earn damn good money doing those god-awful runs, and she obviously wasn't blowing her profits when she got to dock. Prilock was beginning to feel almost guilty about mistrusting the Byahail. He had to admire her determination and ethics. And as for her dislike of humans, well, he could only sympathize with that. He'd always found them difficult to get along with. Even the ones he could respect he had little in common with. He found their interests to be incomprehensible if not downright ridiculous most of the time. And their annoying fixation on mating just about drove Prilock mad. It seemed sometimes to be the main drive of their lives. Even when they had a mate, they still focused on matters of mating incessantly. Prilock could understand the need for companionship. He sometimes felt a bit lonely himself. But humans were never satisfied with just having friendship. They wanted sex, the more the better. It was, as Shaka asserted, disgusting.

The fact that the Byahail was a pansexual was a matter of total indifference to Prilock. She was law-abiding and obviously a being of high integrity, and that was all that concerned him. But no doubt the human trash of the Water Hole would harass her to distraction if she tried to go there to relax and socialize. A Byahail was just too obvious a target. It was a shame for her to have to spend what little time she had at dock in the solitude of her ship, but he understood how it would be preferable to enduring the inevitable crudities and bigotry of human company. The patrons of the Water Hole no doubt considered Prilock to be even more of a freak than the Byahail, but, because he was the Castellan, they wouldn't dare get out of line. It occurred to him that if Shaka Mahdi were in his company they would have no choice but to show her the same respect as well.

"How long do you plan to be docking here?" he asked her.

"Leave in three days. Will be no trouble," Shaka repeated firmly. "Please to finish search of ship."

"I am finished," he said. "It's quite obvious that you have no illicit intentions. I apologize for the inconvenience."

Shaka looked triumphant. "Now are seeing. Shaka is honest."

Prilock nodded. "Yes, I see that." He started to leave. "Captain," he said, pausing, "If you are at all inclined, you are welcome to be my guest at the Water Hole. That is what passes for a hospitality center in this place. I like to keep an eye on things there, but it does get tedious sitting there watching the antics of the patrons with no one intelligent to talk to."

She looked at him suspiciously. "Am not looking for company," she said. "Used to being alone."

"Fine. I merely make the offer. I'd welcome the company. But believe me, I am quite used to being alone, myself."

Her bright eyes narrowed as she sized him up, trying to decide if she could trust him. "Will think about it," she said.

The usual run of fights, burglaries and the apprehension of a smuggler he had had his eye on for quite some time kept the Castellan completely occupied over the next couple of days. He gave little thought to the Byahail freighter captain, except to note that she did not come into the Water Hole any time that he was there. When he reviewed the schedules and manifests of ships due to depart on the following day, he came across the *Chimera* and wondered if Shaka Mahdi might make an appearance that evening, her last chance to do so. He had planned on doing a bit of covert work. Perhaps disguise himself as something prosaic, a chair or a wall fixture. See what he could overhear. He'd keep an eye out for her.

He decided to stretch himself out comfortably among the artificial foliage in a corner of the bar often used by shady characters for making deals. He suspected there was a plot afoot to smuggle narcotics into the port, possibly to be exchanged right there in the Watering Hole. That sort of activity had been common before he had come. Indeed, the former castellan had been suspected of accepting substantial payments to look the other way. Prilock had been approached once or twice, until the word got around that doing so was not a wise idea. Then the silly idiots had tried to do him in. They soon discovered that doing in a creature such as himself was no easy matter. In fact, Prilock wasn't sure if there *was* a way to do him in. He tried not to let it make him too cocky.

So he spent a good deal of his time eavesdropping on anyone he had his suspicions about. It was a marvelously effective method of breaking conspiracies. He tried to be careful not to invade the privacy of honest citizens, not that there were an awful lot of them in Farport, and fewer still who spent their time at the Water Hole. Even so, it was not proper to violate the rights of persons who had done no harm. So he tried to be discreet. An additional bonus to his activities was the fact that it put the fear into criminal types. Simply the fact that they knew he was able to lurk about undetectable as a bit of common furniture kept the patrons on their toes, slightly more honest than they might otherwise be.

So far that night, though, he had learned little of any use. At the table beneath him a couple of well-groomed Northmen in engineer's suits with ranking insignia were involved in a discussion about physics and technology.

"It would be an enormous advantage," one said, "Imagine the radical revolution in transportation if vehicles could be constructed to fly over the swamp the way some insects do."

"Oh, granted, granted," the other agreed. "It would be a fantastic breakthrough. But the fact of the matter is that it simply can't be done. The weight threshold constitutes an insurmountable barrier to flight. Nothing any larger or heavier than a black sparrow is capable of true flight. The kites in the Northern forests do not truly fly, they only glide from tree to tree on air currents. And nothing larger than a kite is capable of even a respectable glide."

"Well, there is the domestic chickbird, which is able to fly short distances."

"The chickbird hardly counts! Even a young, strong hen can barely go more than a few yards. And a full-grown cock is too heavy to do even that."

"That may be so, but I still contend that research can discover methods that nature has not evolved. And the potential for flying vehicles makes it worth the time to investigate."

Flying vehicles indeed, Prilock thought. As if humans couldn't get into enough trouble with the technology they already had. Still, he wouldn't put it past some clever Northman inventor to come up with such a thing. And may the gods help the Moor to keep control of it if they did.

He was about to quietly transform back to his customary human shape when he saw Shaka Mahdi come into the bar. There was an air of challenge about her, as if she defied anyone to try anything. She glanced around the place, probably looking for him, and then found a table in the back, sliding into the chair and lighting up a ginseng. She looked out of place and uncomfortable.

Prilock slid down out of the foliage and resumed his familiar human guise. The two engineers uttered loud oaths of surprise at his sudden appearance. Let that be a lesson to you, he thought. There was a Northman trader with a couple of rough companions at the table just ahead. He overheard the trader making an exceptionally crude and obscene comment concerning Byahail, making clear by gesture what he would do with the particular Byahail who had just walked into the place. Prilock made a point of bumping up against the trader's table as he walked by, spilling a tall drink into the Northman's lap.

"So sorry," Prilock said, as transparently as possible. "How very clumsy of me."

The Northman snarled with rage and started to rise from his seat, but thought better of it when his companion whispered something urgently into his ear.

As Castellan Prilock approached the Byahail's table she looked up with a restrained smile. "Castellan."

"Captain," he said, politely inclining his head in greeting. "May I join you?"

"Would be honored," Shaka replied with relief. Prilock's presence was a guarantee of protection from harassment. It also meant that they were served promptly.

The conversation was a bit awkward at first, since neither of them were much practiced at the art. But it fell into place quite neatly when they hit upon a subject near and dear to them both.

A couple at the bar began arguing loudly. The woman, and then the man, stood up and began hurling accusations at each other until the woman ran out in tears. The man ran out after her, shouting her name.

The Castellan shook his head in disgust. "I have never understood human relationships!"

"Is no sense, true!" the Byahail agreed. "Such trouble are causing each other! Fighting, and anger—"

"The silly, possessive demands they make on each other!"

"Humans do not know how to be friends," Shaka said. "Think friend is just to say hello and maybe trust a bit. Never is there real trust. Never is there patience."

"What do you expect? How could humans trust each other?" Prilock replied. "And frankly, they try my patience severely. I'm not surprised they drive each other berserk."

"And sex! Always sex! But once is sex, then is jealousy!"

"And the nagging! 'Why can't you be more like this?' 'Why can't you act more like that?' If the silly fools wanted someone who acted just so, why did they couple with someone who didn't?"

"Is crazy." Shaka shook her head. She looked at Prilock. "Castellan never had relationship, eh?"

The icy glare with which he responded was answer enough. The very idea. "Besides," he said grimly, "I'm the only one of me there is that I know of. How am I going to find anyone compatible when I can't even find someone of the same species?"

"Hm!" Shaka agreed with a thoughtful nod. "Am seeing problem." She took out a ginseng and lit it.

Prilock was watching a suspiciously furtive character who came into the bar and sat down. But the man didn't strike up a conversation with anyone, and seemed only to want to get quietly drunk. "If you don't mind my asking," he said, "I thought most of your people stayed pretty much together on the Reservation since the Treaty. What got you into the freight business?"

Smoke curled lazily from her mouth and nose. "Is no future on Reservation. So leave on transport ship. Work for passage. Good captain. Treat Shaka with respect. Hard work, but good pay. See many lands. Learn many things." She smiled sadly, watching the smoke rise. "Learn that world of humans is not very pleasant. But is better than starving on Reservation and waiting to die."

"As I recall," Prilock said, "the resettlement onto the Reservation was an attempt to save your people from being wiped out by the Kurlu."

"Humans have more interest in peace than in justice," Shaka replied. "Kurlu refuse to give back land taken from Byahail. So humans of U.P. say Byahail must learn to live in new lands. Not understanding. Byahail live in same valley, in shadow of same mountains, for all time. How can Byahail live somewhere else?"

"I would think you would try, if it meant survival."

"Are not understanding," Shaka insisted. "Byahail are peaceful. Want no trouble. But always humans are attacking, taking slaves, selling people for pleasure, to mock and make joke. Then Kurlu come, take land and try to kill off Byahail. Can fight, many years are fighting to survive. But when all of world is against, how to win? Then time of Treaty comes, and humans of U.P. say, 'Now will be peace. Will give Byahail new lands.' Elders try making humans understand, Byahail cannot live on other lands. But humans do not understand. Not part of land as Byahail are part of land. So all of Byahail go to Reservation. Elders sit down and fight no more. Say, is up to gods. Old gods of Byahail will come and avenge Byahail. Will return Byahail to land. Elders wait for gods to come. Gods never come. Shaka is not believing in old gods anymore. Time of Byahail is gone. People die. Byahail join world of shadows."

The Castellan looked at her with what he sincerely hoped was a sympathetic expression. He wasn't good at making those sorts of expressions, mostly because he used them so little. Then he said, "And yet, you refuse to give up."

"Gods will not save Shaka," she growled. "Shaka will save Shaka. Will make new life, learn ways of humans, become strong and free." She paused, her expression of defiance softening somewhat. "But is hard sometimes. Am alone so much among strangers." She glanced at Prilock. "Is good having someone for talking."

"Yes, it is," he agreed.

Several prostitutes came into the Water Hole. Prilock knew

them. They came in about this time most every night. He didn't like it; the whole notion of prostitution disgusted him. But the U.P. did not explicitly ban prostitution in the territories, so there was little he could do about it unless they violated some other law, such as cheating their clients or harassing the bar patrons. And at least if they were allowed to operate in the open he could monitor what went on to some extent. In nations where prostitution was banned it didn't go away, it merely went underground. The abuses and violence were horrific, and there was little the authorities could do.

Shaka tapped the ash off the tip of the ginseng, rolling it on the edge of the ash bowl. "So, are only one of kind," she said to him. "Where came from?"

"I have no idea where I came from," Prilock said. "Some U.P. scientists found me adrift in an abandoned Kurlu shuttle in the Southern swamp. They are the first intelligent beings I can re-member seeing. They didn't recognize me as an intelligent being until I could figure out a way to communicate with them."

"How came here?"

He laughed bitterly. "I can assure you, it wasn't easy! It took me almost twenty years to convince them that I had a right to a life outside of a laboratory cage. Fortunately, there are some very idealistic people in the U.P. administration with far more integrity than the average human. They've given me a chance to prove my-self here. A remarkably wise decision on their part, seeing as I've succeeded in keeping order here at the settlement when no human governor could." He paused, and then added, "I also think they liked the idea of keeping me stashed away out here where they could keep an eye on me, far away from residential areas. So I won't scare the horses."

"Am not understanding."

Prilock sighed irritably. "Even the most open-minded human finds my natural appearance somewhat revolting."

"Is not this? What is like?"

"Well, to give you some idea, the name 'prilock' comes from a dark, gelatinous pudding commonly eaten by the Moor of the far West. The name stuck."

"Are like pudding?"

"Apparently they thought so. I have also been described by different humans with words like slime, goo, ick, ooze, and a highly diverse but basically unicellular, large, brown, glutinous mass. 'Not pretty' was how one human put it." He sighed. "Still, to be fair, the United Peoples Academy has treated me quite well. They've been a steadfast advocate in my favor."

"Are lucky." She drew a lungful of smoke from the ginseng. "Am trusting humans once. Sell Shaka to brothel."

Prilock arched an eyebrow with disgust. "Really? Typical!"

"Fight hard to get out," Shaka growled. "Finally get away. Never! No human makes profit from Shaka's body! Now, am trusting no one but Shaka."

"A wise policy."

They sat in silence for a few minutes. Then the beast took one last draw on the ginseng and put it out in the ash bowl. She said, "Am thinking maybe can trust another besides Shaka. Am thinking maybe can trust Castellan."

He looked over at her, genuinely flattered. "Thank you, Captain."

"Is Shaka," she said.

He nodded. "Is Prilock, then," he said with the slightest hint of a smile.

The following morning the *Chimera* left dock, precisely on schedule, and Castellan Prilock did his reports and made his rounds. There was, of course, gossip.

Lieutenant Morris printed out the list for the next day's arrivals and departures. The Castellan would want it as soon as he got in. After over a year of dealing with it, Morris had decided that serving under Castellan Prilock wasn't really all that bad. Most of them had hated it at first. They had hated it from the moment they had heard that their superior officer was going to be some kind of weird monster. But the Castellan seemed pretty human most of the time. And he wasn't all that bad. A hard-ass, to be sure. Laser straight and never missed a thing. A little creepy, too, considering what he could do. But they got used to it after a while. And they got so they had to respect him. He demanded a lot from them, and he may have been a supercilious S. O. B., but he always tried to be scrupulously just. And in some ways that was a hell of a lot better than some of the crafty, arbitrary types they'd had giving the orders in the past.

Morris did wonder sometimes if the creature got lonely from time to time. It must have been tough, being the only one of his kind. Being a Castellan in a gods-forsaken tussock in the swamp like Farport was bad enough—it wasn't like you could just go down to the officers' club and hobnob with others of your rank and station. Still, past governors had lowered themselves to seek out what company they could among the merchants and the clean-cut types passing through. The Castellan didn't even attempt that. Probably wouldn't be all that welcome, either, considering what he was. Maybe the creature didn't need company. Maybe his kind, whatever that was, didn't get lonely. Although there was that Byahail that passed through a couple of months ago. The port was all abuzz over that for awhile. What a pair.

Morris glanced over the list to see if there was anything that might be of particular interest to the Castellan. To show that you paid attention and noticed things generally made a good impression. And the fact that Prilock never missed anything meant he didn't overlook good work, either. And that meant promotions would be scrupulously fair.

Hey. Wasn't that . . . ?

Lieutenant Morris couldn't suppress a grin.

Prilock thought it entirely inappropriate for his lieutenant to mention particularly that the freighter *Chimera* had requested permission to schedule a stop at Farport.

"Thank you," the Castellan said frostily, "I'm sure I couldn't possibly have read that for myself." It was quite obvious that the entire port authority crew as well as the security teams were gleefully aware that the Castellan had once spent an evening socially with a Byahail. He could tell from the expressions on their faces that they thought it a tremendous joke. Damned humans!

So he made a point of being otherwise occupied when the *Chimera* docked. He would do nothing to encourage the stupid rumors. And he went into the Water Hole the same time he always did. Not the slightest shift of routine.

Shaka Mahdi was sitting at the bar. Haggus, the barkeeper, was chattering on as he wiped down the bar, making wet circles with the grey rag. "Hell, the only thing you can expect about the Castellan is that he's most likely to turn up when you least want him. Keep an eye on the furniture. If it starts to move, it's probably him."

"Count your change, Captain," Prilock said as he came over.

Shaka looked up and grinned. "Castellan! Is good to see! Am just asking now if are around."

Haggus put his hands on his hips, still holding the bar rag. "So what about my permits, Prilock? A couple of wheels would do wonders for business. It would improve business for everybody in the port."

"No need to nag, Haggus," Prilock replied. "You know how absolutely thrilled I am with the notion of your bringing gambling in here."

"Just trying to make a living," the barkeeper grumbled.

"Hmm. Really. I know how desperate you are for extra cash after I ruined that cozy little deal you had going."

"Hey! I told you! I had nothing to do with those smugglers! You can't prove a thing!"

"Perhaps not. But I know damn well that your snub nose is going to be buried deep anywhere there is the smell of money."

Haggus glared at him and stormed off to the other end of the bar.

"Are keeping humans on toes," Shaka said. "Is good. Not easy, though, eh?"

"Not easy, no," he agreed. "Shall we take a table where we can talk with a bit more privacy?"

"This place," the Byahail said, "Too many humans. All staring. Am not liking to imagine what are thinking. Come, can go to Shaka's ship. No humans staring. Can have glass of brandy maybe, yes?"

He hesitated. Then he leaned over and said quietly, "Listen, Shaka, maybe I should make something clear. I don't deny that I find your company pleasant. But don't get the idea that I'm interested in any kind of . . . relationship." He said the word with distaste.

The Byahail sat back, her black eyes wide. "Why are saying this?" she asked with surprise. "Thought Prilock understood. Shaka comes back here, glad to see Prilock. Am thinking, Good to spend time with Prilock. Is friend. Can trust. Not complicated. Can talk. Pass time. Then, Shaka leave again." She shook her head adamantly. "Not want relationship. If am wanting that kind of misery, plenty of humans to choose from."

Prilock nodded, relieved. "In that case, where is your ship docked?"

From then on Shaka Mahdi made a point of scheduling a stop-over at Farport whenever it was possible. The Water Hole was about the only place she felt at home. She could walk in there feeling like she belonged, because she knew the Castellan, and no one was going to give her a hard time. Prilock himself was very good company, someone she felt she had a great deal in common with. He always managed to put aside a couple hours of time to visit with her in the sanctuary of her ship. He would become so engrossed in their conversations that he would end up spending a couple of hours more than he planned. They felt at ease with each other in a way that neither had ever felt in the company of humans.

Shaka put off asking too many personal questions about Prilock until she thought they knew each other well enough for her to ask. There were a thousand things about him that she wanted to know.

"Never see Prilock having dinner," she said, pouring herself a drink.

"I only eat once a day and have no real need to take in much of anything else."

"Eat in morning? Evening?" Shaka sat down across from him, a ginseng held between her bony fingers.

"Morning, generally. I like to take advantage of the typical human sleep cycle to rest up a bit myself. I find I feel the need for nourishment when I first come out of torpor."

"Is torpor like sleep?"

The Castellan leaned back in the chair. He enjoyed talking about himself to someone who seemed genuinely interested and not just crudely curious. That was one reason he had not minded the company of the U.P. Academy scientists. The topic of conversation was usually him. "Yes, a bit like sleep, I'd imagine. Except, I don't require quite so much of it. A full eight hours of torpor is enough to keep me going for several days. Unless I have to do a lot of transubstantiating. That tends to wear me out more quickly that just maintaining a steady form."

"Transub—" She faltered with the word. "Is when change shape, yes?"

"Transubstantiation. That's what the scientists used to call it," Prilock said. "I return to my natural state when I am at rest."

Shaka drew on the ginseng. Smoke drifted from her nose and mouth as she spoke. What a bizarre thing for a creature to want to do, Prilock thought.

"Am hoping is not rude to ask," she said, "But, what are looking like in natural state? What is Prilock when just Prilock?"

"You mean, you really want to see? Most people would pay money to avoid the experience."

"Yes, if Prilock is not minding," Shaka said politely. "Am most curious."

He shrugged. He avoided being seen in public in his deliquescent state. He normally went torpid behind a firmly locked door in the privacy of his office. It was the only time he felt at all vulnerable. So he kept the rest periods as short as possible and as infrequent as possible, rarely allowing himself more than a few hours every day or so.

He rested his hand on the table next to him. It melted into a dark mass of slime. Shaka stared, fascinated. "All is like that?"

"One big puddle if I relax completely," he replied.

She came over, hastily putting out the ginseng in a bowl on the table. "If is not rude," she started hesitantly.

"Ask, ask. I am what I am and I'm long past being ashamed of it."

"Permit to touch?"

He stared at her in disbelief. "Excuse me? Did you say, 'touch'?"

"Is rude to ask?"

"Not rude," he replied, "Just a bit of a shock. Most people are not terribly eager to shove their fingers into a lump of brown muck."

The Byahail stood up straight, offended. "Shaka is not most people!" she declared. "Is curious about friend. Is new thing, very special. Part of getting to know friend."

He shrugged again. "Feel free," he said. He watched closely for her reaction.

She carefully extended her fingers, dipping them experimentally into the dark ooze that was Prilock's hand. She withdrew them, examining them, seeing that nothing clung to them. She looked at him with concern. "Not hurt?"

"Me? No, and I doubt you could."

She nodded, reaching down to touch him again. She let her fingers linger in the mass, testing the texture, the feeling. "Is smooth, soft," she marveled. "Warm."

"It doesn't bother you?"

"Feel nice. Very nice. Like warm mud where Shaka was born. Brings thoughts of old lands, lands of Byahail, time before humans. Like—" She stopped, frowning. He was about to ask her what was wrong when he noticed something very odd. He was experiencing a soothing, relaxing sensation all around the area she was touching. The longer her hand remained there the more the feeling seemed to intensify and spread. He abruptly withdrew the pseudopod, reforming it into a hand.

"What?" she asked. "Hurt?"

"No," he said, puzzled. "Not exactly."

"Something not normal happen," Shaka guessed. "What?"

"Did you feel something? I mean, besides the sensation of warm goo between your fingers."

"Not sure," the Byahail answered carefully. "Thinking of mud beds where Shaka was born and nurtured. Is making peaceful feeling. Good. Then feeling is strong, more than memory, maybe."

"Hmm." He had had physical contact with humans before in his natural state, especially during all the tests they had run on him, and had been touched occasionally since, usually by accident and with an accompanying grimace of disgust. But never had physical contact induced anything like what he had just experienced. Was it possible he had imagined it?

He reached for her hand. "May I?"

She nodded.

Prilock let his hand melt around her hand, encasing it in his own substance, maximizing surface area contact. "This doesn't bother you?"

"No. Feel very nice." If she was repressing any kind of negative reaction she was doing a magnificent job of it. She gave every indication of genuinely enjoying his touch. Then, there it was. Unmistakably. A sensation of peace and well-being seemed to be flowing from the area of contact into the rest of his body. It would have been alarming if it were not so benign.

"This not happen usually?" Shaka asked.

"No. Not for you either?"

She shook her head. "Many beings have touched," she said. "Sometimes is good. Most of times not so good. But never is this."

"Remarkable!" he murmured. The longer he was in contact with her the more reluctant he was to withdraw. Some part of him was protesting righteously that this simply couldn't be right, that there was something unnatural about it, but he couldn't say what.

Apparently Shaka was having the same uneasy impulses, but acted on them before he did.

"Please to stop," she said.

He immediately withdrew, reforming human appendages.

"Are you all right?"

"Am fine," she said distractedly. She retreated to the other side of the room and relit her ginseng. She looked at him sharply. "Prilock not do that on purpose?"

"I swear to you," he said solemnly. "I had no idea. This is as much of a surprise to me as it is to you."

"Prilock is friend," she said almost pleading. "Would not try to trick Shaka."

"Most certainly not," he said firmly.

The Byahail nodded. "Trust Prilock. Are noble being. Not human. Not try to seduce Shaka with trick."

Prilock looked mildly offended. "You wanted to touch me first, remember? If anything, I should be wondering about your motives."

She took a long pull on the ginseng. "Is true. Look like Shaka try to trick Prilock." She looked at him. "Are trusting?"

He nodded. "Yes. Apparently there is some sort of biochemical sympathy between our two species that neither one of us was aware of."

"Is very strange," Shaka said. She added, cautiously, "But is not unpleasant."

"No, not unpleasant at all," Prilock agreed.

"Very strange," she murmured thoughtfully. "Would not mind to try again?"

He hesitated, and then said, "No, I suppose not. I admit I am very curious about this. But we must agree to break contact immediately if either of us requests it."

"Agreed," she said firmly.

He stood up and met the Byahail in the middle of the room.

He took her hands as before and melted around them. The sensation seemed to come more quickly this time, perhaps because they were expecting it. Distinctly peaceful. Tranquil. All anxiety was slowly being smoothed away. The sense of friendship and mutual comfort was palpable. He couldn't seem to resist the impulse to continue relaxing, melting and oozing up over her wrists and up her arms. The feeling drew him in, soothing, reassuring.

Shaka kept thinking, Just another moment, just one moment more. Then she would put a stop to it. But it felt so wonderful, this contentment, this peace of mind and ease of heart. It had been too many years since had she known this kind of contentment, this relief from loneliness and bitterness. It was beautiful, and she didn't want it to stop.

Several hours later, slowly surfacing from the most restful sleep she had enjoyed in memory, Shaka awoke on the floor enveloped in dark slime. It should have startled her, but she felt so deliciously comfortable and drowsy that she had more than enough time to remember what had happened before she woke up completely. She trilled softly, stretching her limbs and disturbing the jelly that encased them. The jelly rippled, then began to withdraw and form itself into human shape.

"What time is it?" the Castellan asked, disoriented. "Did I spend the night here?"

"Am thinking so," Shaka said, squinting at the chronometer. As soon as Prilock withdrew his touch she began to feel stiff and sore from sleeping on the floor. The tranquil sensation lingered somewhat but was fading.

"I spent the night here!" Prilock exclaimed again.

"What is problem?" Shaka asked, yawning. She stood up with difficulty, flexing her muscles to try to work the stiffness out of them. She craved a good, strong, rich cup of coffee. "Are wanting breakfast, maybe? Time of day when eat, yes?"

"No thank you, " Prilock murmured distractedly. "I have what I need in my office." He shook his head and cried out again in disbelief, "I spent the night here! I completely lost control, went torpid, and spent the night here!"

"What, are afraid for reputation?" Shaka asked with a grin. "Why waste time? Humans always think worst no matter what."

"I suppose," he said, uneasy and unconvinced. "I have to go. I have to review the morning reports. I have to go."

"So, go," Shaka said with a shrug. "Can talk later, okay?"

He left hastily. As soon as he was off the ship he transformed himself into a long, green snake, slithering quickly through the thick brush to arrive at his office, hopefully unobserved.

Haggus scowled at the evening crowd, biting his lip and doing figures in his head. Business was lousy, thanks to that damned castellan the U. P. had installed last year. Ever since that unnatural son of a bitch had arrived it had gotten progressively harder to get any kind of a scam going. Prilock had collared so many operators they had to build an annex on the detention center. Everyone had gotten a lot more cautious, but the Castellan was well-nigh ubiquitous. Instead of staying in his office and sticking to the business of a governor, Prilock had his nose in everything that was going on. The U. P. had sent him to bring law and order to the settlement, and by the gods, he was going to do it, even if he had to bust half the port in the process.

Opening up the cash drawer, Haggus looked through his receipts. Pathetic. He swore foully and stuffed the receipts back into the drawer. He had to find a way to make up the shortfall. But there was nothing he dared to try with that damned, inhuman freak oozing around. There wasn't anywhere you could hide from the bastard. Haggus went in terror of being in a room somewhere, seemingly safe and sound, closing a deal, only to have a wall fixture start to melt and announce, "You're under arrest." Unnatural, creeping monster. The only time you knew absolutely where he was was when you were looking him right in the eye.

Haggus went down to the other end of the bar to serve a customer who had just slouched into a seat. It wasn't that Haggus was a bigot. He'd serve a Northman or a Moor, or a slant-eyed Kurlu. Even that frikking Byahail, for gods' sake. Hell, he'd serve a striped behemoth and its queen if their credits were good. Didn't matter to him. Farport was the last faint toot of civilization at the edge of U. P. territory. All kinds came into the Water Hole, and they were all welcome, so long as they paid and they didn't bust up the place too badly. At the core of it, they were all basically the same, whatever their race. They had one head, four limbs, and if you ran them through with a skelran they would bleed like hell.

Castellan Prilock, on the other hand, had one head and four limbs only when he was in the mood. Or he could be the potted plant in the corner or the chair you just sat on. It was enough to make a man crazy. Where the U. P. had found the monster was anybody's guess. There were some damned strange creatures lurking out there in the swamps. Like the Byahail, for example. And nobody knew what freaks of nature might live in the lands to the far south, if indeed there was land, and not just endless tracts of poisonous swamp. But wherever it was they'd dug up the creature that called himself Prilock, Haggus wished to hell they had left him there.

He set a tall ale in front of the customer, a weary old trader who had been coming in off and on since before the Treaty. Amazing what could happen in twenty years. Time was, half the patrons in the Water Hole would think nothing of slitting the throats of the other half and calling it patriotism. Now they all sat peaceably in the same room sipping their drinks, maybe even slipping in a friendly game of lots, it they could sneak it by the Castellan, which wasn't likely. If there was going to be bloodshed it would be over something important, like somebody caught cheating at lots. Not some ridiculous nonsense like what piece of real estate your mother squeezed you out onto.

As he took the trader's credits, he looked up and noticed an evil-looking crew of Kurlu traders jostling their way into the bar and invading a table. Very rough customers. Haggus hurried to get them served. He glanced nervously over in the direction where the Castellan normally stood and didn't see him. Then Haggus spotted him towards the back, watching the Kurlu. Haggus felt relieved. Much as he resented the way the Castellan ran things, he had to admit there was much less trouble thanks to him. In the old days, half the money he made on the side went towards repairs and maintenance. At least once a week some damned Kurlu freighter captain would decide to bounce his co-pilot off the walls just for kicks. Or a bunch of Northmen would begin using the bottles on the back of the bar for target practice. That wouldn't happen nowadays. Hardly even needed bouncers anymore. The Castellan was the bouncer from Hell. Prilock didn't need to carry a weapon. He *was* a weapon.

And Haggus didn't have to bribe him to get his protection. That, too, he had to admit was a plus. There wasn't the old competition for favors among the merchants and black market traders to get the good graces of the Castellan on their side. When it came to bidding, Haggus didn't have nearly the wherewithal to compete with some of the bigger, nastier players. The fact that Prilock was obnoxiously incorruptible did make the playing field a lot more even.

Haggus noticed the Byahail coming into the bar. Headed right for the Castellan's table, of course. Damnedest thing, the way the Castellan had taken a fancy to the beast. What a pair. A pansexual and an oversized amoeba disguised as a human being. They were fourteen jokes just waiting to be told, each more obscene than the one before.

Of course, they didn't act much like a couple. Didn't act like there was a thing between them, just sitting there talking, casual as you please. But then, that shouldn't be much of a surprise. The Castellan was too much of a tight-ass to admit to having feelings of any sort. At least, never in public. In private, those two were probably doing things that would make a devil blush. Rumor had it that the Castellan had been seen sneaking into his own office early yesterday morning, the implication being that he had spent the night elsewhere. An easy guess where. Did the Byahail know what he really was? Probably. Probably turned her on.

Haggus made a face. The whole notion was disgusting.

And there they sat, for all the world to see. Hell, the Castellan was so damned uptight that Haggus could almost believe there really wasn't anything going on between them. He could almost picture them sitting around all night, all smug and superior, talking about how much better they were than ordinary folks. Too good to indulge in something as normal and natural as sex. He could almost believe it, but not quite. No, they had to be rutting like crazed swamp lizards in the privacy of the Byahail's ship. Just had to be. Disgusting.

Castellan Prilock spoke without looking at his companion, his attention focused on the rowdy group of Kurlu across the room. "I'm sorry I didn't come by last night."

"Is no problem," Shaka said, lighting up a smoke.

"I was quite busy. A lot of paperwork to catch up on."

"Not to make excuse," Shaka said. "Am knowing better."

He glanced over at her. Of course she knew better. What did he think she was? Some kind of silly human whose feelings he had to protect with flimsy lies? He nodded. "All right. To be honest, I needed some time to think. What happened between us, it unsettled me a bit."

"Am glad did not come by," Shaka said. "Needed time to think, too."

The Kurlu were starting to argue amongst themselves. Prilock frowned. He wasn't in the mood to have to break up a fight. If it looked like it might get nasty he'd call a security team to keep an eye on the situation.

"I don't like losing control like that," he said. "I have too many responsibilities."

"Am feeling same way," the Byahail said, turning the ginseng slowly between her fingers. "Make Shaka feel vulnerable. Am not liking that feeling." She paused. "Am glad at least that it happen with someone who is friend."

Prilock glanced at her again. It was refreshing talking to someone who spoke so plainly and simply. It was easy for him to like her. Ironically, that was exactly what bothered him. That, and the uncomfortable knowledge of the biochemical symbiosis between them. This whole thing was starting to smell unpleasantly like a relationship.

"You're scheduled to depart tomorrow," he said.

"Yes. Am going to do Eastlands route. Eight weeks." She took a long pull off the ginseng. She exhaled slowly. "Will miss Prilock. Will look forward to seeing again."

"I'll probably be here," he said, "but no promises. Things could change. After all, there is a lot I don't know about myself. Should I learn some radical truth about my origins or abilities, or should I meet others of my kind, my plans might have to change suddenly. I cannot make any commitments to anyone or anything."

She took the statement in, considering what was not said but was meant to be inferred. She inclined her head. "Understood," she said. "Future is never certain."

A chorus of shouts began to rise from across the room. "There they go," Prilock grumbled. He pulled his radio out of his pocket. "Security, this is the Castellan. Get a team over here to the Water Hole on the double."

"What's up, Chief?" came the reply.

"Kurlu. Seven of them. They might settle down, but I doubt it."

"On our way."

He looked apologetically at Shaka. "You'll have to excuse me. I've got to take care of this."

"Is job," she said, getting up. "Will be on ship if are wishing to talk more. If not, am saying goodbye now. Maybe will see again some day."

"All right—" He intended to say more, but was interrupted by a blood-thirsty bellow and the sound of a crash. He had to take action immediately. Prilock charged towards the Kurlu with the expression of an annoyed lion. A formidable being, Shaka thought regretfully. A noble being.

By the time the security team got there Prilock had more or less gotten things under control. Shaka was long gone.

It was quite late by the time he finished taking care of the business with the Kurlu. It had been difficult and unpleasant, and had ended up in the infirmary. Some people just wouldn't listen until you literally pounded sense into them. He'd had to transubstantiate into something very hard and forceful to get his point across, something that couldn't be bruised by a fist, pierced by a skelran, or seared by a gun. Certain types of flexible metal alloys worked well, but it took an awful lot of effort. It was exhausting.

Then there were some other assorted left-overs of paperwork to take care of. He got matters settled and realized how tired he was. He hadn't felt the need of rest the night before, and it was finally catching up with him. All that fast changing to get those Kurlu subdued.

How nice it would be to wrap himself around the warm, sentient form of Shaka Mahdi and sink into a blissful torpor, instead of sloshing around restlessly in the back of his office, plagued by worries and anxieties, until torpor finally came.

But he shouldn't let himself think about that. It was inviting trouble. Better not to get involved. It could get complicated. Inconvenient. Awkward. It wasn't natural, this thing between them. He didn't like it. Not at all. He had too many responsibilities, too much to think about. His life here at Farport was settled, properly organized, challenging but manageable. No need to complicate it. No need at all.

Still, he would miss the companionship, the pleasant conversation. It had been nice to feel like he had some common ground with another being. There was something about the Byahail that he genuinely liked. He found the creature admirable. A handsome beast. A welcome break from the company of humans.

He wondered if all Byahail were like Shaka Mahdi. Such a brave, honorable creature, who seemed to know the true meaning of friendship.

Yes, well, so it was nice while it lasted, but it was getting too complicated, too involved, and it was just as well that he had put an end to it. Now his life could get back to normal. None of this unsettling, biosympathetic weirdness. He'd be able to relax once she left.

Tomorrow she would be shipping out.

And he would miss her.

Yes, damn it, he would miss her. He could rationalize it to himself as much as he liked, it didn't change the truth of the matter. For the first time in his short and essentially meaningless life, he had really connected, deeply and significantly, with another being. It scared him silly. It shot through his arrogance with a vulnerability that was terrifying. He hated it. And craved it desperately. It also made him intensely curious. There had to be some reason for their symbiosis. It couldn't be utter, empty coincidence. So thus, it was the first real clue as to what he was, where he came from, why he existed at all.

It would be the soaring height of idiotic pride if he turned his back on the Byahail now.

When he arrived at the *Chimera* he had to request access twice before the door opened. Shaka Mahdi looked a little disoriented. "Not expecting," she said as she gestured for him to come in.

"No, I don't suppose I gave you any reason to. Were you asleep?" He followed her back through the cabin to her quarters.

"No, not asleep yet." She seemed a bit unsteady and her voice was somewhat slurred. It dawned on him. She had been drinking. He saw the half-empty bottle on the table.

"You've been doing an efficient job on this," he observed, picking up the bottle.

She sat on the edge of her bunk. "Ship out tomorrow. Must be alert when out of dock. Last chance is tonight."

"So you decided to get good and blind, eh?" He realized how

it sounded after he'd said it and regretted it. What she did in the privacy of her own ship was none of his business.

She shrugged indifferently. "Why not? Brandy is good to make loneliness and old pain go away. Is not as good as friend, but friend is not here." She waved her hand. "Please not to worry, Shaka understand. Relationship is burden to friend. Most important, never to put burden on friend."

"I do apologize if—"

"Not to apologize," Shaka said. She leaned over, reaching for her smokes. "Byahail elders teach, 'Do not ask more of friend than friend can give.'"

"I'm afraid there is little I can give you."

"Little is better than nothing," she said, lighting the ginseng. "And Prilock give Shaka night of peace. Is worth much."

"Yes," he agreed quietly, "That was worth a great deal." He watched the smoke drift up from the ginseng in her hand. "Captain," he said slowly, "I've been thinking." Prilock sat down on the edge of the bunk. "Haggus, the Northman who runs the Water Hole, has been pestering me for a gambling permit. The very idea makes me shudder. It would make my job ten times as difficult. But it could be good for the settlement. It would attract business, and the other merchants would benefit. Properly managed, all the residents of Farport could benefit from it."

She leaned back against the side of the bunk and eyed him thoughtfully, the faintest of smiles playing at her mouth. "Good equipment available in Simpan. Reputation for making good wheels. Maybe barkeeper will be wanting to make order if knowing permits will be granted."

"Mention to him that you have good reason to believe I'll grant the permits. Coming from you, he'll no doubt take it as golden."

Shaka grinned. "More business means barkeeper and other merchants need more supplies. Am knowing to be in right place at right time. This is good fortune for Shaka."

"I'd say it's a stroke of good fortune all around," Prilock said with satisfaction. "I'd just as soon have you handle the shipment of gambling equipment anyway. That way I'd be sure that all the proper forms would be filed, and black market traders wouldn't get their dirty fingers into it."

Shaka blew a long stream of smoke towards the ventilation duct. "Will have to delay departure," she said. "Must talk to bar-keeper."

"Really? How much of a delay?" he asked. "After all, I'll have to make corrections to the official log."

"Not sure," said Shaka. "Will let Castellan know."

"I would appreciate that."

She nodded slowly, smiling at him. "Is good to have friend," she said, extending her hand to him.

"Indeed it is," he agreed, taking her hand and melting around it.

So he wouldn't make it back to his office that night. So let them talk. They probably would anyway.

CHAPTER 2

Dr. Yoshi swatted at the fly, and missed. With all the marvelous technology developed since the U.P. gave the Northmen something to focus their energy on besides killing each other, one would think there would be a more sophisticated way of dealing with flies. In the controlled environment of the cities they weren't a problem. But out here in this godsforsaken backwater flies were just one among many assorted pests. Dr. Yoshi sighed and sipped on his schnapps. To think that at first he had actually been excited at the prospect of doing his public service time at Farport, living on the frontier, meeting strange and exotic peoples and learning their ways and customs. His idealistic illusions had long ago evaporated. Too much time spent treating gunblast wounds and trying to cope with strange and exotic diseases. He never would have been able to stick it out for his full four years of service if the U. P. hadn't sent Prilock out here to impose some kind of order on the brawling chaos that was business as usual for Farport.

Yoshi had seen three administrations come and go since arriving there. The Moor who was castellan when the doctor arrived was dedicated and well-meaning, and a very competent administrator, but much too mild-mannered to deal with the rough customers the port attracted. The Northman they sent as his replacement got himself killed within a month. The next castellan settled right into place. He was perfectly at home dealing with the pirates and black marketeers; he was just as corrupt as they were. Then the U. P. in an act of desperation had sent out this odd creature to take over the job of castellan. They had contacted Dr. Yoshi before Prilock arrived and advised him that the new governor at Farport was going to be a bit, well, different. It was an experiment, they said. Dr. Yoshi's observations would be most appreciated, but they asked him to please be patient and give the new castellan an adequate chance before passing judgement. Yoshi had formed a firm opinion of Prilock within the first week, and that opinion had remained essentially unchanged ever since.

The fly landed on the corner of the doctor's computer screen. Yoshi crept up on it stealthily and then smacked it. He achieved the minor victory of smearing the fly across the screen. One should not have to contend with flies in a modern medical facility, he thought furiously as he cleaned the mess up with a sterile pad. He tossed the pad in the direction of the waste bin and missed. The doctor swore mutedly. He took another sip of schnapps and continued working on his reports. He reminded himself that he should count his blessings. If it weren't for the U.P.'s public service program he wouldn't have been able to afford medical school in the first place. And his term of service here would be over soon. Another year and he could get on with his career. Establish a practice back in the northwest, in Malowi or Sebu, where he could concentrate on health maintenance and the occasional broken bone sustained in a playground accident, instead of patching up ill-tempered traders who'd taken a skelran through the tattoo in a barroom brawl.

He entered the last line of data, checked his work for accuracy, and then printed out a paper back-up of the reports. He didn't trust the computer. It had a nasty habit of crashing at the most inconvenient times, another annoying feature of life out here in the middle of the swamp. His work done, he could either take a meal in his quarters and retire early, or he could get some dinner down at the Water Hole and take in a bit of entertainment. With any luck he would be able to get through the evening peacefully without an emergency call to patch up some belligerent idiot. Word was apparently getting around. There were fewer fights in the Water Hole, and when one did start, Prilock could usually settle matters without having to resort to extreme means. The regulars, at least, had learned the futility of arguing with him. Yoshi was very grateful for that.

The doctor drained the last of the schnapps from the glass and decided to go down to the Water Hole. Perhaps he would attempt to extract two words of small talk out of the Castellan. Yoshi was intensely curious about Prilock, but it was next to impossible to draw the creature into conversation. Tonight, however, he might be in a better mood. His friend the Byahail was in port. Yoshi was very curious about her, too. The Byahail were an odd, reclusive race. They were dying out now, despite efforts to get them established on a reservation far from Kurlu aggression. Shaka Mahdi was the first specimen he'd ever seen, and could well be the last. Few people ever saw one except in pictures. To actually sit down and talk to one was precisely the sort of opportunity he'd hoped for in coming to Farport. But the Byahail was damn near as anti-social as Prilock was.

Yoshi turned down the lights and locked up his office. He had only been broken into once since Prilock had come. Prior to that, break-ins had occurred with tedious regularity. The Castellan had made a substantial difference, one could not deny it. The doctor wondered where the creature had come from. Apparently it was a total mystery even to Prilock, himself. Nothing like him existed anywhere in the known world. Supposedly, there was a great mountain range beyond the Valley of the Byahail. And there were still vast tracts of swamp in the far south that even the Kurlu hadn't explored. There were all sorts of legends told by Kurlu traders concerning strange beasts and unnatural monsters which came down from the mountains or out of the swamps. Perhaps some of the legends were true. But how some hypothetical monster from the South could end up in an abandoned Kurlu shuttle a thousand miles from the nearest Kurlu outpost was a puzzle.

Regardless of what Prilock was and where he came from, he was here, obviously intelligent, and thus fully entitled to the civil rights of any other intelligent being. The great mission of the United Peoples was to bring peace, prosperity and justice to all the races of the world, and although they had not succeeded universally in that mission—failing miserably in some cases, such as that of the Byahail—they were determined to succeed in the case of Prilock. And Dr. Yoshi had to admit, they had certainly allowed him to make good use of his potential. Yoshi might not personally care for the Castellan; in fact he thought him arrogant, egotistical, and abrasively self-important. But the doctor respected him a great deal. And his reports to U.P. headquarters had reflected that. As far as Yoshi was concerned, Prilock was the best damned castellan Farport had ever had or ever could have.

The Water Hole was a bit more crowded than usual. A lot of the crowd looked to be Kurlu. A fleet of merchants must have docked. Dr. Yoshi hesitated, wondering if he should reconsider his plan. The Kurlu tended not to be a particularly pleasant crowd. Then he spotted the Castellan sitting at the bar, the Byahail next to him. That was unusual. Normally they sat at some secluded table, eyeing the other patrons fishily from a distance. And it seemed that Prilock was actually carrying on a conversation with the bar-keeper, Haggus. This, also, was too unusual to be ignored. And too good an opportunity to pass up.

Dr. Yoshi made his way towards the bar. He noticed Shaka Mahdi had a ginseng smoke in her hand. The doctor shuddered to think what that was doing to her lungs. And she damn near chain-smoked them. Nasty habit. Prilock didn't seem to give a damn about it. What an odd relationship they had. Understandable that they might gravitate towards one another, both being freaks in a human world. Yoshi wondered if it were true what everybody said about them—that they were far more than just friends. The doctor tended to pay little attention to Water Hole gossip, but it was pretty much common knowledge that the Castellan didn't sleep in his office when Shaka Mahdi's ship was in dock. It was difficult to resist the temptation to speculate as to what such a bizarre pair of creatures might do in private, but Yoshi reminded himself sternly that he was above such things. And, at any rate, it was none of his business.

A chorus of shouts erupted from a table as the doctor walked past, startling him. He looked over to see what the commotion was. A crew of Kurlu freighter merchants was tossing lots on the table. That sort of thing was strictly prohibited, but Prilock apparently hadn't noticed it yet. The doctor wondered if he ought to point it out to him, or if that, too, was none of his business.

As he settled himself next to the Castellan at the bar he realized why Haggus was being granted the privilege of an extended conversation with Prilock. They were discussing the rules and regulations regarding the newly installed but not yet operational gaming wheel that Haggus had purchased.

"Why should I limit the size of the wagers?" Haggus demanded irately.

"Because those are the rules as clearly specified by the U.P. Gaming Commission," Prilock explained. He turned and nodded a polite greeting to Yoshi as he sat down. "Good evening, Doctor."

"Good evening, Castellan. Haggus, a glass of schnapps, please."

"Right away, Doc. Listen, Prilock, I should think it would be the patron's own business how much he wants to bet." He continued the argument as he served the doctor.

"Thinking has never been your strong suit, Haggus," Prilock retorted, "So just obey the rules and don't try to get creative."

"Dammit, Prilock! My customers have certain expectations! Here you go, Doc."

"Thank you. On my tab?"

"Sure, no problem."

Prilock said stubbornly, "If you can't obey the law I can very easily revoke your permit and have Captain Mahdi dismantle the equipment and load it back aboard her ship."

"Sure," Shaka said, blowing a stream of smoke towards the ceiling. "Is fine with Shaka. Get paid for shipping both ways."

"All right! All right!" Haggus cried out in exasperation. "But you and your security teams are going to have to help me enforce your damn rules!"

"That is what we're here for," Prilock replied.

"They aren't going to like it," Haggus grumbled.

"That is not my concern."

Another chorus of shouts rose up from the table where the illicit game was in progress.

"What the devil is going on over there?" Prilock exclaimed irritably, looking over in their direction. The doctor thought it might perhaps be politic to mention something.

"I'm not sure, but I think they might have a game of lots going."

"We'll see about that," Prilock said, straightening his uniform and striding over to the table. Shaka turned around to watch, leaning a bony elbow on the bar, grinning as she took a long pull on the ginseng. By the time the Castellan got to the table most of the rest of the bar was watching, too. When they weren't the object of his attention, the patrons enjoyed watching him in action.

"Excuse me," Prilock interrupted the players in a voice impossible to ignore, "But unlicensed gambling is not permitted on these premises."

The Kurlu paused in their play to look up at him, incredulous that he would dare to interfere with them.

"What did you say?" one of them asked. They grinned at one another.

"I said," Prilock repeated clearly, "Unlicensed gambling is not allowed on these premises."

"Gambling?" said one with a noticeable number of missing teeth and an ugly scar on an already ugly face. "We're not gambling. Just a friendly game of lots. Eh, men?"

"Nevertheless, it is not permitted," Prilock said. "That is the law."

The biggest of them stood up menacingly. So did the one with the missing teeth. "I don't think I like your laws," he said.

"Liking the laws is not required," Prilock shot back. "Obeying them is."

The Kurlu took a step towards Prilock. "I am Commodore Fenrire," he snarled through a contemptuous leer, "And when my men and I are in port we entertain ourselves as we please!"

"Delighted to meet you, Commodore," Prilock replied. "I am Castellan Prilock, and when you and your crew are in Farport, you will obey the law."

The rest of the crew rose slowly to their feet. Fenrire's eyes glittered nastily. "And who will make us?"

Prilock sighed. He took his radio out of its pocket. "Prilock to security."

"Morris here."

"Send a team to the Water Hole. I've got, let's see, ten Kurlu who seem inclined to be obstinate concerning our rules about gambling."

"Only ten Sir?" Morris replied. "Are you sure you need our help?"

"Lieutenant!" Prilock snapped warningly.

"On our way, Sir."

"Good," Fenrire sneered. "You'll need a team of men to find all the pieces when we're done with you."

Prilock arched an eyebrow. "Terror is oozing from my every pore."

"You're not big enough to talk to me that way," Fenrire snarled.

"How big would you like me to be?" Prilock inquired, and grew himself up to about half a head taller than the Kurlu commander. "Will this do?"

The other crew members yelped in surprise and jumped back a foot or two, stumbling over chairs and against tables. Other patrons grabbed their drinks and scurried for the corners. Fenrire stared at Prilock in shock, his gap-toothed mouth hanging open. Then he resumed his belligerence. "It's a trick! Nothing more! And I'm not going to fall for it!" He cocked his fist back but before he could throw a punch something hit him like a steel bar across the jaw. For all practical purposes, that was indeed what had hit him. Prilock transformed his arm back into a normal human appendage. Fenrire fell back against the table and slid to the floor, stunned.

"Well," Prilock observed, resuming his normal size, "We now

know what you will fall for." The security team arrived, joining him. "Thank you, Lieutenant. Just in time. Would you kindly escort these gentlemen back to their ship?"

"Yes, Sir."

He addressed the Kurlu crew. "You may collect your commander and your lots and leave. You are all welcome to return when you feel more inclined to behave yourselves. Good evening." He turned and strode smartly back to the bar leaving the security team to herd the murderously muttering crew out of the bar.

The doctor finished his schnapps with a gulp. Thank the gods he's on our side, Yoshi thought as he ordered another.

According to what the transport engineer had told her in the bar last night, she could increase the output of her engines by almost twenty per cent by installing a phase adjustment unit and realigning the fuel flow to account for the difference in input. She had the unit in place and was working the spanner in, careful not to touch the coil. She got it halfway into place when a stray charge from the coil zapped her hand and she dropped the spanner. It slipped through the netting and down behind the console.

She swore furiously. She'd have to take the whole damn console apart to retrieve the spanner. Shaka sat back and set down her tools, picking up a ginseng smoke and lighting it. Maybe while she had the console out she should take a look at a few things. Maybe make some more modifications. Possibly improve the efficiency of the fuel flow.

She'd been spending a lot of time and credits customizing her ship. It was a sleek, handsome craft. Fast, with precision handling, able to negotiate the most twisted, overgrown canal with no problem. She could bid routes at half the time of conventional freighters. The next major project would be to upgrade the weapons systems. She had been taking some rather risky jobs, carrying shipments through waters known to be haunted by pirates. But the money was good and Shaka had confidence in herself and her ship. A couple of on-board blasters and she would need to fear no

one. Her application for heavy armaments was already on its way
to the U. P. Commercial Regulatory Agency with a letter of
recommendation from Prilock. She ought to receive and answer
within a month.

Things had worked out remarkably well between her and the
Castellan. Prilock was truly an exceptional being. A real friend in
the Byahail sense of the word. Shaka trusted him absolutely. He
placed no burdens or demands on her, and she asked nothing
burdensome of him. What they shared, they shared because it
satisfied the needs of them both.

Thanks to him, Shaka Mahdi had become more or less a regular fixture at Farport. As she became acquainted with the humans
who lived and regularly visited there, she became accustomed to
them. They treated her with a certain respect, and some were even
friendly towards her. She learned how to make small talk in the
Water Hole, striking up conversations with the patrons, often picking up valuable information and ideas from other people in the
freight and transport business.

As dependable as sunset, Prilock would show up at her
ship after he had made his last rounds and finished his reports.
If he worked exceptionally late, which he often did, Shaka
would putter about the ship or study the International Commerce Law manuals until she was tired enough to doze off. She
would be startled awake by the sensation of something soft
and warm flopping down over her. "It's just me, go back to
sleep," he'd say, and she'd settle back with a sigh, letting the
feeling of contentment and security wash over her. No matter
what indignities, insults, and aggravations plagued her, she
knew that she could go home to Farport, to a kindred spirit
and friend, and when she lay her head down to sleep, comfort
and serenity would lie down with her. No more sleepless nights,
tossing with anxiety, gnawed by loneliness. Prilock had once
apologized that he could offer her very little, but his friendship had given her everything she could possibly ask for.

And although he seemed satisfied with the arrangement, she

regretted she had not been able to give him that which she knew he wanted most: Some clue as to his own identity. If her people knew of creatures such as he, she had never heard of it.

She put out the ginseng and rummaged around among her tools for a boltpuller. She heard someone coming aboard the ship and she looked up, and grinned. "Castellan! Is good timing! Have lost spanner behind console. Please to reach."

"Certainly," Prilock said. He leaned over and stretched his arm into a slender tentacle, groping for the spanner. "Are you sure it's back here? Ah, there it is. Here." He handed it to her. Prilock avoided such displays of his ability in front of humans. He had learned that it was better not to do anything to remind them that he wasn't one of them if he could avoid it. Over the years he had worked to mimic the behavior of humans, including facial expression, gesture, and colloquial communication, in an effort to better interact with them. When he was granted the Farport assignment, he had carefully chosen and crafted his appearance to command the most authority possible. Dramatic performances like the one he had put on for the benefit of the unruly Kurlu were very useful for the purpose of intimidation. It kept the troublemakers in line. But in his every day dealings with humans he attempted to handle all situations as a human would, albeit a human of superior intellect and ethical standards.

In front of Shaka Mahdi, however, he behaved as he would if he were alone. She put him completely at ease. No human he had ever met accepted him as he was with such complete matter-of-factness. She was always pleased to see him, yet she made no demands on his time. She was easy to be with, a being with whom he had an understanding, a being who shared his sense of honor, his passion for order and justice, and his contempt for the general wallow of humanity. It was with genuine pleasure that he anticipated the end of the day when she was in port. Whether he felt the need of torpor or not, he did not pass up the opportunity to be with her, simply for the pure pleasure of it. Those precious few hours of serenity made it easier for him to face the rest of the day. And her company in the Water Hole made the business of having to deal with the idiots and drunken scum a whole lot less tedious.

It was unusual for him to drop by her ship in the middle of the day like this, but he had something in particular on his mind.

"I see on the manifest that you are taking a route through the Snaketree Waters to the Lower Kai Peninsula," he said, scanning the data board.

"Yes," she replied, trying once again to insert the spanner and get the unit properly aligned. "Is good money."

"I've been seeing a lot of reports on pirate activity in the Snaketree area. How is your ship equipped for defense?"

"Could be better," she admitted, carefully withdrawing the spanner and checking the output. "But ship is fast. Am careful. As soon as permits come through, will put in blasters."

Prilock nodded, frowning. "I'll feel better when you do. Damned bureaucracy. Everything takes forever. How long has it been since you sent the forms to Malowi? Never mind, can't be helped." He checked something off on the databoard. "Just as a precaution, I am requesting that all ships passing through hazardous waters maintain a strict schedule and close communication. If there is trouble, I want to be able to notify the U.P. as soon as possible to send rescue craft out."

Shaka shrugged. "Okay. Sounds like good idea." She gave a grunt of satisfaction as the figures on the readout lined up just the way she wanted them to. She scrutinized her work. Perhaps she'd take the ship out this afternoon as see what sort of effect her tinkering had on the performance.

"Haggus is starting up the gambling operation tonight. I can hardly wait," he said ironically.

"Barkeeper has found someone to run wheel already?"

"So it would seem." Prilock frowned, shaking his head. "A professional from up North. Something about her doesn't ring quite true. I'm going to have my security people check her out very thoroughly."

He looked up from the data board. "My guess is she's on the run from something. Will you be dropping by the Water Hole tonight?"

"Not sure. Bar will be very crowded. Kurlu merchant fleet still in port."

"Mmmn," he frowned, examining the data board. "They aren't due to leave until tomorrow. Lovely. I wonder if Fenrire will put on an appearance?"

"Am not liking that Kurlu. Am coming to bar only if Prilock is there," Shaka said, getting to her feet with the help of her tail.

"Oh, I'll be there, don't you worry," he assured her, "Although you might not see me. I intend to keep a very close eye on things. Including on my own security teams," he added grimly. "That damned Lt. Morris will probably be placing bets every time he thinks I'm not looking."

"Is only human," she said. "What are expecting? Should not be so hard on that one."

"Since when are you so quick to defend a human?" he asked testily.

"Expect little of humans," she said, pushing the access panel into place and securing it with a gentle kick. "Am not disappointed often."

"Unfortunately, I have to expect a great deal of them," Prilock replied. "Much as I might prefer it, I can't run this place without relying on them."

"Maybe will come by," she said, "maybe not."

"If not, I'll see you back here after hours." He tucked the data board under his arm and strode purposefully out of the ship.

Shaka decided to go a get a bite to eat before taking the ship out. She realized she had been so intent on her work that she hadn't stopped for lunch. So she packed up her tools and headed out. The walkway into the settlement was well-beaten, but still heavily overgrown on either side. The machete crews were constantly at work trying to keep the jungle of the swamp at bay. It was difficult to keep up with the grasses and vines which grew very quickly in the humid, fertile climate, filling in every empty space and crawling up the sides of every exposed wall.

Shaka heard the thick foliage moving beside her. She stopped, looking into the thicket of green and dark red but saw nothing. Her instincts were prickling, though, and her nostrils flared. A group of Moor traders passed her going the other way down the walkway towards the dock. She started walking again, her tail lashing back and forth uneasily. She saw something move out of the corner of her eye. There were four of them.

Dr. Yoshi was in the middle of doing a diagnostic on his main life support unit when he got a call from the security team.

"Security to medical."

"Yoshi here."

"We're bringing in four assault suspects for treatment. Two with superficial injuries, one serious, one critical."

"Excuse me," Yoshi said into the radio, "Did you say assault suspects or victims?"

"Suspects," Morris replied.

"Prilock," Yoshi sighed, shaking his head. When would those idiots learn not to mess with—

"No, not this time," Morris replied, a trace of amusement in his voice. "The intended victim, if you can call her that, is coming in, too, but reluctantly. She's got only minor injuries."

Moments later the security team came in, amidst much commotion, herding two rather battered looking Kurlu who were supporting a third, and carrying another on a stretcher. Shaka Mahdi was being escorted politely but firmly. "Am fine!" she protested loudly. "Only have cut! Is nothing!"

"Well, well, well," Yoshi said and called for the nurse. The assortment of broken bones and contusions was impressive, as was the gore covering the Byahail's boots. The skelran cut on her face was certainly not nothing; a nasty deep gash from just below her eye down to her jaw line, and it was bleeding profusely. But it was clear who had gotten the worst of the skirmish. Dr. Yoshi gave a quick examination of the man on the stretcher and realized he needn't waste any time on him. The man's chest cavity was crushed.

There was nothing to be done. He turned his attention to the others while the nurse, Christina, briskly overruled Shaka's protests and worked on closing the cut on her face.

Prilock burst into the room with an impatient demand of, "What's all this then?" Morris started to explain but Shaka cut him off.

"These ones ambush on walkway to port!" she cried. "Grab, say, 'Tell Castellan this is for Commodore Fenrire!' Then start to hit. So Shaka hit back!"

"So I see," Prilock said, assessing the damage done to her would-be assailants. He looked expectantly towards Lt. Morris.

"The team was out on routine patrol," Morris said. "They heard a commotion down by the docks, so they went to investigate. They discovered Captain Mahdi kicking the snot—pardon the expression—out of these Kurlu crewmen. When I heard what was happening I came immediately."

"Cowards!" Shaka spat, glaring at the Kurlu with contempt. "Are knowing are no match for Prilock, so try to avenge Commodore by attacking Shaka! Cowards! No honor!"

"And precious little sense," Prilock observed. "You are all right, I hope, Captain Mahdi?"

"Of course," she said, fidgeting as Christina tried to finish treating the cut. "Is nothing."

"How about them?" Prilock nodded towards the crewmen, who glared back in venomous hate.

"Well," Dr. Yoshi replied, "One was pretty much dead on arrival. I've got one here with a concussion and severe abdominal injuries, but he'll make it. The other two can be released any time."

There was the faintest trace of a smile on Prilock's face. "Very good. Lieutenant, take these two into custody and place a guard on the doctor's patient. I will inform their commander of the situation."

"Human filth!" Shaka spat at the prisoners as the security team led them out. "Cowards! And Commodore is even bigger coward! Tell that! From Shaka Mahdi!"

"I think you've made your point," Prilock said to her, not without a certain feeling of pride. The Byahail could take care of herself quite well. A most formidable beast.

She walked with a bit of a limp—she had apparently pulled a muscle in her leg during her encounter with Fenrire's crew— and her face hurt badly, but Shaka made an appearance at the Water Hole anyway. It was almost a matter of pride at this point to show up. But the crowds made her uncomfortable. She glanced around as she came in the door, assessing the situation. It was still a bit early, still a few empty tables. A number of locals had gathered around the gaming wheel, laughing and daring each other to give their luck a try. A woman in an elaborate and alluring costume was acting as croupier. That must have been the woman Prilock had mentioned, the one he felt uneasy about. She had dark skin and almond-shaped eyes like a Moor, but had the straight hair and narrow nose of a Northman. Her appearance was striking and she used it to good advantage, flirting with the patrons without encouraging them to familiarity, keeping their attention and directing it to the wheel. Obviously a professional.

Behind the bar was Haggus, pleased with himself and delighted with the success and profit he anticipated. There was also a woman Shaka did not recognize behind the bar. Apparently Haggus was so confident of success that he had hired an assistant.

Prilock was no where to be seen.

Shaka made her way towards the bar, resolved to stay and show no discomfort. She belonged here. She had a right to be here. They weren't going to drive her away. She passed a party of mixed Moor and Northmen who had already imbibed enough of Haggus's best to be exceedingly jolly. As Shaka made her way by one of them looked up and whistled. "Well, look at that! Do you believe it?"

"I'll be damned! Hey, fullserve!"

Shaka felt the feathers in her mane stiffen in rage at the crude slur.

"Turn around, fullserve! Let's get a look at you!"

Shaka spun around to snarl at them, "Human filth!"

The scruffy group laughed heartily, and one said, "Hey, that's no way to talk to a paying customer!"

"Yeah," said another, "Your boss pays you to be nice to us, remember?"

"Am not employed here!" she spat.

"No? Well, come on over! We'll give you some work!"

They all laughed in great whoops. Shaka trembled with rage but bit back on it. She had learned that striking back in such situations accomplished nothing. Besides, in the eyes of the law it would be she who was in the wrong if she struck the first blow, no matter what the verbal provocation. The best thing to do was simply walk away. She turned her back and did so, with forced, measured strides, squelching the urge to lash out, to break something or someone. She hated humans. How she hated humans!

She took a seat at the bar, glowering.

"Good evening, Captain!" Haggus said cheerfully. "What can I get for you?"

"Brandy," she growled.

"Sure thing! Say, that's a nasty cut. Somebody give you a hard time?"

"Humans!" she snapped. "Always are giving a hard time!"

"Hey," Haggus protested as he set the glass in front of her, "Have I ever given you a hard time?"

"No," she admitted. "Barkeeper show respect. Is true."

"Damn straight! I'm no bigot. Shall I put this on your tab?"

She nodded, taking a sizable sip. She turned to scowl briefly at the table that had harassed her. "But some humans!" she growled.

"You think it's bad now," Haggus said, "You should have seen the place before Prilock got here. Somebody like you wouldn't have lasted five minutes!"

"Castellan is strong and noble being," Shaka said proudly. "Make Farport place of law."

"Yeah, I got to hand it to the son of a bitch," Haggus said.

"Barkeeper is not liking Castellan."

"No, I don't particularly like him, and he knows it," he replied. "But I'll give him credit where credit is due. And unlike some of the bastards who have tried to run this settlement, he doesn't think he's above the law. He expects the same from everybody, including himself."

"Has much honor," she agreed. "Is good friend to have."

"Lucky you. I wish I knew how to get on his good side. He's been riding me ever since he got here."

"Barkeeper does not respect law. Break rules. What are expecting?"

"Listen, I'm only trying to make a living!" Haggus protested.

"Hah! Are just lazy. Is not easy to live by rules. But can be done. Must work hard and have honor."

"Oh, sure! And I suppose you always obey the rules all the time."

"Always," Shaka said firmly.

"Gods!" Haggus exclaimed, rolling his eyes, "No wonder the Castellan likes you!" He excused himself to go wait on another customer.

Shaka sipped on her brandy, keeping a wary eye on her surroundings. The Kurlu were starting to come in and that made her uneasy. She knew Prilock was around somewhere, carefully concealed. And she doubted anyone would pick a fight with her after the pasting she'd given Fenrire's would-be avengers. Word of such humiliations got around fast. Still, she hated sitting there by herself.

Shaka had just finished her first brandy and was debating whether to order another or give in to her uneasiness and leave, when she noticed that odd little Moor doctor coming over. He would not have been her first choice for a conversation, but she would have been hard-pressed to pick a second choice after Prilock, anyway. The doctor would probably do as well as anyone.

"Good evening, Captain!" the doctor said cheerfully. "How's that cheek doing?"

The question annoyed her. He had only just inspected it a few hours ago. That side of her face ached, and the cut itself stung every time she moved her facial muscles. It was unpleasant but it would heal. What more was there to say? "Is fine," she said.

"I must say, Captain, I am impressed with your fighting skills! Is that Byahail training? Or did you learn how to fight after leaving the Reservation?"

"All Byahail must know how to fight," Shaka said. "Thanks to humans."

The implied insult didn't seem to register. The doctor simply assumed an expression of sympathy. Shaka knew that expression. She had seen it on the faces of many U.P. people who tried to salve their guilt over what humans had done to the Byahail by expressing great concern over the Byahail history and situation. Their sincere but impotent concern did about as much for her people as the old gods did.

Haggus greeted the doctor and he ordered his usual schnapps. Shaka ordered another brandy. At least concern was better than indifference or contempt.

"I must say," Yoshi said, "I admire your courage. You must have faced incredible odds, coming off the Reservation as you did and trying to make your way in the world."

She shrugged. "Is same as Castellan. Always must be proving honesty. Proving worth."

"Yes," Yoshi said, nodding, "I guess you both have that in common. Not being human, I mean. Still, you've managed to overcome the handicap."

"Is not handicap," Shaka retorted. "Would not want to be human."

"Yes, of course." He was caught a bit off-balance by that. "Considering some of the humans I know I wouldn't blame you. But we're not all bad. Surely there have been humans who gave you a break, who played fair with you."

She thought of the freighter captain she had worked for. He had found her hiding in his ship after she had escaped from the brothel. He had let her stay on board, found work for her to do, and finally made her a regular member of his crew. He had always treated her with respect. And then there was the woman at the U.P. Credit Bureau who helped her get a loan to purchase her ship, carefully helping her with the paperwork, and pushing things through when prejudice got in the way. And then there were the people who first hired her, taking a chance on her, giving her the references that gave her legitimacy as a freighter captain. Yes, there had been humans who had treated her honorably.

"Is true," she said. "Is also true sometimes win on gaming wheel. Odds are not much different." She returned to quietly sipping her brandy.

"There you go, Doc," Haggus said. "Sorry it took so long. Had to open another bottle."

"No problem. Looks like you've got a big crowd for opening night."

"Yeah," Haggus said with a grin. "This is gonna be fantastic for business. In fact, I hired an assistant. Maggie, her name is. She married that character who runs the food store down by the rooming house."

"Ah, yes! Brock, I think his name is. Just moved in last year."

"That's the guy."

Yoshi nodded over towards the wheel. "Where did you find the croupier? She looks like a real pro."

"She is," Haggus said proudly. "Came in on a transport a couple of days ago. Heard we were putting in a gaming wheel and wondered if we had anybody to run it. I said no, and she said she used to work at a big Casino up in Malowi. So I said I'd give her a shot at it. And look at her! Slick as you please."

"Yes, she seems marvelous," Yoshi agreed. "A real way with the crowd. And what a beautiful woman!"

"Ain't she a dream? Her name's 'Pousse.' Man, I can't believe my luck at getting somebody like her! If she works out, she'll be worth every credit of the salary she wants."

The doctor shook his head. "I wonder what the hell she's doing looking for work in a place like this?"

"I wondered the same thing," Haggus said. "She claims she had to leave Malowi for personal reasons. That's good enough for me."

Shaka looked over at the croupier. "Castellan is suspicious," she said. "Is checking references."

"Oh, great!" Haggus groaned. "If they find something, I'll scream."

"You know Prilock," Yoshi said with a smile. "If she has any kind of record at all he'll be on her like a buckfly. Speaking of whom, I wonder where he is? I'd expect him to have a front row seat to keep his eye on things."

"Oh, he's around, all right. You can bet on that. Probably disguised as a light fixture or something, listening to our every word. Eh, Captain?"

"Prilock is here." Shaka disliked the flippant way they talked about the Castellan. It was not respectful.

Haggus looked up and raised his hand in a mock salute of greeting. "Lt. Morris! Good to see you! I'd offer you a drink, but I know you must be on duty."

"Unfortunately, yes. The Castellan's called out the whole royal guard to be sure things don't get out of hand. Good evening, Doctor." Morris glanced politely over at Shaka. "Good evening, Captain. That was a hell of a good fight you fought today."

It was, wasn't it? Shaka thought, secretly pleased. "Thank you," she said to Morris.

"So, what was the trouble?" Haggus asked.

Damned busy-body gossip, Shaka thought.

"Haven't you heard?" Morris exclaimed. "Remember that Kurlu commodore the Castellan put in his place last night? Well, four of his crew—four of them, mind you, and all of 'em big and ugly as a striped behemoth—jumped Captain Mahdi earlier today. She put three of them in the infirmary and one of 'em in the morgue."

"No kidding?" Haggus said, impressed. "You didn't tell me that, Captain."

"Is not true," she said. "Only put one in infirmary. Two are released. Only minor injuries."

Haggus exploded into laughter. "No kidding! Damn! You're almost as dangerous as the Castellan! Have another brandy, Captain! On the house!"

She inclined her head in polite acceptance of the offer, permitting herself to enjoy their admiration. Human company is not so bad sometimes, Shaka thought.

One of the security people told Pousse that as soon as she was off-duty the Castellan wanted to see her. It was late, and she was tired, but one did not refuse the Castellan. She had a feeling she knew what he wanted to see her about. Pousse had hoped that a backwater dive like the Water Hole wouldn't check her references too closely. Apparently, no such luck.

She had seen him watching her later in the evening. Even without the uniform she would have known who he was. Cold, flinty eyes and a chiseled, angular face; his scowl could wither frivolity at a glance. Haggus had warned her about him. He wasn't human, although he looked human enough, and everyone she talked to was very evasive about what he was if not human. So Pousse felt more than a little nervous as she went into his spare, rigidly neat and well-lit office.

"You wanted to see me, Sir?"

He looked up at her from behind his desk. Most men she felt confident she could charm and soften with just a little effort. But she could tell immediately her best efforts would be wasted on Castellan Prilock. He was steel and ice.

"Yes," he said, holding up a data board and looking it over. "You were less than candid on your application for employment at the Water Hole."

"I put down nothing that wasn't true," she said.

He fixed her with a frosty stare. "That may be so, Madam, but what you conveniently neglected to mention was that you were convicted of a serious offense, paid a heavy fine, and served three years in the Kaywa Correctional Facility. Isn't that so?"

She winced mentally. There was no point in trying to deny it. "I served my time, Sir," she said. "I've paid my debt. I just want a chance to leave my past behind and start over."

"One cannot leave one's past behind, Madam," Prilock said sharply. "One's actions have consequences and one must learn to live with them."

"Yes, Sir. I know I made a mistake, but—"

He cut her off. "You were involved in a conspiracy to cheat the customers and defraud the Casino. By law, this sort of conviction bars you from ever working in a gambling establishment again."

"I realize that, Sir," she tried to explain, "but I thought since Farport is located in a territory—"

"You could have applied to me for a waiver. But you didn't do that, did you? You chose instead to falsify your employment application and mislead your employer. This choice of action does not inspire great confidence in me as to your sincerity."

"I apologize, Sir," she said, trying to keep her voice calm. The son of a bitch. The hard-ass son of a bitch. "I realize I have handled this badly. Perhaps I could start over. I really do need this job, and it is the only work I know."

"You could learn another trade," Prilock replied.

"But I am very good at what I do! You can ask Haggus—"

"I am not concerned with your job performance," he said shortly, tossing the data board onto the desk. "I am concerned with keeping the peace and upholding the law."

Son of a bitch. Bloody, heartless son of a bitch. "Please, Sir, just give me a chance. I promise you'll have no trouble from me."

"I am already having trouble with you," he retorted. "You may remain in Farport if you choose, but you will have to find some other form of employment. I don't want to see you in the Water Hole again except as a patron."

"But Sir—!"

His forbidding expression silenced her immediately. "Be glad that I don't intend to bring charges against you for falsifying your application," he said. "That is all. You may go now."

Pousse choked down anger. They were right. He wasn't human.

"Yes, Sir," she said coldly and turned to go.

Shaka had just about given up waiting for Prilock to get in. She went to the upper deck of the *Chimera* for one last smoke before going to bed. The ship was moving slightly in the water. There must have been a heavy rainfall somewhere that was raising the level of the swamp. The storm would probably reach them by daybreak. From the upper deck she could see through the thick foliage to the settlement. Most of the lights were out. It was well past closing. She wondered what business was holding Prilock up. Then she saw him coming down the walkway towards the dock.

"Is late," she said, coming down to the main deck to meet him.

"I had a bit of unpleasantness to clear up," he said, following her into the cabin. "That croupier I told you about. It seems my suspicions were justified."

"Pousse? Is too bad. Everyone is liking. What is wrong?"

"She has a felony conviction that bars her from working in a gambling establishment. That's why she couldn't work in the Northwest." They went through the cabin to the back, Shaka talking over her shoulder to Prilock.

"But Farport is in territory. Castellan can make exception, yes?"

"Yes, I could have, if she had approached me. But she didn't. She tried to get away with lying to Haggus instead." He sat down on the edge of the bunk. Shaka leaned against the support.

"Haggus does not care," Shaka said. "Is liking Pousse a lot. Good croupier is good for business."

"That's not the point," Prilock said. "The course of action she chose to take indicates to me she can't be trusted. If I let her work in the Water Hole she might very well start in with her old tricks. And if she gets caught, it all comes back on me."

"Is not such a big thing, is it?"

He leaned back against the wall. "For an ordinary administrator, no. But I am under special scrutiny. There are a number of high-level officials in the U.P. who raised hell at the notion of me being assigned the post of castellan here. There are those who opposed the notion of me being granted basic civil liberties at all. They would be far happier if I had remained safely contained in the labs, spending my time doing tricks for the researchers."

Shaka nodded. "Are watching carefully, eh?"

"Exceedingly carefully," Prilock said. "I'm sticking my neck out by granting Haggus a gambling permit. If I let him hire a former felon as a croupier and she takes off with half the profits, there are going to be all sorts of triumphant howls about my lack of judgement and integrity."

"But, Prilock makes Farport place of law. No human castellan ever do that. No credit for that?"

"Oh, I've gotten plenty of credit for that. But if I make a serious blunder, all that credit is spent. One more mistake and it's back to the labs for the U.P.'s famous Anomaly Number 35719."

Shaka nodded. "Am seeing problem." She sat down on a chair and began to pull off her boots. "Am thinking," she said, "Pousse will be hard to replace. Hard to find good croupier to work in place like Water Hole. Is too bad. Good croupier mean good business. Good for Haggus. Good for Farport. People make much money, all legal. Is good to make easy for humans to make money legal. Humans are lazy. Little honor. If can't make honest living, will cheat."

Prilock sighed. "I know. And I can't help wondering if Pousse will simply take her talents to the black market if she can't earn a living legitimately."

"Not problem of Castellan," Shaka said, tossing her boots aside.

"No, I suppose not. But as you are so fond of pointing out to me, humans are only human and one cannot expect them to be otherwise. If this woman is sincere in her desire to reform herself, and I frustrate her instead of encouraging her, she might well become bitter and say to hell with trying to play by the rules. I can't expect her to do as you or I would do, sticking to what is honorable and honest in spite of the difficulties. Most humans simply aren't that way."

"Is true." She stripped off her suit and sat down on the bunk next to Prilock. "Have advice for Castellan," she said. "Go to sleep. Make decision in morning."

"I've already made my decision," he said. "I can't very well go back on it. It wouldn't look good."

"So what?" Shaka replied. "Is more important to do right thing than to look good. Change mind if is right thing. Is more honorable to admit mistake."

He nodded reluctantly. "I suppose you are right about that, too. Well, to hell with it for tonight. A few hours of peaceful torpor will do me a world of good." He grumbled as he began to melt over her, "It's hell sometimes being a superior being."

"Is better than being human," she replied, lying back on the bunk with a contented sigh.

Bright and early Prilock was at the Water Hole as Haggus opened for business.

"Good morning, Barkeeper," he said as he came in.

"That's a fine joke!" Haggus snarled. "Thanks again for screwing up my life, Prilock!"

"I take it you've already spoken to Pousse."

"Yes I have! Do you realize what a bloody, roaring, pain in the ass it's going to be to replace her? What have you got against me, will you tell me that? Why do you take such bastardly pleasure in making my life miserable?"

"Because you respond with such gratifying fury," Prilock replied smoothly. "Unfortunately, my delight in your misery is going to be short-lived. I've changed my mind regarding Pousse."

Haggus froze in his tracks. "You have?"

"Yes. I've decided that keeping you honest just isn't enough of a challenge anymore. I think it would be marvelously stimulating to complicate my job by allowing you to hire a former felon as a croupier."

"You're kidding."

"About it being marvelously stimulating? Yes, I confess you're quite right. I actually think it's going to be a wretched headache."

"Gods damn it, Prilock!" Haggus exclaimed. "Are you saying you'll grant Pousse a waiver to work here?"

"If she still wants to work here and is willing to ask me for it, yes. Although why she'd want to work for a blustering trout like you is beyond me."

"Maggie!" Haggus bellowed, "Watch the register! I gotta catch that transport before it leaves!" He tore out of the Water Hole, his feet barely touching the ground.

Prilock nodded with satisfaction and left to go on his usual rounds.

CHAPTER 3

"Sir, we've got three ships scheduled to dock this afternoon which haven't called in as required."

Prilock looked up from the papers on his desk to address the intercom. "Are they registered for hazardous routes?" he asked.

"Yes Sir. All three are coming in from the far Southeast, two freighters and a transport."

"How late are they?"

"The transport has missed one checkpoint, the freighters both missed the last two."

"Give me their names and registries. I'll call it in to U.P. Rescue." He picked up a pen.

"Just a moment, Sir." There was a pause. Prilock tapped the pen impatiently. "The transport just called in. They apologize for being tardy."

"Note the name of the captain," Prilock said. "I'll want to speak with him when the ship docks." There was a reason for these regulations, Prilock thought irritably. "What about the missing freighters?"

"We've got the Marellen, registration UPFT 678-39, captain is Fritz Morn. And—"

"Yes," Prilock asked impatiently, "What about the other?"

"It's—it's the *Chimera*, Sir."

Prilock followed the stretcher as they brought it off the patrol ship and hurried it to the infirmary. The commander of the patrol boat walked with him, matching the rapid pace. "We found her adrift in a weed-choked waterway off the main channel," the commander said. "The ship was pretty much stripped. They took everything they could pry off it. Almost certainly it was pirates."

"What about Captain Mahdi?"

"Can't tell you, Castellan. My medic never worked on Byahail before. We didn't even think it was alive at all until the crewman carrying the body insisted it didn't feel dead. Our medic can't verify its status either way. Maybe your doctor can do better."

Dr. Yoshi was ready for them. They pulled the blanket away and moved her onto the table. The doctor felt sickened by what he saw. What the pirates had done to her was brutal beyond belief. She can't be alive, Yoshi thought, and almost thought it a mercy. But she didn't seem to be dead, either. He couldn't detect a heartbeat or any kind of respiration, but the flesh was still resilient, and blood still oozed wetly from the innumerable cuts and gashes. He'd feel silly trying to patch up a corpse, but maybe there was something about Byahail physiology that he didn't know, and it would be a tragedy if he gave up on her before she was really gone. So he dutifully began an intravenous drip and began patching up the holes.

"Doctor?"

Yoshi looked up at Prilock. The Castellan was standing there, to all appearances as cool as ever. But Yoshi noticed an unnatural brightness in his eyes. And he seemed to be trembling very slightly. "I don't know," Yoshi said. "I'll do what I can."

Prilock turned towards the U.P. commander. "Is there any way of finding out who is responsible for this?"

"I'm afraid not," the commander replied. "Like with most pirate attacks, they covered their tracks. The way the ship was looted and stripped was pretty typical. The assault on the captain was unusually violent, but not unknown to happen sometimes. It was a Byahail, after all."

"What the hell difference would that make?" Prilock exploded. But he knew damn well what difference it made.

The commander's expression was sympathetic. "I understand the captain was a friend of yours. I'm sorry."

"It doesn't matter who the captain was. This outrage demands justice!"

"Of course. We'll do whatever we can. But unless Captain Mahdi recovers enough to give us some kind of lead, I'm afraid we won't have much luck."

Prilock nodded curtly. It was obscenely clear. There would be no justice done.

"You'll have to excuse me," the commander said. "We still have to try to find that other missing freighter."

Prilock barely acknowledged the commander's departure. It was catching up with him fast. If she had simply disappeared, or even just been killed, neat and cold, he could have handled it. But this, seeing her dying right in front of him, her body slashed and hacked apart, it was too much.

"May I be alone with her?" he said, too loudly, too abruptly.

Yoshi shrugged. "It can't do any harm. I've done all I can for her. " He motioned the nurse to follow him. The door swished quietly shut.

Prilock was trembling so badly he could barely hold his form. He would find the ones who did this. He would resign his post and spend the rest of his existence hunting them down. He stood over her, enraged and bewildered. How could any thinking, feeling being do this to another living thing? What kind of monster would commit such an atrocity? Such a monster deserved to die in the worst way possible. And more was the pity that such a monster could not die more than once.

Prilock reached down and touched her face, melting his hand over the skin exposed between the bandages. Instead of the old familiar sense of comfort the physical contact gave, he felt an intense void, like a bitter cold that drew the warmth from his hand. The hungry cold drew him down to her. Without hesitation he relaxed his form, covering her gently like a blanket, letting her draw in the warmth from him.

The doctor waited as long as he dared before going back in to check on his patient. He didn't want to disturb the Castellan, but there was a chance that, with diligence, he could pull her through. So, his eyes lowered respectfully, he went back into the treatment room. He was not prepared to see his patient lying encased in dark brown jelly.

"Blessed gods!" Yoshi gasped. The jelly hastily oozed off onto the floor and transmuted back up into the familiar form of the Castellan. The doctor rushed over, staring in astonishment at the medical indicators. "What did you do?" he demanded.

Prilock started to stammer, "Why, I was—I was just—" Then he stopped, following the doctor's gaze, inexpertly trying to read the indicators. "Is she improving?"

"I'm getting a pulse and respiration! It's pretty weak, but it's a hell of an improvement on nothing! Whatever you did, it worked!"

"I'll be damned," Prilock murmured.

The doctor examined her carefully. Sure enough, all her vital signs were beginning to register where he'd been getting nothing before. "What did you do?" Yoshi pleaded. "What were you doing when I came in?"

It wasn't something Prilock particularly cared to discuss with an outsider. It was intimate business between Shaka and himself. But there seemed no way to get out of it gracefully. "It seems," he explained stiffly, "That her species and mine share some sort of sympathetic biochemical compatibility. When I am in my neutral state, physical contact between us induces a state of tranquility and a sense of well-being." He added, "It seemed worth a try."

"Fascinating!" the doctor breathed. "I've heard of such things but I've never seen an actual example of it. If it—"

He was distracted by a slight movement. Shaka shifted uneasily. Her raw, cracked lips formed a word, breathing it rather than speaking it: "Prilock."

"I'm here," he said, bending over her and melting his arms over her. The doctor watched in mixed astonishment and disgust at the spectacle of the Castellan turning into slime all over his patient. Her eyes flickered but she couldn't open them. Her lips moved again soundlessly. Prilock leaned close, putting his ear next to her mouth and sharpening his hearing as much as possible. She spoke two syllables and then sighed back into unconsciousness. The doctor couldn't hear what she said. But it was clear enough to Prilock. And it filled him with a fierce sense of fury and purpose. It was all he needed to know. She said, "Fenrire."

It was quite simple to track down Fenrire. He was, after all, the commander of a large and wealthy merchant fleet. Less than an hour of discreet research gave Prilock the information he required. He then put in for a leave of absence. He expected it would be readily granted. He hadn't taken so much as a coffee break since he was assigned there. He disliked leaving someone else in charge, and reluctantly settled on Lt. Morris. The chief of security was a logical choice, and although Morris could be irritatingly frivolous at times, and entirely too prone to horseplay, he was in Prilock's estimation the most competent officer available. The Castellan fully expected the mice to come out and play gleefully in his absence, but it could not be helped. Prilock had to take care of this matter himself. Nothing in the laws of the U.P. would supply the justice the situation required.

As soon as he received approval for his leave he arranged for a private transport. Then he called Lt. Morris into his office to brief him. Morris listened quietly to what he was told, nodding periodically to the list of duties he'd be expected to perform in the Castellan's absence, answering firmly and confidently when asked if he understood. At the end of the briefing, as Prilock was putting his desk in order, Morris spoke up.

"You're going after them, aren't you, Sir."

Prilock looked up sharply. "My business is my own," he replied, and continued sorting his paperwork into neat piles.

"Of course, Sir," Morris said firmly. "It's absolutely no business of mine where you are going. Will there be anything else, Sir?"

"Just keep the vandals outside the gates, Lieutenant, and don't get creative," Prilock replied. "And make damn sure the reports get filed on time, got that?"

"Yes, Sir. You can count on me."

"I hope so," Prilock muttered, picking up his case and walking towards the door.

"Sir?" Morris said as he walked by him.

"Yes?"

"Good luck," Morris said quietly.

Prilock looked at him evenly. "They are the ones who are going to need the luck," he said with quiet intensity, and he strode out the door.

He stopped by the infirmary one more time before he left.

"As usual," Yoshi said, "she improves while you're with her and her progress levels off when you're gone."

Prilock melted his hand against her cheek. She felt much better to him. The cold hunger was gone. But true warmth and responsiveness hadn't yet returned.

"She told you something, didn't she?" the doctor asked. "Somehow she communicated something to you and you think you know who her attackers are." Prilock ignored him. The doctor raised his voice. "I'm right, aren't I? That's why you're leaving, isn't it?"

Prilock looked up at him coldly. Still he said nothing.

"Has it occurred to you," Yoshi said angrily, "that your presence here, with her, might do her a whole lot more good than vengeance will? I can keep her alive, but there doesn't seem to be a whole lot more that I can do. She needs you!"

"I will be back," Prilock said, looking down at Shaka's still form, heavily bandaged. Heavily damaged. Barely breathing. "Just keep her alive until I return."

Dr. Yoshi slammed his hand down on the desk. "Damn it, Prilock! If you know something, then for gods' sake turn it over to the proper authorities and let them handle it!"

Prilock drew himself up, freezing the doctor with a stare as cold and unreachable as an Arctic peak. "I don't expect you to be able to grasp the nature of my understanding with Shaka Mahdi, but you had better realize that it takes precedence over human business. When I return I will be your damned castellan again. I'll conform to your damned human rules and enforce your damned human laws. But as of now and until then, I am not your creature!" Prilock picked up his case and left.

After sagging in defeat for a moment or so, Yoshi went over to check Shaka's vital signs. The brief surge in cell regeneration had begun again to slow to a crawl.

Yoshi began to study everything he could find in the medical data base about Byahail physiology. But the more he read, the more puzzled he became. Nothing in all the research he checked could explain why Shaka Mahdi was alive. And the more he looked the more jarring were the discrepancies between the records and the tests he'd done on his patient. It just didn't make any sense. The Byahail were not human, but they were still mere flesh and blood creatures, subject to the same general physical laws as any other creature. The failure of a major organ meant death to the organism. That was all there was to it.

Microscopic analysis of Shaka Mahdi's tissue raised more questions. The tissue was noticeably different from the samples in the textbooks. There were elements that were completely atypical for a Byahail, or any other known organism. He couldn't figure it out until, just for comparison, he called up and began to examine the records of Anomaly Number 35719, a.k.a. "Prilock." Abruptly things began to fall into place. Tests on the tissues of the anomaly showed, instead of cells, innumerable tiny threads which all interconnected to form a fluid whole, and which, it was theorized, could be manipulated to mimic the structure of virtually any kind of matter. How it actually was done the scientists of the U.P. laboratories had no idea.

Tiny threads identical to the ones in the samples from Anomaly 35719 were distributed thinly all through the tissue samples from Shaka Mahdi.

Intensely excited by his discovery, Yoshi kept working, making comparisons, trying to figure out how it worked until finally exhaustion caught up with him. He felt himself sagging, his eyes burning from staring at a computer screen and the fine print of texts. He was about ready to call it quits and lie down for at least an hour or two when he was jolted wide awake by an eerie high-pitched keening. It was inarticulate, or perhaps it was a language he did not recognize. It was coming from the infirmary. Shaka Mahdi had regained consciousness.

"Shaka, it's all right! You're safe, now. You're among friends—" He tried to take her hand to comfort her. She recoiled weakly, wailing, "Not to touch! Not to touch! Not! Not!"

"All right," he said, hastily backing off. "It's Doctor Yoshi. Do you understand? Do you recognize me?"

"Am ruined!" she cried in that thin, high voice, so utterly uncharacteristic and disturbing. "Am ruined! Is pain! All is pain and ruin!"

"No, you're going to be all right," Yoshi insisted in a reassuring voice. "You are healing, getting better. We didn't think you were going to make it, but you're doing just fine."

"Stupid human. Never fine. Never again. Ruined. Am destroyed. Am destroyed." Her voice fell away into faint keening.

"I can give something for the pain," Yoshi said. "I might have been too conservative with the dosage—"

"Is no use," she whispered, shaking her head slowly from side to side. "Future is torn out." She closed her eyes. "Am destroyed."

"Shaka, I'll do whatever I can—" Yoshi said gently, helplessly.

"Too many to fight," she whispered. "And that one."

"Who was it, Shaka? Who did this to you?"

Her eyes opened again, one still swollen partially shut, the other bright and black and filled with horror. "Fenrire," she said.

Dr. Yoshi now understood Prilock's departure.

The security guard came to the end of the long corridor and checked the locks on the large double doors. He flashed his light with a briskness born of tedious routine, glancing to either side of the stacked crates. Then he turned and headed back down the corridor, pausing here and there to check beneath the great suspended drums of chemicals, or behind the metal shelves. The motions were all habitual; he looked without really seeing, thinking of the credits he had lost at lots last evening and how he was going to win them back, and whether he was going to get lucky with the new barmaid he had his eye on. Only the presence of something obviously out of place— like another human being—would have jerked his attention back to his job.

The guard's footsteps receded into the distance, echoing off the high ceiling of the warehouse. A puddle of brown ooze flowed out from under a palette. It ran up the side of a crate, sending tiny feelers into it, then running down the other side. It flowed up and down the aisles of crates and barrels, testing, seeking, searching. Its modified sensory organs easily spotted the tight beams of the security system, avoided them, sliding under and around them. It seeped under doors and into locked cabinets, silently and swiftly, leaving no trace behind, nothing to alert even the most wary investigator that it had been there. When it heard the guard approaching again on his rounds it sank into a drain, waiting, perfectly still, until the guard was gone. Then it emerged and resumed its steady, systematic search.

Concealed in crates with prosaically misleading labels it found the evidence it was searching for. Parts from a customized single pilot freighter, hastily dismantled, all ID marks carefully effaced, but still bearing signs of the distinctive handiwork of Shaka Mahdi. Her endless, meticulous tinkering over time had made her ship unique. Anyone familiar with the *Chimera* would have recognized the components.

True justice demanded more proof than mere circumstantial evidence, no matter how damning. There must be no mistake. No other possible explanation. No room for reasonable doubt. There was more work to be done.

The brown ooze flowed up and out of a vent in the roof, running down the wall onto the ground, then through the mesh of the fence. It paused for a moment, alert, and then it took the form of a large, dark brown dog with baleful yellow eyes. The dog loped off through the night towards the lights of the town.

Dr. Yoshi was asleep in his chair with his head on his desk when Christina came in that morning. She greeted him and asked how their patient was doing.

"Well, she finally regained consciousness last night," he said, stretching and twisting stiffly.

"No kidding? That's great! I'm going to make myself a cup of coffee. Bet you could use one, too."

"Gods, yes!" Yoshi groaned, trying to stand up. "Don't bother to put it in a cup, just prepare an IV for me."

"So, Shaka Mahdi came out of it, eh? How is she doing?" She took the coffee paraphernalia out of the sterilizer where they stored them and began setting up on the counter.

"About as well as you'd expect. Pretty traumatized. But she did tell me who assaulted her."

"Oh? Who?"

Yoshi pushed some papers aside and sat on the edge of the desk. "Remember Commodore Fenrire? Came through here a while ago with a fleet of Kurlu merchant ships. Prilock had a run-in with him in the Water Hole, and a couple of Fenrire's men decided to take it out on Shaka Mahdi."

"Oh, yeah! How could I forget?" Christina said, looking up from measuring coffee into the filter. "It was four against one and she still beat the daylights out of them. So, they decided to get even, is that it?"

"Something like that, I would assume," Yoshi said. "I'd say there was a bit of escalation involved, wouldn't you?"

"A bit, yes." Christina shook her head with disgust.

"Anyway, she is pretty devastated. She won't eat, all she does is lay there and moan. I don't know, somehow I expected the Byahail to be more of a survivor than this."

Christina looked up sharply. "A tough exterior can hide some real weaknesses sometimes," she said. "Besides, we can only imagine what they put her through. Somehow I don't think hers is an unreasonable response." She returned her attention to the coffee. It began to drip, the smell filling the room.

"Of course, of course," Dr. Yoshi said hastily. "I didn't really mean to imply it was unreasonable. It's just that I don't know what to do. How to reach her. She doesn't want to live. And I'm not sure why."

Christina took a deep breath, letting it out with measured patience. "How do you think you'd feel if you'd been humiliated, raped and tortured? Just filled to bursting with joie de vivre, I'm sure!"

"Christina, for heaven's sake, stop twisting around the meaning of what I say! Is that coffee ready yet?"

"Yes, help yourself. I have an errand to run."

"Where the hell are you going?" he demanded. "You just got here!"

"Listen, I'll be right back. In the meantime, just do me a favor and stay out of the infirmary. Let me handle Shaka Mahdi, okay?" She scurried out the door.

"I can't stay out of the bloody infirmary!" he shouted after her, "I'm the bloody doctor!"

It was good to be back in home port.

Commodore Fenrire sat back in his chair, one hand on the table wrapped around the handle of a mug of fine ale. Below the raised deck where those of true rank and wealth sat, was the floor of the alehouse, where the ordinary rabble drank and whored. There were exclusive clubs where many officers went where they could avoid the rabble altogether. Fenrire didn't feel comfortable in those sorts of clubs. Too stuffy. Here he could get together with others of his rank and kind and really relax. Swap gossip, which was mostly lies, and news, which was mostly gossip. Here a man could tell a really blue tale and not have to worry about some elitist type acting insulted. And here the whores were whores, and didn't try to act like proud ladies. This was the sort of atmosphere Fenrire preferred.

The commodore was a hands-on person. He liked to do things personally, instead of hiring someone else to do his dirty business for him. Of course, he enjoyed flexing his power by making other people do things for him. But he often disciplined his men personally, settled his debts in person, and preferred to procure his women himself. Whores didn't fight back convincingly.

It was this personal touch that got him his prosperity. He saw to it things got done right. Screw-ups answered directly to him, and he made sure they didn't screw up again. And if he wanted something, he went after it, he didn't wait for somebody to give it to him. He had acquired a good deal of wealth. But that didn't eliminate the need to acquire more. Wealth was like women: The true pleasure was in taking possession, not in the having afterwards. And the more fiercely competitive the battle, the better. Fenrire enjoyed the taste of blood in his encounters with both men and women.

"Ever get to Sebu these days?"

"Not lately," Fenrire replied. "Import agents in Karzan pay as good a price as the ones in Sebu, and I save my fleet a day's travel."

"Is that so? Who're you dealing with?"

"Why should I tell you, you old pirate!" Fenrire sneered. "You'd only try to cut into my business!"

"Enough talk of business," another growled. "We're here to relax!"

"Aye! Where can a man find a decent whore in this town? I don't want one filthy with pox!"

"In this town? God's prick! You'd have to catch 'em coming out o' their mother!"

"Yeah, Fenrire's spoiled 'em all!"

"If they're walking the streets, they're fair game," Fenrire said. "That's what I figure."

"Had a right tawny one from Simpan on my last trip. Couldn't have been more 'n twelve, but she filled out a corset like a matron. Sweet as honey she was. Had that shy look when she spread 'em. And the prettiest moans you ever heard."

"You're a romantic, you are, Carper!" said a captain from further east. They tolerated his company because he was free with his money. "If I don't hear 'em scream I figure I ain't pushin' it in deep enough."

"Some o' the whores I've seen you could bloody crawl up inside 'em and they'd hardly notice."

They all laughed and snorted, and drank to that, and waved to the serving wench to bring another round.

Fenrire broke a lull in the conversation. "I had a piece of something my last time out that I'm willing to wager none of you buggers have ever had."

"That's quite a brag, you old liar!"

"Let's hear it! Make it good."

"Any of you pox-ridden old sinners ever have a Byahail?"

They responded with hoots of derision.

"By the tit of the goddess, that's the worst lie you ever told!"

"Aye! Where the hell did you manage to find a fullserve?"

"What did you do, raid the Reservation?"

"This is no yarn," he said smugly, sipping his ale. "It's fact that you can read in the U.P. police reports."

Interest at the table picked up. "All right, Fenrire," said the captain, "You've got our attention. Let's hear the story."

"Well, this fullserve dared to raise itself up on its hind legs and pretend to be as good as human. Wore a freighter captain's uniform, had a ship, and was taking business away from real freighters."

"Aye! I've heard o'the beast! Hangs around Farport in U.P. territory."

"That's the one."

"Hah! I've seen it!" another snorted. "Proud as a cock it is and full of airs. And a scrapper. I don't believe you had a piece of it! In fact, I hear the beast took down four o'your best men. The bloody fullserve would cut it off before you could get it in!" The others chuckled.

"Oh, it put up a fight, to be sure," Fenrire acknowledged with a wolfish grin. "But in the end, I got my piece. And more. I did it up and did it in. Finest bit of fun I've had in a good long time. You see, it was personal. A man can't just take an insult to himself and his crew and let it go. Something has to be done, or he loses respect. But I had a special reason to do that fullserve up right and leave it for the U.P. to find. You've all heard of the castellan of Farport, haven't you?"

"Aye! A nasty piece o' work that whore's bastard is! Who hasn't heard of him!"

"Threw five o' my men into his bloody jail and wouldn't let 'em go 'til I paid a ridiculous fine! Poor sots weren't guilty o' nothing but just having a bit o' fun."

"He ain't human, though I'll be hanged and sunk in the swamp if I know what in bugger-all he is!"

"If you took him down a notch or two I'd buy you a keg!"

Fenrire casually sipped his ale, enjoying the distinction the tale was bringing him. "I expect he was pretty upset when they brought in his pet all used and busted up."

"The fullserve was his?"

Fenrire nodded.

"You don't say?"

"Well, I'll be bloody damned!"

"So, Commodore, is it true what they say about fullserves?"

"They come by the name honestly," Fenrire replied. "When the gods were handing out equipment, fullserves got in line twice. And still weren't satisfied!"

They howled with laughter, and someone asked, "Tell us! Was it as good as they say it is?"

"You'll never know how good!"

"Damn you, Fenrire! You always get all the luck!"

He shrugged and replied, "I just make full use of my opportunities. So, how about that keg, Carper?"

"Send your boy to see my boy tomorrow," Carper replied heartily. "It's well worth it to be able to lie in my bed tonight imagining the expression on that bugger Prilock's face when they brought his beast in!"

They bought another round to toast Fenrire and the trumping he'd done to the castellan of Farport, the unnatural son of a bitch. Then the captain from farther east turned to the stranger sitting beside him, a smartly dressed commodore none of them recognized. Each of them had just naturally assumed that someone else knew him and had invited him to the table. The captain clapped him on the back and said, "You've been pretty quiet this evening. Surely you must have some story you can tell us."

"Aye," said another. "What's your favorite brothel?"

"I've never paid for it in my life!" the stranger declared, and they all laughed heartily in appreciative disbelief.

The hour grew late and they each said their goodnights and went their separate ways. Outside the ale house the stranger paused, standing in the shadows. He spat once with disgust, and then melted down into a brown dog with baleful eyes which trotted purposefully off into the night.

Shaka Mahdi struggled up from yet another nightmare of help-lessness and terror. As she shook herself awake she could hear a gentle voice saying, "It's just a dream. You're safe now. No one can hurt you here."

Christina sat by the bed, putting a book aside. "I've been waiting for you to wake up. I wanted to be here when you did."

Shaka looked at her with weary despair. "Why are caring?"

"I want to help you if I can."

"Let Shaka die." She closed her eyes, lying back.

"I know that must seem like the only answer right now," Christina said, "But you must believe that it will get better."

"Never get better. Am destroyed. Am cripple. Am killed inside. Future is torn out."

"You're still alive. And part of you wants very much to live, or you wouldn't have made it this far." The nurse leaned over to a table, taking an insulated bottle and pouring out some of the contents into a cup. "Good. It's still warm. Just the right temperature, in fact." She put a straw into it and offered it to Shaka. "Try some."

"Don't want."

"It will make you feel better, I know it. It's warm and sweet and delicious, and entirely too rich. But when I feel miserable I make myself a huge glass of it and drink it all myself."

"What is?"

"It's made with chocolate and cream. Try a sip."

"Don't want."

"Just a sip. I'll nag you until you do, but if you'll just try it, I promise I won't push you to drink any more." She held the cup and the straw to Shaka's lips. She saw the Byahail's nose twitch, tempted by the rich smell. Reluctantly, she took a sip.

"Is good," she admitted softly.

"There, you see? I'll hold it for you. You take as much as you want."

"Is no point," Shaka sighed.

"Your body badly needs strength right now," Christina said. "I'll admit this isn't the most nutritious substance known to man, but it will help. And it will make you feel better."

"Is nothing can make Shaka feel better. Is only pain. Is only fear."

"I know it seems that way now," Christina said. "It's hard to imagine you could ever want to live again. But it does get better."

"What does human know?" Shaka said with weak resentment. "Know nothing. Stupid human."

Christina put the cup aside. "Shaka, when I was a lot younger, seventeen, in fact, I used to sneak out of the house at night to meet with my friends and do all sorts of daring things that our parents wouldn't allow us to do. I'd been warned about hanging around places like the Water Hole and talking to strangers. But I didn't listen. And one night I paid for it. I'm not sure how many of them there were. I tried so hard to block the memory that now I'm fuzzy on a lot of the details. But I was raped repeatedly and left in an alley by the docks." Christina felt herself beginning to shake as she spoke, but she forced her voice to stay steady and to speak of the thing that still had the power to make her cry uncontrollably if she thought about it too much. "I was afraid to tell anyone what had happened to me. I was afraid of being punished for going out, that everyone would say I asked for it, that it was my own fault." She took a deep breath. "I couldn't live with the memory of it. It made me sick. I tried to commit suicide twice. The second time my parents took me to a doctor to try to find out what was wrong with me. Finally the truth came out. I began to heal. But it took me a long time to put my life back together." There, she had said. it. She had gotten it all out. She looked over at Shaka. The Byahail was watching her intently. "Anyway, Christina concluded, "I know that what happened to me wasn't as bad as what happened to you. Not nearly. I wasn't beaten or tortured. But I think that because of it I have some idea of how you feel. I think I can begin to understand in a small way."

Shaka continued to watch her silently for a few moments. It was impossible to guess what she was thinking. Finally she asked, "No justice for Christina? Not punish ones who do horror?"

Christina shook her head. "No. By the time I finally could talk about it they were long gone. And I don't think I could have identified them anyway. And even if I could have, I don't think I could have stood to look at them."

Again there was a long silence. Then the Byahail asked, "Christina not lose future?"

"I'm not sure I understand what you mean," she said, suspecting the word had more significance to the Byahail than its usual definition.

"Future," Shaka said, and then sighed. "Is no matter. No future for Byahail anyway. Not without lands. But, while can have future, is hope. Is maybe. No hope now. Future is torn out. Am ruined. Ruined."

Suddenly it dawned on Christina—what meant the future to any being: Future generations. "I guess physically I'm still perfectly able," Christina said, "But it won't ever happen. Because of what happened to me I can't stand the idea of anybody ever touching me. So I guess it's pretty well impossible. There won't be any future for me."

"Byahail are different. Can make future with another if wanting, but can have alone. But is nothing for Shaka. Nothing ever." She shivered. "Is horror—all horror and pain. How to live with?"

"Because my attackers didn't cut me up the way yours did, the physical pain passed fairly quickly for me. For me it was the emotional pain. I felt like I had been ripped open with a knife. Like everything that was me had been pulled out and stomped on. I felt like a house with the front door kicked in, so any vandal could just walk in and help himself."

"Destroyed," Shaka whispered. "Ruined."

"Exactly," Christina said nodding. "All I wanted to do was die. It was all I could think of to make the pain stop. But I'm glad I didn't succeed in killing myself. You can come to enjoy life again if you try."

"How to? Keep seeing, too many to fight. Keep seeing, keep seeing—" Her voice fell into a whimper.

"I'd wake up at night, dreaming about it. I thought I'd lose my mind."

"Dream, yes. Cannot sleep because of dream. But awake cannot make evil memory stop."

"With help and support, if you can endure it, it will get better. But you have to let other people help you." Christina smiled, reaching over for the cup. "And you have to drink lots and lots of chocolate." She offered it again to Shaka, and this time the Byahail hesitated only slightly before taking the straw.

"That's right. Now, I just want you to know that I'm going to stick with you through the worst of it. I'll talk you through and distract you from the memories and bring you anything you need. I'll try to keep you going until Prilock gets back."

The mention of the Castellan's name did not have the positive effect Christina expected. Instead, Shaka seemed to sag.

"What's wrong?" she asked.

"Is end of friendship," Shaka sighed, closing her eyes.

"What do you mean?"

The Byahail opened her eyes again gazing vaguely into space. "Am cripple. Am burden. Must not be burden to friend. Is not good."

"A true friend would never turn his back on you because of something like this, and I know the Castellan is your true friend," Christina said confidently.

"No, would not turn back," Shaka said. "Prilock is noble being. But still, must be end of friendship."

"Shaka, I can't believe—"

Shaka sighed heavily. "Humans do not understand friendship. In living, are many burdens. Many problems. Is often struggle. Is hard. But friend is easy. With friend, is no struggle. Is good to have friend. Like having place of peace. Is trust. Is pleasant. Is easy. When troubles come, must face alone. Must not burden friend. Friend has trouble enough. Does not need troubles of another."

Her logic seemed odd but not incomprehensible. And it made sense for them. How else could two such emotionally suspicious creatures maintain a relationship? Christina tried another approach.

"Would it be all right to accept help from a friend if it were freely offered?" she asked.

"Maybe," Shaka said carefully. "Must not ask for help. But may accept if help is offered. Still, is not good. Not good to be dependent on friend. Makes friendship difficult. Is wrong."

"Then it is important for you to become strong and independent again, isn't it?"

Shaka shook her head wearily. "Never be strong again."

Christina spoke firmly. "As a nurse, I know for certain that we can help you to heal and become strong again. I'll be honest with you, we can't make you perfect. But we can help you to learn ways of overcoming whatever weakness your injuries leave you with. Certainly you can become independent again."

"How to fix what is in here?" Shaka asked, gesturing towards her chest. "Will always be fear. Will always be memory. Is true for Christina, eh?"

Christina hesitated. Yes, it was true. She would never again be the brassy girl who feared nothing. There would always be the fear. But she had overcome it. She had found ways to live with it, and now she rarely even thought of it. But what could she say to convince someone to whom the pain was starkly real that it would, in time, recede?

With someone like the Byahail, there was only one way Christina could think of.

"Shaka, if I could do it, you can do it. Your experience may have been worse than mine, but you are a much stronger being."

The compliment caught Shaka off-guard and got her attention.

"I'll admit I don't know you well," Christina continued, "so I could be wrong. But I see you as a being of great strength and spirit. I should think your chances of overcoming something like this would be much better than any human's."

"Is maybe true," said Shaka thoughtfully.

"Anyway," the nurse said, "I should think a brave and noble creature like yourself would do your best to try. I'd hate to think that a contemptible monster like Fenrire could defeat you."

One corner of Shaka's scabbed mouth curled into a weak smile. "Are talking like Doctor. Try to shame Shaka into trying to get better. Am not child. Am seeing what are doing."

Christina smiled apologetically. "All right, I confess. But you have to admit, it is true, isn't it? Think about it. Everything I'm saying is true. You are a brave and noble creature. And much stronger in spirit than most humans. More than most Byahail, too, I'll bet. You wouldn't accept defeat without a fight."

"Is true," Shaka agreed, eyeing the nurse.

"In fact, I'll bet you'd fight to recover out of sheer defiance, just to spit in the eyes of those who tried to destroy you."

"Enough, silly human!" the Byahail said. "Am not needing silly flattery. Am needing more of favorite drink."

"There!" Christina said, reaching for the bottle. "Told you it would make you feel better."

Fenrire disliked office work. Most important men in his position hired accountants to take care of inventories, shipping schedules, calculating profits, expenditures and the like. And in fact, the warehouse crew foreman handled a lot of it. But the top level paperwork Fenrire trusted to nobody. The fewer people knew about his little indiscretions, the better. And if anybody was going to fudge the books for profit, it was going to be him.

The unpleasant consequences of this policy was that he had to spend at least one or two evenings a week in the office at the warehouse. On this particular night he had quite a bit to do. He was shipping out in the morning and he wanted to be sure his paperwork was in plausible order. He had most of the customs agents in his pocket, but there were a few on the U.P. side of the swamp whom he hadn't been able to buy. And there were the occasional prize bastards like Castellan Prilock. Fenrire grinned at the thought of Prilock. A pity he couldn't come right out and crow in the bastard's face. The pleasure would almost be worth the trouble it might cause him.

Intruding on his concentration was the sound of regular clicking. It was coming in through the open office door from the warehouse. He looked up from the stack of invoices. The clicking sound paused, then continued, getting closer. It dawned on him: it was the sound of an animal's claws on the hard, bare floor of the warehouse. Fenrire remembered seeing a big brown dog hanging around the gate. But how could the animal have gotten in? And where was the security guard? The Commodore muttered an oath of irritation. Getting up from the desk he went to the cabinet to get his blaster. He'd take care of the animal. And then he'd find that damned security guard and fix him for goofing off on the job.

He went out into the main warehouse and listened for the sound of the dog's movements. It seemed to be off to his left. Probably trotting down the main aisle. But when he got there the aisle was empty. He listened. Then he heard it somewhere further down. Tick-tick-tick-tick-tick . . . .

Fenrire walked quickly towards the sound. The damned guard

probably had sneaked out the door, going someplace he had no business going, and accidentally let the dog in. Son of a bitch was history. Fenrire would close the books on him personally. But first, the dog. Where was the damned thing?

He got to the other end of the warehouse. Still no visible sign of the animal. Fenrire swore foully, looking around. He listened. Nothing. He started back up the aisle, stopping to look down each row of crates. Then he thought he heard something behind him. The Commodore spun around and nearly dropped the blaster in utter astonishment.

"Good evening, Commodore."

"How in bloody hell did you get in here?" Fenrire sputtered furiously.

"A more challenging question might be how in bloody hell would you keep me out?" Prilock replied.

"Aye," Fenrire snarled, "You're just full of tricks, aren't you? Well, you're a bit out of your jurisdiction, Castellan!"

"I'm not here in an official capacity," Prilock replied. "This is personal."

A malicious grin spread across Fenrire's face. "I can't imagine what you could mean."

"No doubt," Prilock said with chilled sarcasm. "And you are no doubt unaware of the stolen freighter parts in those crates behind you."

"Are they stolen?" Fenrire exclaimed in mock dismay, looking around. "Well, what do you know! I bought 'em all in good faith. Guess you just can't trust anybody nowadays, can you?"

"Not even your employees, it seems. Someone has mistakenly labeled the crates as refrigerator components. Terribly careless."

"Oh, terribly!" Fenrire agreed with a sneer. "But you can't really be all that concerned with my inventory problems. What's your business here?"

"It concerns Captain Shaka Mahdi."

Fenrire's grin broadened. "Can't say I recognize the name."

"That's very peculiar," Prilock said, biting down on fury and continuing to speak in an arctic and rigidly controlled voice. "She identified you as the one who assaulted her."

The grin faded. "That's impossible."

"Oh? And why is that?"

Fenrire hesitated.

"Go ahead," Prilock taunted him. "You're just dying to brag about it to my face, aren't you? Yes, of course you are. You said as much in the alehouse."

The Commodore looked distinctly uneasy for a moment. Unnatural bastard. How could he know . . . ? Sneaky goddamned monster. Fenrire felt a surge of hate.

"All right," he said, "What does it matter? You can't prove a thing. And I know you're bluffing about the beast having survived. It was dead as a slab of meat. I made sure of that personally. After we'd had our fun!"

Prilock's eyes glittered with hate and triumph. "You will pay for that, Commodore!"

Fenrire threw back his head and laughed. "Will I really? And how do you intend to make me pay? The Kurlu Empire has no use for the U.P.'s little minions of justice! You have no power here!"

"Oh, don't I?" Prilock said with quiet, deadly intensity.

"Whatever power you have, you subhuman freak, this blaster cancels it out!" Fenrire brought up the gun and fired.

Prilock had been watching him very closely, waiting for the slightest muscle twitch that would indicate he was about to shoot. When he did, Prilock reacted, springing upwards with all his strength, hitting the ceiling with a splat and adhering there. The gun blast narrowly missed him, striking the suspended drum behind him instead. The drum ruptured, spilling out its contents.

Fenrire barely had time to utter a single shrieked curse before the spray of highly corrosive chemical hit him.

Prilock waited until the liquid had stopped spraying and had fallen into a trickle. Then he crept across the ceiling and dropped to the floor. He wasn't sure if the corrosive chemical would damage his substance or not, but he wasn't taking any chances. Acid was one of the few things he was really wary of. He stepped carefully, avoiding the noxious puddles that were leisurely eating their way through the floor.

Fenrire was writhing on the floor, screaming in agony, trying to wipe the acid off and succeeding only in spreading it further and getting it all over himself. Prilock stood placidly over him, his hands folded behind his back.

"How does it feel?" Prilock inquired.

"You whore's bastard!" Fenrire shrieked, struggling to get up and flopping helplessly back down into the fuming mess of his own dissolving clothing and flesh. "You sadistic, inhuman, bloody monster!"

"Praise from Caesar," Prilock replied.

Fenrire clutched at the floor with claw-like fingers which were quickly turning into wet sinew and exposed bone. He choked and gagged inarticulately. Finally, after several minutes of twitching and gurgling he collapsed inert on the floor, the flesh still bubbling and fuming.

"As you have done unto others," Prilock murmured softly. And he turned and walked away.

Prilock took his time coming back over the swamplands. He needed time to think. He anchored and spent a few uneasy hours in torpor, missing the peace he was accustomed to. Then he resumed the slow journey, standing at the controls, frowning.

First of all, he had to decide if he should make a full report of what had happened to his superiors. If word got back to them through some other route they would no doubt demand an explanation, which would be awkward to say the least. And yet making a full report would be just as awkward and difficult. He ultimately decided against it. He had always done his best to co-operate as much as possible with his human benefactors, if one could really call them that. But the events of the past few days were no one's business but his own. There was no need to toss it out for the bureaucrats to play with.

Besides, Fenrire's death had been completely self-inflicted. Prilock had done nothing beyond a few minor indiscretions. What really was there to report?

But there was more than just the problem of how to deal with the U.P. officials. There was the problem of how to deal with himself. With the deed accomplished, an odd numbness had set in. He could look back at what had happened with a certain objectivity. From the moment they had brought Shaka Mahdi in he had been possessed by a single-minded fixation. He could think of nothing else but to bring terrible swift justice to the monster who was responsible. And at the point of triumph, watching his enemy die in agony, he felt joy. Tremendous joy, not just at seeing Fenrire die, but at seeing him suffer.

For an intelligent, rational, and highly civilized being to revel in the sufferings of another, no matter who that other was, was insane. It was beastly emotions out of control. Not justice, but vengeance.

Control had been the meaning of Prilock's life ever since he had learned he was capable of it. To maintain his form, to accurately mimic subtle manipulations of speech and expression, to command authority, to achieve dignity, to outwit his opponents and oppressors. The key was reason and control. He did not like at all feeling his control slip.

As it had with Shaka the night they had discovered their symbiosis.

The curse of relationships. Dependence. Loss of control. It was all happening.

And face it; he could not get a decent torpor without her.

But wait. Before he blamed it all on the poor Byahail, he had to think for a moment: Why was all that control necessary, after all? What was the true source of both his difficulties and those of Captain Mahdi?

Humans. Damned humans. What would the world be like if there were no humans? A hell of a lot more peaceful.

He pulled in to the official dock at Farport and turned over the transport. Technically, his first responsibility was to the office.

But he could see that the building which housed the governor's office was still standing and any catastrophes that Morris hadn't been able to handle in the Castellan's absence had waited this long and could wait another hour or two.

Two steps into the infirmary he could hear that Shaka Mahdi was alive and well.

"Not to touch! Not to touch!"

"For gods' sake, Captain, how can I get you back into bed if you won't let me lift you?"

"Only Doctor Christina!"

"Thank you," came the quieter voice of the nurse, "but I'm not a doctor yet."

"Better doctor than that one! Stupid human!"

"Well," she replied awkwardly, "in any case I can't lift you by myself."

"What in blazes were you doing out of bed anyway, dammit? You aren't strong enough to be trying to walk yet." Dr. Yoshi sounded tired and exasperated.

"How to get strong if not try? Doctor Christina is saying Shaka must try to get strong."

"Yes, yes, but within reason! And not unsupervised! Now just let me—"

"Not to touch! Not! Not!"

"All right! Sit there on the floor! See if I care!"

Prilock opened the door and went in. "Can I be of help?"

Yoshi looked up, painfully grateful.

"Prilock!" Shaka whooped joyfully, trying to lurch upwards. Her legs refused to support her and she fell back onto the floor.

"Now just wait a minute, don't make a spectacle of yourself," Prilock said as he came over to her, scooping up her bony frame effortlessly and setting her on the edge of the bed. She looked emaciated from loss of muscle tissue. Her body was still fragile from the rigors of near-death. Some of her bandages were off, scarred tissue puckered vividly. It was distressing to see her like that. But better than when he had left.

"I can't tell you how glad I am to see you!" Yoshi exclaimed. "Maybe you can handle her!"

"Oh?" Prilock inquired. "Has Captain Mahdi been a less than ideal patient?"

"Well, that's putting it mildly," Yoshi replied.

Shaka spoke up shrilly. "Doctor keeps Shaka locked up here! Will not let to have smokes! Will not let to go to ship!"

"Your ship has been stripped! It's uninhabitable!" the doctor insisted.

"Then must repair," she retorted.

"You can't even stand up!"

"Most repairs not done standing up."

Yoshi threw up his hands in despair. "All right. Go ahead. I'll be happy to be rid of you for a while. If Prilock wants to take you, I'll get an ambulator."

"No need for that," Prilock said, picking Shaka up again, carrying her easily. She lowered her eyes unhappily. "Am sorry to be burden," she said in a low voice edged with shame.

"Not a problem," Prilock replied briskly, "Just don't make a habit of it."

"Take the whole afternoon, please!" Yoshi said. "Just get her back here by tonight so I can check on her. Sooner, if there's any sign of trouble."

"I will bring her back when she is ready to come back," Prilock replied loftily. "You said yourself that I can do more for her than any of your medicine."

"Fine!" Yoshi snapped, and turned on his heel, storming out of the room muttering, "Sometimes I wonder why the hell I ever became a doctor!"

"Don't worry about him," Christina said, "He hasn't had much sleep lately. Shaka, if you need me you know where to find me."

"Am knowing, Doctor Christina."

"Shall we go?" Prilock said to Shaka, and she nodded adamantly.

For just the briefest moment Christina could see it, a gentleness in Prilock's expression, a trust in the way Shaka rested in his arms. An understanding. A symbiosis.

More than just friends.

CHAPTER 4

Farport prospered.

Unlikely as it might have seemed to those who had lived there for all the long and unglamorous years, Farport had, by word of mouth, acquired a reputation as the latest undiscovered tourist spot for the adventurous. It was, so they said, a wild frontier port where strange and colorful traders—and maybe even pirates—came and went. Exotic goods could be bartered for duty-free, since Farport was in a territory, not a sovereign nation. And because it was a territory, completely cosmopolitan and diverse, only the basic laws of the U.P. Treaties applied. Gambling was legal. Prostitution was legal. All manner of exotic foods, beverages and intoxicants could be purchased, and whatever restrictions on purchase and use might be in force in the port, in the privacy of one's ship, one could do as one pleased.

What really let the floodgates open was an article published in a widely read and respected Northwest travel journal. The author described his adventures, "at the far edges of civilization, deep in the unchartable wastes of the swamp." The port was, "a modest, primitive settlement, narrow roads and crooked houses, all built askew of spare parts and United Peoples' donations." He went on to describe the quaint shops, and the outdoor market that the locals held on holidays, where one might find, "fresh eels, hand-made baskets, mats woven of swamp grass, and statuettes carved from the teeth of the striped behemoth. The air is filled with the smell of graincakes cooking in hot oil, and the cries of the sellers, calling out in the accents of a dozen different lands. Barefoot children run laughing through the narrow, twisting streets, and crews of Kurlu merchants, on shore leave and impatient for amusement, walk among the stalls looking for a bottle of opium wine and a woman who will entertain them for a price." He went on and on like that, digressing for a paragraph or two to emphasize that the U.P. made certain that the port had a quite decent medical facility and quite reasonably modern docks, and that the local eating establishment was quite wholesome. He also praised the Castellan of Farport for the efficiency of the government, both in maintaining law and order in such a wild place, and in managing the brisk flow of traffic in the port facilities. Then he returned to his flowery, romantic rhetoric, describing Prilock as "a grim-faced and mysterious man of awesome countenance and astonishing abilities, whose rule is iron, stern and just." He implied that officials in the U.P. were very evasive in their answers to questions about Prilock, and the locals whispered the wildest things about him. Often, he said, the Castellan could be seen in the company of a tall Byahail freighter captain who walked with a limp and whose face was fearfully scarred.

The tourist transports couldn't haul them in fast enough.

Almost overnight the stunned but delighted merchants of Farport began raking in the credits. They expanded their businesses, whether it might be a rooming house or an eel stand. Artisans from miles around made the trek across the swamp to Farport to peddle their wares in the thriving outdoor market, which had expanded to include nearly all of the main street. The Water Hole was packed every night, and continued to be packed even after Haggus knocked out two walls and doubled its capacity. He was hauling in money so fast that he didn't scream in outrage when Prilock imposed a temporary surtax to fund an expansion of the harbor. Most of the merchants affected by the surtax didn't squawk at all; the U.P. would provide matching funds, and an expanded harbor meant more business. Farport was a boomtown.

Prilock hated it. He hated the crowds, the increase in corruption and crime, the decadence, the noise, and the absolute impossibility of imposing order on the catastrophe. The best he could do was keep a rein on the situation to keep it from bolting wildly out of control. An even greater challenge was to keep a rein on his temper, which was increasingly a problem as the frustrations mounted. But most of all he hated his own unwanted and unavoidable notoriety. He tried to keep a low profile, transmuted only under the most dire circumstances and in the most discreet way possible, and delegated a lot more of the patrolling and monitoring duties. He got a promotion approved for Morris and increased the security staff. Even so, he was working harder than he ever had before. There was little time to spend on Shaka's ship, his refuge, the only peace he could get. And she went out less and less, hating the stares and the oppressive crowds. Her body was healing well. Physically she was as much recovered as she was going to be. She could function pretty much normally, although she would always walk with a limp. There was no reason why she could not go back to work. Her ship was repaired. Not as good as it used to be, but functional. She needed to go back to work to pay off the credits she had borrowed to make the repairs and to support herself while she healed. There was certainly work to be had. But Shaka had not yet gone back to work.

The thought of sailing out into the great, vast swamp alone terrified her. Yet she refused to hire any kind of crew. She could not stand the idea of sharing her ship with humans. Her dislike and distrust of them had, if anything, increased. Paradoxically, she had acquired what she considered to be her first and only true friend among humans. Christina came by to see Shaka from time to time, and she did not mind. They would talk. And afterward Shaka would feel it was good that they had. Sometimes she needed to talk about certain things that Christina understood. Somehow it made those things less fearsome.

But there were other things that all the talking in the world could not help with. Dr. Yoshi had tried to explain to her what he had discovered, the little threads of Prilock's substance which had spread throughout her body, how they had kept life going on a cellular level until medical attention could begin to correct the terrible injuries. But it still made no sense to her. What did this mean, that there was some of Prilock within her? What did this mean, that she was alive because of it? Was she now immortal? Could nothing kill her? Could it be undone? Would she age? If life became unbearable, was there no chance ever of release?

Sometimes she felt afraid even of Prilock, afraid of the changes he had caused in her. Their relationship confused her, but it was the only connection she had to any life beyond her own. She feared his touch, but also craved it. When he was with her the confusion evaporated, peace returned, fear was banished. But when he left again the doubts began to gnaw at her. She wanted to run, to flee, but there was no place to go but out into the swamp or back to the Reservation. She would pick up a bottle of opium wine, wanting to drink until all thought and all memory were obliterated. But then she would think of Prilock, coming to her ship and finding her passed out, and she felt ashamed at the disgust she knew he would feel at her weakness. The burden of living seemed unbearable, yet she knew she had to bear it uncomplaining because of him.

Each day she rose determined to resume working and living normally again, and each day she put off acting until the day was over. She read, she studied, she tinkered with her ship. But most of all she exercised, lifting weights, straining muscles, pushing, pulling, practicing precise routines, working herself into a panting, dripping sweat. Then she would rest and shower herself off, and then go back at it again. She grew stronger, broader, her arms became more powerful, her kick more deadly. But still the will to act, to go out and live again, remained crippled and weak.

Prilock did not push her. He did not ask her when she intended to go back to work. He quietly paid her bills for her—certainly he had nothing else to spend his governor's wages on—and wrote off the rent due on the docking space for her ship. She could pay him back when she was able, however long that might take. It made no difference to him. He was simply glad that she was still alive, that he still had her ship to go to at the end of the day. If she never became again what she had been before he would be sorry for her, but her presence in his life was all he really needed. Her company and a few precious hours of peaceful torpor were all he required of their friendship. It was not up to him to judge or make her life's decisions for her. And yet at some nagging inner level, it did annoy and concern him that she did not at least try to resume her responsibilities and work.

"Are all bets placed? Very good! May the Lady of Fortune be with you!" Pousse stepped back and let the wheel spin. Cries and pleas and shouts rose from the crowd as it slowed and finally settled. Several patrons swore furiously and one whooped with joy.

"Congratulations, Brother!" Pousse said. "Here are your vouchers. The Lady seems to be with you. Would you care to try again?"

The croupier of the Water Hole was quite pleased at the way things were turning out for her. She had been able to move out of the dismal little room she had rented when she had first come to Farport and into a new and lavish suite in a hotel just built to accommodate the booming tourist trade. She had demanded and received a handsome raise in salary and gone out and bought an entire new wardrobe more suitable to the greater numbers and sophistication of her clientele. She had two assistants working for her to take care of the more tedious duties associated with the job, but she supervised them closely, and only she operated the wheel. There was talk of getting a second gaming wheel, and some other games as well. Pousse insisted to Haggus that she be given complete control over the operations. There would be no irregularities, she was determined to see to that. The damned Castellan and his lackeys were constantly sniffing around, and she made absolutely sure they would find nothing amiss. Never mind the law; keeping the games honest was in her best interest. The reputation of the Water Hole brought in even more business, since the patrons were assured that their odds of winning were exactly what they ought to be. Pousse was the mistress of the games, and their success was making her wealthy and famous. She had no intention of letting anything spoil that. She had been taken in once before with sweet talk and promises, and it had led to catastrophe and ruin. She had lost everything. Now she was beginning to regain some of the status and self-respect she had had before. No one and nothing was ever going to take that away from her again. If Farport continued to grow and prosper, so would she. She was the most glamorous, desirable woman in Farport, a pleasure made even more pleasant by the knowledge that she had no need to exploit it. Pousse was in control of her life.

Coming to this place was unquestionably the best stroke of luck she had had since the disaster in Malowi that had sent her to prison. Haggus was a tolerable employer, although she had to watch him carefully and could not trust him to add two and two honestly. The clientele still could be rough at times, but it was improving. And Captain Morris had really been quite nice to her, unlike his boss. She had never forgiven Prilock for the cruel welcome he had given her. In spite of the fact that he had let her stay, her opinion of him had remained unchanged. He was a cold-blooded, unfeeling creature whom she neither understood nor wanted to. She once asked Captain Morris how he could stand serving such a creature, and he laughed.

"You get used to it," he said. "Prilock isn't so bad once you get to know him. As long as you follow the rules and do your job everything is fine. And he doesn't play favorites. If anybody ever gives you a hard time, just let him know. He'll come down just as hard on them as he did on you."

Pousse was determined that she would never, under any circumstances, go to that damned monster for anything.

It was time for her to go on her break. She apologized to the patrons for the inconvenience and promised to return in fifteen minutes. She locked the wheel securely so it could not be tampered with in her absence and went to the bar to sit for a moment and get a drink. Maggie had a glass of wine waiting for her. "How's it going?"

"Just fine," Pousse said, grateful to get off her feet and sip something to cool her throat.

"It looks like we may set another record for business tonight," Maggie said.

"If we do, I shall certainly demand another raise. And so should you!"

"Not likely!" Maggie laughed. "The Castellan has ordered another surtax increase to cover the cost of upgrading the sewerage system."

"Really? Isn't he taking enough of a cut as it is?"

"Too much by half, to hear Haggus talk," Maggie replied, "But you've got to expect it. All those shiny new toilets in all those fancy hotels have to empty somewhere."

"I suppose," Pousse sighed.

"Besides," Maggie said over her shoulder as she went off to take care of another customer, "We're serving fifteen times the drinks we were serving last year—where do you think that's all going?"

Pousse smiled, putting the glass to her lips. The wine had improved in quality, too. It was as good as anything she could get in Malowi. All in all, Farport had come a long way from the dive it had been when she first came. She supposed it was inevitable that the taxes should go up.

"Mind if I join you?"

She looked up, frowning. Pousse had a firm rule about fraternizing with the customers, especially when she was working. But the man smiling down at her gave her pause. She normally didn't care much for Kurlu types, but he was strikingly handsome. His skin was a rich olive tone, instead of the usual sallowness of his race. His large, dark eyes were bright and intelligent, his bearing showed refinement, his speech showed education. His black hair was neatly groomed and slicked back, his cheeks cleanly shaven. He wore the uniform of an officer of the Elite Corps, clean and well-pressed, with numerous decorations. Pousse could not help herself. "By all means," she said, "Do sit down."

"Thank you," he said. "May I introduce myself; I am Commander Marcus Lars."

"Delighted to meet you," she replied, meaning it. "I am called Pousse."

"What a lovely name! Quite enchantingly simple." He signaled to Maggie, ordering a straight whiskey by gesture. He said, "I couldn't help noticing how well you handle this crowd of ruffians. I would expect to see a professional of your charm and expertise in Malowi, not in a place like this."

"Thank you. It's a long story." She countered, "I would hardly expect an officer such as yourself to be in a place like the Water Hole. Do you have business here?"

"I'm afraid I do," he said. "Rather unpleasant business, too, although it is the sort of business that someone must take care of, and my government has entrusted me with the dubious honor."

"Really?" Pousse said, sipping her wine. "I am intrigued."

He smiled at Maggie as she set the whiskey down in front of him. Pousse noticed she had poured him the select, not the ordinary bar whiskey, a prudent decision she had made no doubt based on his appearance. He gave her more than sufficient credits to cover it and told her to keep the change.

"Yes," he said to Pousse, tasting the whiskey and nodding slightly with approval. "I don't suppose you have ever heard of a creature called a 'shadow-slayer'."

"No, I must confess I haven't."

"It is hardly a surprise, and not at all to your discredit. Ordinary citizens of the Kurlu Empire are only just becoming aware of this terrible menace. My government has been attempting to take care of the matter without alarming the general public, but unfortunately the creatures are becoming more aggressive, and have proven extremely difficult to wipe out."

"What sort of creature are they?" Pousse asked.

Lars frowned. "I wish that you did not have to know. It was the hope of the Kurlu Empire that we could contain the threat and neutralize it before it spread to U.P. territory. But I fear that may no longer be possible. I fear that at least one of the creatures is already among you."

Pousse glanced nervously around the bar.

"It began," the officer said, pausing to take another sip of whiskey and then continuing, "when the Kurlu settled the lands to the south of us, incorporating them into the Empire and beginning development of them. At first, we lost only individuals. Then entire outposts were decimated. The creatures were unlike anything we had ever encountered, deadly, ruthless, and devilishly clever. They were called 'shadow-slayers' because they seemed to come unseen, out of the very shadows themselves, killing with terrifying swiftness. Our best scientists studied what little evidence they could find, and our best soldiers and hunters tried to fight back. After many years we have finally discovered enough about these monsters that we can effectively track them down and destroy them. But only one at a time, when we can isolate one in our territory. We cannot reach their stronghold, which we think is in the Byahail Mountains of the Far South. And so the slaughter goes on."

"How awful!" Pousse exclaimed. "And you think there is one here at Farport?"

He nodded, looking at her gravely. "As I said, the shadow-slayers are extremely intelligent. Worse still, it seems they can assume any shape they wish. When they are wounded, or mercifully dead, they revert to what we believe is their natural form—a kind of dark jelly. But when they are alive and alert, they can appear as anything. Even a man."

Pousse caught her breath. A certain, incredible possibility was forming in her mind. "How can you tell when one is near?"

Lars smiled at her. "With this," he said, taking a small device out of his breast pocket. It was slender and rectangular, like a little calculator, but it had only three buttons on it and a narrow window. "Shadow-slayers carry certain rare elements in their bodies which this device can detect. Those elements do exist naturally, but not in the concentrations and combinations that occur in the mass of the creatures. Should this window begin to turn red, I know one is coming near. If it comes closer than twenty feet, the device will beep an alert. Thus the creature cannot take me off-guard."

"Fascinating!" Pousse exclaimed. "What can you do then to defend yourself?"

"Well that you should ask," Lars replied, slipping the device back into his pocket. "They are not easily killed, these creatures. Crude weapons, such as knives or clubs, are useless against them. Projectile weapons, such as bullet guns, are equally useless. Even the most powerful blaster is unreliable, because the creatures can move with incredible swiftness, and are able to evade the beam. Flame-throwers can work, but are obviously too bulky to be carried around. So our scientists devised this weapon." He drew from the holster on his hip a strange-looking gun unlike anything Pousse had ever seen before. It had a funnel-shaped barrel and two large plastic cartridges attached to it.

"How does it work?" she asked.

"These cartridges contain a powerful corrosive," Lars explained. "It is a highly concentrated form of an acid used in industry for etching metal. The acid is projected at high velocity out of the barrel at a wide angle of dispersal. Even a small quantity is enough to mortally damage a shadow-slayer by rapidly dissolving its very substance. We have observed that the loss of as little as a tenth of their mass is enough to kill them."

"I see," Pousse said, nodding. "But, what makes you think one of these horrid creatures is here?"

Lars smiled at her knowingly. "Surely you've heard strange rumors about your Castellan. Have you never wondered if he were quite human?"

Pousse felt a hot rush of excitement. She looked up at the clock behind the bar. "Dear me! I should have been back at the wheel ten minutes ago! Talking to you has made me completely forget the time! Please excuse me, Commander, I must get back to work. But we certainly must talk more about this later." She rose with calculated haste and walked silkily back to her post at the gaming wheel. What a fascinating development! she thought as she considered how best to use it.

Prilock added up the figures and scowled at the print-out. If estimated revenues continued as projected there should be more than enough funds available to take care of the essentials. There might even be enough to consider doing something about the main street so it didn't turn into a river of mud every time they got a heavy rainfall. But he ought to try to get some feel for how the majority of merchants and residents wanted their money spent. Expansion of the port facilities, utilities and sewer systems was essential. Beyond that, expenditures would be discretionary. Perhaps some sort of town council could be organized. What a headache that would be.

Then there was the matter of how to handle the port traffic while construction of the new docking facilities was in progress. Another major headache. Prilock wished he could just push it all aside for the night and close up the office. The thought of spending an evening of peace and quiet in the sanctuary of Shaka's ship was awfully tempting. But he still had to go over the manifests for the next day, and there was a stack of official documents that needed to be looked over and signed. It all had to be done before he could think about leaving.

The com unit beeped annoyingly. "Yes?" he snapped.

"Castellan, this is Morris."

"Morris? Aren't you off-duty?"

"Yes, Sir, but something has come up. Lt. Tamri wasn't quite sure how to handle it and contacted me—"

"The last time I checked I was still in charge here," Prilock interrupted. "Why did the lieutenant see fit to get you out of bed instead?"

"Well, Sir, it's a rather awkward situation."

"Oh, I see," Prilock replied sarcastically. "Gods know I'm not used to handling awkward situations."

Morris continued evenly. "It seems there's a Kurlu officer of the Elite in the Watering Hole."

"Really?" Prilock frowned. He should have been aware of

someone of that sort of rank visiting Farport. There were matters of protocol. "Have you any idea what his business is?"

"That's the problem, Sir. He's been making inquiries regarding a creature he calls a 'shadow-slayer.' He talked with the croupier, Pousse, for quite some time. One of my undercover people managed to catch a good deal of the conversation. These 'shadow-slayers' are supposed to be elusive killers, a real problem in the Empire, but virtually unknown here in the West. The officer is here as an agent of the Kurlu government, with orders to track down and destroy one of the creatures rumored to be here in Farport."

"Why the devil wasn't I informed of this?" Prilock snapped. "If we have some sort of dangerous creature running loose here—"

"Sir," Morris interrupted him carefully, "according to the officer these shadow-slayers can assume any form, even human." He paused. "He's been asking about you, Sir."

The true significance of what Morris was telling him hit Prilock solidly. "I see," he said quietly.

"He's got some sort of weapon, an acid gun designed to kill the creatures." Morris paused again and said, "Under the circumstances, Sir, I think it might be a good idea if you didn't come down here until we've had a chance to straighten things out."

"Nonsense," Prilock said briskly, "The sooner I confront this Kurlu officer the better. I'm on my way." But his voice lacked its usual firm conviction. He was too much distracted by the damnable implications of what Morris had told him.

Shadow-slayers. Unknown in the West, but abundant and pernicious enough that the Kurlu government had armed and trained an Elite officer to track them down and destroy them. Able to assume any shape, even human.

The first clue he had ever had of his origins and his kin, and it came in the form of an assassin sent to kill him.

He started to get up from his desk and then sat back down again. Suddenly, he couldn't seem to move.

He stared at his hands, carefully crafted appendages designed to look precisely like human hands. He was so used to maintaining their form that he didn't even need to think about it anymore.

Shadow-slayers.

I have worked hard, he thought. I have obeyed and enforced their laws. I have always acted in a manner as honorable and just as I possibly could. I have been accepted, entrusted with a position of authority, and I have performed my duties in an exemplary manner. I am a citizen of the United Peoples. Law and order are on my side. They have no right to . . . kill me.

Prilock stared hard at the imminent possibility of his own death. Who would defend him? Shaka Mahdi, certainly, had she been well and able. But she was not the strong being she had once been, and she would only be one against an armed killer. Who, then? The humans who had always hated and resented him? Morris, he trusted. But could he depend on the other men? He knew what they all thought of him. They would most likely sing at his funeral and dance on his grave. The Kurlu would confirm all their worst prejudices concerning him. They would cheer the assassin on. Far from standing in his way, they would part like the waters of the Naryl Canal. They would applaud the execution and all chip in to buy the assassin a parting gift. Thank you, friend, for ridding us of that damned inhuman Castellan!

Shadow-slayer.

He heard someone coming into the office. Immediately he tensed. Was this it? The assassin walking in with a map to the office provided by the good people in the Water Hole? For an amazingly long fraction of a second Prilock examined his feelings about mortality.

The door opened. To his surprise, it was Pousse.

"Madam?" he greeted her curiously.

"Castellan," she said coolly. She stood in front of his desk. "I haven't much time. I must get back to the Water Hole. But I've come to warn you."

"I'm listening," he said.

"There is a Kurlu Elite officer by the name of Marcus Lars in the Water Hole. I have reason to believe he has come here to kill you. He is armed with a weapon that shoots a highly corrosive acid, and he has a device—" She paused as Prilock held up his hand.

"I know," he said softly.

"You know?" she echoed.

"Captain Morris just contacted me about the matter."

"Oh," she murmured awkwardly. "Well, if you know, then I need not stay any longer. I'd best get back." She started to turn to go.

"Madam." Prilock stood up. She turned. He asked, "Why did you come here? I would have thought you'd be among the first in line to shake his hand when he took me down."

She held herself erect, her chin in the air. "That shows how little you know me," she said.

"Enlighten me," he replied. "Why did you come here to warn me?"

She hesitated, realizing that in spite of the fact that her news had been scooped, the gesture was still quite meaningful. "Because I didn't have to," she said, "And I wanted you to know it and remember that I did."

He nodded slowly. "I will remember, Madam."

She found herself taken back for a moment. His eyes, they seemed so human. His expression, it almost seemed like gratitude.

Then she nodded and turned to go.

Prilock watched her leave. He quickly sorted and straightened the papers on his desk. He checked to make sure the reports were ready to go out, then he turned off the lights and locked the office door.

Marcus Lars finished his whiskey and set the glass down on the bar. He waved the bartender away when she offered to refill it. Lars estimated there were five, possibly six undercover guards in the bar presently, in addition to the four uniforms who had just arrived. They were on to him, he was quite sure. The croupier had slipped out and then returned a few minutes ago. No doubt she had gone to warn the Castellan, the silly, treacherous bitch. But it didn't really matter. He anticipated one of two things happening. If the security guards didn't realize the Castellan's true nature, a public revelation as to what the creature was could be enough to turn their loyalties. Surely even these soft-bellied Northmen and Moor had sufficient humanity in them to rebel at the thought of protecting a monster whose race routinely slaughtered innocent people. If, on the other hand, the guard knew full well what the creature was, but lacked the spine to rise up against it, they would no doubt welcome a liberator who would do the job for them. Either way, Lars was assured that the guard would give him little trouble once he exposed the creature for what it was. As for the civilians, he had talked with enough of them to know there was a general dislike and even downright loathing with regard to Farport's governor, coupled with vague suspicions and uneasiness about his inhuman qualities. Marcus Lars was quite confident that the people would be on his side.

Would the monster come himself? Or might he sent some agent to deal with Lars while he remained remote and safe? No, the monster would come. Shadow-slayers were all ego and arrogance. They knew no fear. They did their killing themselves, without shame or remorse, whether the victim was a distinguished merchant fleet officer who had incurred their displeasure, or a village full of women and children slated for slaughter in revenge for the execution of one of their own. Still, this creature was unique. It had passed as human, had functioned and been treated as human. It walked as a man, and would come in here and face him as a man, speaking with a man's voice and using a man's gestures. The reports said that the thing known as Prilock was so perfect an imitation that the sham was impossible to detect. The thing had fooled countless people with its masquerade. But tonight Prilock would be revealed for the revolting creature it was, not even remotely human.

Lars knew that Prilock was about ready to make his move when the plainclothes security guards began going around from table to table, quietly asking people to leave. Then the door opened and the Castellan came in, flanked by six uniformed guards including his chief of security. Lars had been determined not to be impressed, but when he finally actually laid eyes on the Castellan he was impressed in spite of himself. Prilock was tall, broad-shouldered, with iron grey hair, eyes of steel and finely chiseled features that commanded attention and unquestioning respect. He walked with a smooth stride of absolute confidence and coiled strength, pure authority personified. Lars reminded himself, the thing made itself look this way, it carefully chose its appearance to have just such an effect, but knowing that did little to diminish the awesome effect.

Prilock stopped and stood several feet away from Marcus Lars. "I understand you are looking for me."

The device in Lars' pocket began to beep. Lars smiled. "Yes," he said, drawing the device out and noting the deep red glow in its window, "I am." He held the device up. "Do you know what this is? It warns me that I am in close proximity to a killer."

"I'd think that in your own company that would be constant," Prilock said.

Lars laughed appreciatively. "Very good, Castellan. Clever, but inaccurate. You see, I am a public servant. I have been entrusted by my government with the responsibility of hunting down a particularly fiendish and brutal kind of killer. I have no idea what your kind calls itself, but we call you 'shadow-slayer,' for your talent for concealment, disguise, and sudden attack." He raised his voice. "Have you people wondered who he was, this Castellan of yours? Have you noticed his unnatural abilities, his inhuman nature? I will tell you: he is a monster from a race of monsters. They come down from the mountains of the far south, they come in the night, unseen and unknown, and when they come, people die. I have seen entire settlements wiped out, not a single baby spared, all brutally slaughtered by these creatures from Hell!"

The room was absolutely silent. No one spoke. They listened with rapt attention to Marcus Lars. Even Prilock could not help but listen, horribly fascinated.

"These monsters," Lars continued in a voice dramatically quieter, "can assume any shape at will. That is why I carry this device, to warn me that one is near. In their natural state they are nothing more than amorphous, brown slime. A disgusting, foul mass of living ooze. But they can easily disguise themselves as anything they wish. They can even walk among you, as this one does. What is your plan, shadow-slayer? To infiltrate human society? To win our trust, gain our confidence, worm your way up to the top and then take what you know back to your kind so that they can do the same? And ultimately, what? Begin replacing people with your own foul kind? A frightening thought, isn't it?" he shouted to the room.

"You are very good," Prilock said, "at telling stories designed to frighten. But the plain fact of the matter is that there is no conspiracy. It is quite common knowledge among those who know me that I know nothing about the others of my kind. Whatever accident delivered me into human society left me completely cut off from others like myself. I had no idea they even existed."

"Do you really expect us to believe that?" Lars cried out incredulously, gesturing as if he spoke for all others present. "Do you really expect us to be that naïve? You may think humans are easy prey, but I assure you, we are not!"

"I expect you to accept the truth," Prilock shot back, "And the truth is that I am nothing more than I appear to be!"

"Shadow-slayers are never what they appear to be," Marcus Lars replied. "They are creatures of deception and death. And there are countless Kurlu graves to attest to the truth of that!"

"I am not responsible for anyone's murder!" Prilock retorted angrily.

"Oh, really?" Lars sneered. "What about Commodore Fenrire?"

"He caused his own death," Prilock replied, suddenly finding himself on the defensive.

"And I suppose you had nothing to do with it, eh? I suppose it was merely coincidence that you had taken a leave of absence from your post here at Farport at the time Fenrire was murdered?"

"I don't deny that I was there, but it was he who fired the shot—"

"Oh yes!" Lars thundered, "How nicely you set it up! Such a precious touch of irony that Commodore Fenrire died an agonizing death from acid spray! And you claim you have no contact with your kind? Was your choice of execution for Fenrire mere coincidence or revenge for those of your own kind whom we had hunted down? Do tell us, please!"

Prilock had been trapped neatly. No matter what he said it would sound lame. He shook his head slowly. "My business with Fenrire was personal. I was seeking justice for a crime he had committed."

"Of course," Lars said mockingly. "As I recall he roughed up a favorite pet of yours."

"Captain Shaka Mahdi is a citizen of the United Peoples who Fenrire brutalized, tortured and left for dead!"

"And so you took the law into your own hands and executed him without trial or defense? Is this your justice?"

Prilock forced himself to remain calm. "I did nothing but confront him. He fired the shot that brought about his own death."

"Well, I expect we have only your word for that, don't we?" Lars said.

"Yes," Prilock replied, "And as all who know me will testify, I never lie."

"Shadow-slayers are nothing but lies," Lars hissed. "Your very appearance is a lie. Your entire life is nothing but a grand fabrication, an inhuman creature trying to pass as human. If these people could see you as you truly are, they would reject you immediately. They would turn away in disgust and horror!" He leered at Prilock mockingly. "Shall we tell them how your foul kind perpetuates itself? Eh? How you implant a seed into a living human host? How that seed grows, living off the host like a demon parasite, growing and feeding, until it drives its victim mad, until nothing remains but a thin shell of skin filled with vile brown slime?"

Prilock felt sickened by the revelation. It couldn't be true, could it? Was that how he, himself, came to be? Great gods, it couldn't be true!

Abruptly the center of attention was snatched away from Marcus Lars as someone entered the room, the only person the security guards would have allowed to pass. Many of the people in the public house had not seen her since before the assault. They stared at her now with open mouths. She seemed taller. She seemed huge. Her great mane was thin and limp; much of it had not grown back. Her face was distorted by scars which curled her lip and narrowed one eye into a squint. Her body was slightly twisted, one leg did not quite match the other, so as she came in she limped oddly, her frame lurching slightly with each step. There was nothing feminine left about her. All gender had been stripped from her. To use the feminine pronoun now would be mere habit, linguistic default.

Shaka Mahdi stood before Marcus Lars and said in a voice of ice, "Kurlu assassin is not wanted here."

Lars stared at her in utter astonishment, and then burst out laughing. "Is this what all the fuss was about? A Kurlu officer died because of this ugly beast?"

Her voice remained low and cold, and in its lack of volume was a menace doubly threatening.

"Is Kurlu who is ugly," she replied. "Ignorant and ugly. Cruel and ugly. Disgusting and ugly."

"Captain," Prilock said gently, "This isn't your fight." He touched her arm to draw her out of the way. But she would not move. She did not take her eyes off of Marcus Lars, remaining immobile as stone.

"Is not Shaka's fight?" she retorted sharply. "These Kurlu, kill Shaka's people, take land, take lives, take everything. Is no justice for Byahail. Am beaten, am destroyed, am made sick and empty by Kurlu. Now this one comes. Comes to kill. To take away again. Comes hunting only noble being who seeks justice one time for this one Byahail. Ugly, cruel and ignorant one comes to kill that noble being. Not Shaka's fight? Is."

Lars' expression was filled with contempt. "What do you want, Beast? My pity? Yours is a primitive, inferior race. It was inevitable that it should fall before the expansion of an advanced and civilized people. The Kurlu Empire took what was justly ours, a rich land inhabited only by savages, and we made it productive. That valley where your species lived its barbarian existence now supports and enriches the glory that is our civilization. You and your bestial race are no more deserving of my pity than the eels and flies that are destroyed when we fill in a swamp to create farmland!"

"Okay, that does it." Taking a deep breath, Captain Morris stepped out to stand beside Shaka Mahdi. "I've heard enough," he said. "I know the Castellan, and I know Captain Mahdi, but I don't know you. And from what I've heard so far, I don't want to."

Lars shrugged with elaborate indifference. "You're opinion of me isn't at issue here. I know where the sympathies of you bleeding heart U.P. types lie. What matters is what you intend to do about this monster living in your midst. Do you intend to continue to be the puppet of this inhuman thing? This enemy of all humanity?"

"Listen, Mister!" Morris retorted angrily, "It'll take a hell of a lot more than your melodramatic oratory to make me turn against the best commanding officer I've ever served!"

Marcus Lars' eyes narrowed. "I can see he's got you both in his pocket. But what about the rest of you? I've told you what he is. I've told you what his bloodthirsty race does. You people aren't willing to be his dupes, are you?"

"Hey!" Haggus shouted from behind the bar, "I don't give a good goddamn if he crawled out from under a rock behind the latrine and has a brother that eats babies raw for breakfast! He made Farport what it is, and without him this place would go straight to Hell in record time! I don't know about the rest of you, but I'm not about to stand here and let this Kurlu son of a bitch take out the one person who can keep this knot of swamp grass from being overrun by rats, pirates, and black market bandits!"

There was a general rumble of agreement. Then the owner of

the new hotel down the street spoke up more succinctly, "Hell, Castellan Prilock may be a bastard, but by the gods, he's our bastard!" His comment elicited a concurrence of appreciative chuckles.

"Besides," somebody else said, "Why should we believe you? Who the hell are you?" Several people thumped on the tables and stamped on the floor for emphasis, with a muttered, "Hear, hear!"

There was just the faintest trace of a smile on Prilock's face. "It seems," he said to Marcus Lars, "that your business here is finished."

The Kurlu's expression was cold and grim. "My congratulations, Prilock," he said, "you've consolidated your position very effectively. You shadow-slayers are a formidable lot, I'll grant you. But in the end, we will defeat you."

"I think we've all heard quite enough of your empty rhetoric," Prilock replied. "I suggest that you take your show on the road, preferably back to more receptive audiences in the Empire. Captain Morris, would you kindly provide our departing guest with a diplomatic escort to his ship?"

"Of course, Sir," Morris replied, picking out four of his finest to perform the task.

Lars smiled coldly, snapping his heels together in a slight formal bow. He began to walk towards the door. Morris watched him uneasily. As a precaution he kept himself between the Castellan and the Kurlu, giving the assassin no opening for a parting shot. He noticed Captain Mahdi doing the same, matching his defensive movements. Neither of them would feel comfortable until they'd seen the wake of Marcus Lars' ship disappear into the swamp.

They had excellent reason to be uneasy. The broadcast of the acid gun made accuracy unnecessary and the trained assassin cared little about collateral damage.

Prilock saw it coming and reacted first, grabbing Morris and throwing him against Shaka Mahdi, sending them both to the floor and diving after them. The guards reacted a split second later, knocking the gun out of Lars' hand and throwing him against the wall, pinning his arms behind him. But Lars had timed it just right. He was able to draw the gun and get off one good shot before they nailed him.

It was pure pandemonium.

Morris scrambled to his feet, flushed with adrenaline. Swearing furiously, he tore off his uniform jacket before the acid could burn through to the flesh. All around him people were milling and shouting. He didn't see the Castellan. Bellowing to make himself heard, he began giving orders.

"Tamri! Estes! Find out who got hit and get all affected clothing off them! If anybody got it on their skin, get them to running water! Maggie! Haggus! Pousse! Help get these people treated! Get them to a sink! Smett! Get the rest of these people out of here! If they aren't injured I want them out!" He looked across the room to where the four guards were holding Marcus Lars. The grin of smug triumph on the assassin's face infuriated Morris. "Byron, get that Kurlu son of a bitch to detention! Strip-search him and lock him up!"

"Yes Sir!"

Morris pulled out his radio. "Medical emergency! Dr. Yoshi to the Water Hole immediately! Repeat, we have a medical emergency here! At least a dozen people with chemical burns!"

"Acknowledged," Yoshi's voice replied, "On my way."

"Security!" Morris barked into the radio, "All back-up units to the Water Hole! Put a guard on the door! I don't want anybody but the medical team coming in here!"

He turned around to do a quick survey of the situation. People were gradually being herded out the door, going reluctantly, staring back into the room in morbid fascination. Fortunately, a good percentage of the crowd had been persuaded to leave before the incident, a prudent precaution on the Castellan's part. But enough curious folks had remained to create bedlam. Several people were babbling hysterically while the guards tried to calm them down and see how badly they had been hit. One woman was wailing in pain as they gently pushed her face down to the bar sink, trying to wash the acid off her cheek. In the area where most of it had fallen there were dots of smoking damage all over the floor and furniture.

Morris kicked a table out of the way and saw Shaka Mahdi kneeling on the floor, bent over a shuddering, shapeless dark mass. A few feet away was a fuming puddle of the dark stuff, bubbling and rapidly dissolving.

So that's what he really looks like, Morris thought. He knelt by Shaka Mahdi. "How bad is he?"

She looked up at him. "Is bad," she said. "Very bad."

"Look, you've been hit, too. Your shoulder, and the leg of your pants."

She shook her head. "Must not let go of him."

"Okay, just hold still. I'll cut the cloth off of you." He pulled a knife from a sheath on his belt. "Tamri! Soak a towel in water and bring it over here!" He carefully cut through the tough material. It tore along the holes where the acid had burned through it. Morris grimaced; the skin underneath was already beginning to blister. "Damn!" he whispered.

"Is nothing," Shaka said distractedly.

He nodded towards the fuming puddle. "Is that part of him?"

She nodded. "Part that was hit."

"He must have sloughed it off to try to save himself."

She nodded again.

Tamri came over with the dripping towel. "Bloody gods!" he exclaimed. "Is that the Castellan?"

"What's left of him," Morris said grimly, taking the towel and washing Shaka's burns. "Quit staring and get back to work."

"Yes, Sir," Tamri said, tearing his eyes away from the gruesome sight with difficulty.

"Where the hell is that damned doctor?" Morris complained, and no sooner were the words out of his mouth but Yoshi and Christina burst breathlessly into the room. "About time," Morris muttered. He stood up, glancing down at the dark, bubbling pool with a shudder as he walked past it. He must have taken the worst of it, Morris thought guiltily. It should have been me. I should have taken it, me and Captain Mahdi. But he took it himself. Ten percent, the Kurlu said. Ten percent or more is fatal. Dear gods, is that ten percent? It looks like more—

"What the bloody hell happened here?" Yoshi demanded.

Shaka could barely hear the doctor's voice. She was vaguely aware of a searing pain somewhere on her body. But more and more it seemed too distant to be her body. More immediate were the waves of intense nausea and anxiety washing over her. Prilock was in mortal agony, clinging to her with an intensity that was cutting off the circulation in her arms. An odd numbness was spreading through her. Dizziness fogged her thoughts. Take, Friend, she thought dreamily, whatever are needing, take. Am giving willingly . . . .

"There you go," Christina said to the woman with a smile. "Now, you come by first thing tomorrow and we'll change the dressing and see how it's healing."

The woman touched the bandage on her face timidly. "Will the scar be very bad?" she asked anxiously.

"We'll do the very best we can to make sure there is as little scar as possible," Christina assured her. "Now, because you know your own face so well, you'll probably notice it more than anyone else would. But by the time we've finished treating you, anyone meeting you for the first time wouldn't notice a thing!"

The woman smiled tentatively. "Thank you, Nurse."

Christina got up with a sigh after the woman was gone. "Well, that's the last of them," she murmured to herself. Just then the door opened and Morris came in. She was relieved to see that it wasn't another patient.

"Hello Christina. Any news?"

"I was just going to check," she said. "Come on." She beckoned him into the other room. Yoshi was standing by the bed where Shaka and Prilock lay, scowling at their vital signs. "Damnedest thing!" he muttered.

"Any change?" Christina asked.

"No better, no worse," he said. "Prilock's vitals don't make a damn bit of sense, but then again, they never did. And Shaka seems stable. She's running a slight fever, that's about it. Still, this can't be any good for her after what she's been through. I don't like the fact that she's unconscious."

"I'm not about to try to separate them," Christina said, "Are you?"

"Hell, no!" Yoshi replied. He shook his head. "I can't get over the biochemical compatibility of these two. They're completely different species, and yet they fit together like two halves of the same organism. It's crazy!"

"As long as they're both still alive." Morris hoisted himself up onto an empty bed and lay down, stretching out with a heavy sigh. "What a day! Bloody gods, am I beat!"

"Watch yourself," Yoshi said, glancing up, "Christina's likely to come by and stick an IV in you."

"Fine," Morris said, raising one arm up. "Fill it with top shelf whiskey."

Yoshi picked up a data board. "I estimate he lost approximately eighteen percent of his body mass in the attack."

"Eighteen?" Morris exclaimed, sitting up. "But anything beyond ten is supposed to be lethal."

"It probably is if you don't have a Byahail handy to do life support," Christina said. "I wonder how she knew to be there? It couldn't have been a coincidence. She's hardly left her ship in weeks."

"I radioed her while I was waiting for the Castellan to get there," Morris said. "I figured she ought to know, and it was a sure bet he wasn't going to call her. I know him. Never bother anybody else to handle something when you can risk your own neck handling it yourself."

"Between the two of them they've got more lives than a cat," Yoshi said. "Morris, you hear anything back from U.P. headquarters?"

"Gods!" he sighed, laying back down. "The fox is sure in the chicken coop there! I thought Admiral Hiro was going to have a stroke when I told him that an Officer of the Kurlu Elite had tried to assassinate the Castellan. But I submitted your request to the

Science Commission. Probably won't hear anything back before morning, though. It's after midnight their time."

Yoshi sat down, tossing the data board onto the desk with a clatter. "Gods! I'll be glad to be able to get back to Malowi and practice nice ordinary medicine!"

"You'll be bored," Christina said.

"Ah, boredom!" Yoshi said, his eyes closing in bliss as he savored the thought. He opened his eyes again. "But I'd almost sacrifice another four years of my life in this place to know what the Kurlu know about these 'shadow-slayers.' There's got to be some kind of connection between them and the Byahail."

"Supposedly they have a stronghold in the far South, in the Byahail Mountains," Morris said. "At least, that's what Lars said to Pousse."

"Aha! How much you want to bet the attacks on the Kurlu outposts started shortly after the Byahail were driven off their land?"

Christina shook her head. "Listen, even if there is a connection, wouldn't Shaka have known about it? I mean, if the Byahail know about the shadow-slayers, wouldn't she have recognized Prilock for what he was?"

Yoshi sighed, rubbing his eyes. "You'd think so, wouldn't you?"

"Listen, folks," Morris said, "Let's just call it a night and go back to work on the puzzle in the morning, okay?"

"Sounds good to me," Christina said. "Do you want to do shifts, Doctor, or shall we let the monitors do their job?"

Through a haze Shaka could hear them talking. Their words drifted into her conscious mind filtered through gauze, their meaning slowly taking shape and then drifting randomly like a drop of dye in water. The Byahail Mountains—

—Byahail Mountains—am remembering—so long ago—rising above valley, sometimes purple, sometimes grey and mist, sometimes all dark—so far away, so high—in warm days of soft rains—kalistra would bloom—air would be sweet with smell of kalistra—on clear night when moon is bright and high, elders would put on beautiful clothes with beads and tiny bells—put on soft shoes

with beads and tiny bells—wrap flowers on staves—flowers in
manes—gather up bundles of bread and fruit and cheese—take
skins of wine and walk path up to Mountains—in moonlight,
sweet smell of kalistra, elders would go singing with sound of little
bells—walking up ancient path to Mountains to meet Chimera—
to meet ancient gods—to commune with Chimera—to renew ancient covenant—older than memory—older than time—Chimera—
gods of Byahail—all village would dance in moonlight, even little
ones—put flowers in mane and bells on feet and arms and tail and
dance in moonlight—sing and play flutes and drums—feast on
sweet breads and fruits and rich cheese—drink wine and sing and
dance until morning—even little ones—to honor ancient gods—
to honor Chimera, who dwell in Mountains, so far and high—am
remembering—am remembering—

—but then humans come—killing—burning—Byahail cry,
'Where are Chimera? Why do gods not protect us?'—elders say,
'must not be dependent on gods, must protect selves—fight—but
is too many—too strong—such great and evil weapons—cannot
win—so much death—day comes can fight no more—must leave
home—must go to Reservation—Where are Chimera?—'Be patient,' say elders, 'Covenant will be honored'—but gods do not
come—years go by—nothing changes—cannot live on Reservation—no birthing mud—no kalistra—no sweet fruits—seasons are
wrong—cannot go to Mountains—elders set festivals by stars—
but is no singing—is no dancing—is only dying—and Chimera
do not come—are only myth—there are no gods—no gods to save
Byahail—time of Byahail is gone—dark age of humans has come—
end of old ways for all time—am remembering—

—but Shaka Mahdi refuses to die—refuses to remain on
Reservation waiting—will go forth—will learn ways of
humans—will get ship—ship will save Shaka Mahdi—ship will
be hope and deliverance—ship will be "Chimera"—like gods of
high Mountains—ancient gods of Byahail—am remembering—
am remembering—

"Chimera."

Christina looked up. "Did you hear something?"

Yoshi paused, his hand poised to shut off the desk lamp. "Yes, I thought I did."

"I think it was Captain Mahdi," Morris said as he pushed himself off the bed. "I think she said, *Chimera.*"

Yoshi went over to her. "No change," he said. "She must have been talking in her sleep."

"You probably heard right, then," Christina said to Morris as she gathered up her bag and sweater and headed for the door. "That ship means more to her than anything else in her life."

"Except the Castellan," Morris said, joining her.

"Except the Castellan," she agreed with a smile. She looked back. "Coming Doctor?"

"I'll be right there," he said. He double-checked the monitors to be certain they were set properly to trigger the alarm if there were any changes in his patients' status.

Shaka sighed softly in her delirium. "Chimera," she whispered, and smiled.

CHAPTER 5

"Well, he certainly doesn't believe in excess comfort," Admiral Terat complained, looking critically around the official reception room.

"I don't imagine the Castellan of Farport receives many visiting dignitaries." Ambassador Soru set his glass down on the somewhat battered table. At least the wine was good.

The door opened.

"Williams!" Soru said pleasantly, rising to greet the Assistant to the Minister. "I was wondering if you were going to make it."

"Damn transports are so unreliable out here in the middle of nowhere," the younger man said, shaking Soru's hand.

"Farport won't be the middle of nowhere much longer, the way it's growing," Soru said. "You know Admiral Terat, of course."

"Of course. Good to see you, Sir."

Terat hurrumphed a greeting. He did not get up.

"You read the briefings, of course?" Soru said.

"On my way down," Williams replied. "Quite a tricky turn of events, isn't it?"

"It's a bad business, Williams," Terat said grimly. "Damned awkward."

"Where are the others?" Williams asked, setting his brief case down on a desk and opening it.

"Bital is down in the wretched excuse they have for a detention center," the Admiral answered, "talking to Commander Lars, the Kurlu Elite officer. Dr. Fellows, I would imagine, is in the infirmary. Fellows has been working with the local doctor—Yoshi, I think his name is—on nursing the anomaly back to health."

"Any luck?"

"Unfortunately, yes," Terat grumbled. "It might have been a lot simpler for us if the damned thing had died."

"What about the Kurlu Ambassador? Have you heard when he's expected?"

"He should be here any time."

Williams grinned. "And then we all get together in one room and discuss it like gentlemen, eh? Hope you have plenty of security on hand."

"We've brought reinforcements," Terat said. "Don't like the Chief of Security here. Don't like his attitude. Impudent puppy. And a bit too tight with that creature, too. Roughed up the Kurlu officer a lot more than was necessary if you ask me."

"Understandable, I might think," Williams said. "After all, Lars did open fire in a room full of people. Ten people injured, besides the Castellan."

"The man's a commander of the Kurlu Elite, for the love of gods, man! You don't strip-search him and throw him into a common jail cell, no matter what he's done!" Terat exclaimed. "Besides, no one was seriously hurt."

"I don't believe the Kurlu Government intends to make more than a nominal fuss about it," Soru said.

"From what I've read in the reports," Williams went on, "the anomaly has done quite a job here. He's well respected by the citizens and by his staff and subordinates. It seems he has inspired quite a bit of loyalty."

"Ridiculous!" Terat snorted. "The creature plays a good game of it, that's all. From what the Kurlu minister told me, they are all damned clever, these creatures."

"True," Soru said. "The Kurlu ambassador emphasized the danger they represent. He was most apologetic for not informing us about the matter before sending out their agent, but they were concerned that prior notification of the U.P. might have alerted the creature to the fact that they were on to it."

Williams looked at Terat. "So we are accepting their version of things, eh?"

"We can't very well afford not to, can we?" the Admiral replied.

Williams inclined his head. "You know the Academy has an entirely different slant on this. Based on the years they worked with the anomaly, they are convinced that Prilock is exactly what he has been claiming he is. And in fact they think he might be a valuable ally, a creature who is on our side and may be able to communicate and negotiate with the others of his kind."

Terat snorted. "The Academy be damned! They pushed to have that thing recognized as an intelligent being with civil rights, and then rammed him down our throats. Castellan indeed! I was opposed to the whole absurd notion from the beginning!"

Williams found a chair and sat down. "Well, you must admit, Prilock has performed every task given him admirably, and running Farport has certainly not been any exception. He's done nothing to cause us the slightest bit of suspicion or uneasiness."

"Well, he wouldn't, would he?" Terat replied. "An enemy agent trying to infiltrate our society would do everything in his power to gain our confidence, eh?"

Williams inclined his head. "I suppose that is true. Nevertheless, I expect Fellows will be arguing strongly for the Academy's position. After all, he does have a vested interest in this matter. He was on the original team that studied the anomaly and has been one of its greatest advocates."

"Dr. Fellows is an ass," Terat grumbled. "Most of those highbrow types are. No sense of perspective. Heads in the clouds. No understanding of harsh realities."

"Well," Williams said, "The Minister has authorized me to act on his behalf to clear up this matter in the most expedient way possible. Naturally, since Farport is under your authority, Admiral, I shall give your recommendations the greatest weight. Of course, as to the larger issue of what to do about the situation with the creatures in general, nothing can be done until a full session of the Council of United Peoples can be convened."

"Of course," Terat said. "I will make my complete recommendations then."

"As to this situation in particular," Soru said, "we must be extremely careful to maintain the best relations possible with the Kurlu. We will have to rely on their information and good graces in dealing with these creatures."

"Of course," Williams said. "We have quite a bit of information, ourselves, and we can use that as a bargaining chip. After all, we had an actual specimen under observation and study for twenty years."

"An excellent point," Soru said.

A knock came on the door, and a guard came in. "Sir, the Kurlu Ambassador's ship has just arrived and is docking."

"Excellent," Williams said, getting up.

"We really ought to have the Elite officer ready and on hand," Soru said, "As a gesture of good faith. It wouldn't do to have the Ambassador see him in the context of a common jail cell."

"A very good point," Williams agreed. "Admiral?"

"Naturally, naturally. Lieutenant," he said to the guard, "Get down to the detention center on the double and tell Bital the Ambassador is here. Have them meet us at the dock."

"Yes Sir."

Williams closed his brief case and picked it up. "Well, here we go. May the Lady of Good Fortune smile on us."

Soru frowned uneasily. "I do hope the anomaly doesn't make any trouble for us."

"It had better not!" Terat growled as he walked out of the room, "At least now we know how to deal with the filthy beggars."

Dr. Fellows nodded as he read the data board, smiling. "You've made excellent progress, Prilock. You've recovered about ninety-nine per cent of your original mass. How are you feeling?"

"I've had better days," Prilock replied, glancing into the mirror critically. "This memory loss bothers me. I keep noticing gaps in what I ought to know. I had to work all morning at remembering how to make my legs work, and it used to be second nature to me."

"Well, that's to be expected," Fellows said. "You're basically a unicellular being. When you lost eighteen per cent of your body mass, you lost eighteen percent of your mind, too. Are you having any trouble re-learning things?"

"No," Prilock said, "But it's damned annoying. And I keep wondering what I've forgotten that I don't remember that I've forgotten. If you know what I mean."

Yoshi chuckled. "I think so. You'll be happy to know that I've just run a complete physical on Shaka Mahdi, and she seems to be none the worse for her part in this ordeal."

"Good," Prilock said, relieved. "She's been through enough."

"I am truly fascinated by this compatibility between you and the Byahail," Fellows said. "When we have an opportunity, I'd like to talk to you more about it."

Indeed, that compatibility was what had saved Prilock's life. The doctors had tried everything to get the missing body mass to regenerate, and nothing seemed to work. It wasn't until Yoshi had told Fellows about the traces of Prilock's genetic matter he had discovered in the Byahail's body, evidently passing into her tissue by osmosis during intimate physical contact, that they hit upon the solution. Filtering out those bits from the Byahail's blood had been a tricky business, but when the tiny threads were returned to Prilock's body in a nutritive medium, he immediately began to gain weight. He now seemed, to all appearances, back to normal.

Prilock looked over at Fellows uneasily. As glad as he was to see the doctor, who was an old and trusted acquaintance, one of the few humans he felt a real measure of respect for, he didn't like discussing his relationship with Shaka with anyone. Fellows was among the first of the scientists to treat him like a person, not like a lab rat. Prilock hoped Fellows would understand, if any of them would, that he had a personal life that did not warrant scientific scrutiny. He changed the subject.

"Well, provided I remember where my office is, which I think I still do, I'd like to return to my duties as soon as possible."

"Good!" Fellows said. "If you feel up to it, your first duty will be to deal with the gaggle of diplomats and assorted political flotsam that has converged on Farport."

"In my honor, no doubt?" Prilock said.

"This little incident has caused quite a stir," Fellows said. "In about a half an hour there is to be a summit of sorts."

"Hm! Who is going to be there?"

"Oh, our ambassador, their ambassador, and all the other self-important little hangers-on that swarm to such occasions. Including our old friend Admiral Terat."

Prilock grimaced. "How charming. And is he calling for my head?"

"On a platter, I'm afraid."

Prilock turned and looked hard at Fellows. "Seriously, Doctor. Terat has been looking for an excuse to lock me up again ever since your people managed to get me released. What do they intend to do about me?"

"Nothing has been decided yet, as far as I know," Fellows said lightly. "Don't worry, old man, we'll get through this."

Prilock's cold expression did not lighten. "They're relieving me, aren't they?"

"Now, I don't think we should jump to any premature conclusions about what they might or might not do—"

"Damn it, don't patronize me! I want the truth!"

Fellows dropped all pretense of joviality. He had direct orders not to say anything to the anomaly that might alarm it. Keep it calm, persuade it to cooperate, that was what he had been told. To hell with his orders; he couldn't be that big a hypocrite. True, things hadn't officially been decided, but he had a damn good idea how it was going to go. No matter what he said at the conference, no matter how eloquently he argued, paranoia would prevail. He had seen the way bureaucrats and diplomats operated for too long to seriously expect anything else. They would play it safe and do the stupidest thing possible, locking up and probably completely alienating the one being who was their best chance, their ace trump, in dealing with the unknown creatures.

He had worked with the strange and remarkable being they had called "Prilock" ever since it had been brought to the Academy laboratories. He knew its behavior patterns intimately. It was extraordinarily intelligent, logical and rational. It had a strong, apparently innate, sense of honor, an aversion to falsehood, and although situations of extreme frustration could provoke outbursts of temper, it did not have a violent nature. If anything, Fellows considered the anomaly to be a superior being who had been extraordinarily patient, all things considered, with the foolish humans it had had to deal with. And he was afraid its patience was about to run out.

He felt he owed Prilock the truth. And if he were completely candid, including about how desperately they needed Prilock's help, in spite of the ignorance of the idiots in charge of this fiasco, maybe the being wouldn't abandon them all in disgust.

Fellows sighed heavily. "Dr. Yoshi," he said grimly, "Would you excuse us, please?"

It was the first time Shaka had felt confident enough with Prilock's recovery that she felt she could leave him and to go back to her ship, shower and change clothes, and spend a few moments of much-needed solitude. He seemed pretty much back to normal, and the doctors seemed satisfied with his progress. Still, Shaka was uneasy leaving him alone for too long. She allowed herself this respite, but was anxious to get back to him within the hour.

She had noticed a change in him as she had begun to come out of the strange delirium. The desperate intimacy of their contact had made her unusually in tune with him, and as she had sensed his agony and terror when he was first wounded, she could sense a vague emptiness, a weakness, an irretrievable loss of some kind. His return to consciousness paralleled hers, and as they came out of the hazy, feverish state, the sensation of loss faded and vanished. Shaka knew it was still there somewhere, buried within him. Prilock's scars were invisible, but were just as cruelly permanent as hers.

The doctors had explained to her what they had done, using her blood to help heal Prilock. The doctor she did not know, the one from the U.P., seemed nice enough, and seemed truly concerned with doing the best he could for Prilock. But Shaka disliked him. There was something in his manner which made her feel that he did not respect her, like so many humans. At least Dr. Yoshi was apologetic that they had taken liberties with her body in trying to heal Prilock. Of course she was glad to give all she could, but she did not like being taken for granted. Dr. Yoshi told her that he would have been happier if he could have gotten her prior permission before doing the experimental procedure. It had not been possible, given her state of delirium, and he guessed that she would want them to do whatever they could. She assured him that it was all right. And she respected Dr. Yoshi a little more for having made the gesture.

She also disliked the questions the strange doctor asked her. His attitude towards her was too clinical. He had no business inquiring into the personal aspects of her relationship with Prilock. She resented it. Dr. Yoshi could be very stupid sometimes, but at least he had never been so indiscreet. But Prilock seemed used to the strange doctor's rude questions. They knew each other from a long time ago, from when Prilock still had to live in the Academy laboratories, being studied. Prilock told her that this doctor had been one of the ones who had worked to get Prilock his freedom, and he trusted him and did not mind his questions. Prilock asked her to be patient with the strange doctor, because he was a good human, as humans went, and an ally. So she tried to be polite. But still, she refused to answer some of his questions.

She stood on the deck of the *Chimera*, smoking a ginseng, allowing herself a few more moments of solitude before returning to the medical center. She thought about how she felt, no longer isolated and unable to act. It had been the call from Morris that night that had done it. That had motivated her, sending her out of her ship for the first time in weeks. She could not let her friend face such a danger alone. She could not trust the humans to protect him. And now that she was out, the habit of impotent inactivity broken, it was easy to keep going. Especially knowing the hidden vulnerability that lay deep inside her friend. A sense of protectiveness made her fierce, cold towards her old fears. And now she knew Prilock was more than just a friend, more than just a fellow outsider in the strange world of humans. He was Chimera.

Chimera. What perfect and obvious sense it made. It explained everything neatly: the easy rapport between them, the symbiosis, the necessity of their friendship. Her relationship with Prilock was not a disturbing mystery anymore. In fact, everything was changed. The Chimera were not a myth. They were very real, and they had come down from the Mountains to honor the covenant. Whatever strange set of circumstances had caused Prilock to stray, amnestic, away from the rest of his kind, it did not matter to Shaka. The gods were real. And one of them had somehow, miraculously, fallen into her care.

There was an official U.P. patrol boat moving past her on its way to the military docks. Shaka frowned. It was the fourth one she had seen. She flicked the stub of the ginseng over the edge of the ship. It hissed briefly as it hit the water. She walked off the ship and up the footpath to the main street. She could smell it in the air—the stink of bureaucrats and diplomacy. Strange guards in blue U.P. uniforms were patrolling the streets. She also saw the grey and brown of the Kurlu diplomatic guard. Then she saw the delegation coming up the street, surrounded by guards both uniformed and in plain clothes. Marcus Lars, free as a dragon fly, was among them. Shaka wrinkled her nose as the stink got worse. It was the sickly-sweet smell of hypocrisy.

She ducked out of sight and hurried on her way to the medical center. She felt a renewed sense of urgency. Prilock had enemies. They had smelled his blood and they were gathering around, smiling with their white, perfect teeth.

There were more guards around the medical center, but they let her by without question. "It's the Byahail," one said knowingly to another, "It's okay." They stared at her, of course. Shaka hated them but she did not fear them. She could not afford fear. Not while the Chimera was in danger.

She went into the doctor's office and saw Yoshi and Christina, restlessly waiting.

"What is with guards?" she asked.

"Oh, you noticed them?" Yoshi snapped sarcastically. "Beats the hell out of me. Nobody has told me anything. But you can bet they aren't there for Prilock's protection!"

"Where is Prilock?"

"In there," Yoshi said, gesturing towards the other room. "Talking to Fellows. I've got a feeling Prilock is going to wring some answers out of him."

"There's going to be some sort of big conference in a half an hour," Christina said. "All sorts of officials in attendance."

"Just saw delegation," Shaka said, glancing over her shoulder. "Did not like look of any of those ones."

"And none of them up to any good," Yoshi said. "You can bet on it!"

Shaka frowned. "What are thinking those ones will do?"

Christina shrugged unhappily, and Yoshi cried, "If you ask me, the bastards'll probably—

He was interrupted by a furious shout from the other room. Prilock's incredulous voice was demanding something about having to sit at the same table with the bloody assassin. Fellow's less audible voice was pleading conciliation. Apparently whatever he said was ineffective. The next thing they heard was a loud crash.

"Dear gods, don't let him wreck my infirmary," Yoshi prayed, bolting for the door. Shaka was already there and had it halfway open.

"Please, Prilock, I urge you!" Fellows was begging, "You'll only destroy your own credibility if you resort to violence!"

Yoshi groaned, seeing a CPR unit in pieces on the floor. Prilock stood above it, shaking with rage, his eyes blazing. "What the bloody hell is the use?" he thundered. "I've been playing their insane, ridiculous game for twenty years! What has it got me? The sons of bitches are ready to lock me up at the first damned bloody Kurlu rumor!"

"It's only temporary—" Fellows started, backing up and beginning to look a little afraid.

"Ready to lock me up while that bloody assassin is treated like a guest of honor!" Prilock shouted, and he hurled another piece of equipment against the wall. Fellows winced recoiling further.

"Prilock, no! My equipment—" Yoshi cried, starting towards him. He froze when he saw the insane rage in Prilock's expression.

"To hell with you and your equipment!" he roared. "You damned bloody humans! I'd like to give you all a real reason to fear me!"

Yoshi retreated hastily to the doorway, hovering there next to Christina, both of them staring in horror at the fearful creature whose terrible power they had always taken for granted as benign. Shaka saw through it down the cold, hidden scar within him. She knew what he was feeling. She knew it all too well. And knowing where it came from, she knew how to deal with it.

She strode over to him, putting her hand firmly on his arm, restraining him from grabbing anything else to throw. "Prilock!" she said sharply, "Rage is not thinking! Who are hurting with anger? Who are hurting with things broken? Doctor who healed! Humans of Farport who need doctor and equipment! Humans of Farport who spoke up for Prilock on night that Marcus Lars came! Humans who defended, who would defend still! Think! Who is hate for? For those ones?"

"No," he said softly, "Not for them." Rationality returned slowly to his expression.

"See," Shaka said gently. "See what are doing. Hurt wrong humans. Make fear in humans who have done no harm. This is not justice. This is not noble. Are great and noble being. Do not do these things."

The fire went out of his eyes and the tension left his body. He looked over at Fellows, then at Dr. Yoshi and Christina. His expression became remorseful. "Forgive me," he said. "Please forgive me. My outburst was inexcusable."

"Quite all right," Yoshi said with relief.

"Most certainly," Dr. Fellows sighed, wiping the perspiration from his forehead with a handkerchief. "I can appreciate your frustration. But we must handle the situation calmly and rationally if we are going to succeed."

"Of course," Prilock murmured. "If I could just have a moment to compose myself."

"Naturally," Fellows said. "I will wait for you outside. But do remember, we have to be at the conference in—" he glanced at his watch, "less than twenty minutes."

"I'll be ready," Prilock said.

"Good!" Fellows, his own composure regained with small difficulty, managed to leave with a fair amount of dignity. Yoshi followed him out, saying, "I want to talk to you!"

Christina, her momentary apprehension completely past, went over to Prilock. "What on earth did he say to you to make you so upset?"

Prilock felt too defeated to be angry anymore. The sources of his anger were too far removed. "There's to be an official inquiry into the allegations being made by the Kurlu government," he said wearily. "This conference is ostensibly to decide what is to be done about the situation in general, and me in particular. Except Fellows is quite certain—and I expect he's right—that a decision has already been made. That's how these people operate. They make their decisions privately and informally, behind closed doors, then go though the official motions for the sake of appearances."

"And what have they decided?" Christina asked, afraid she knew the answer already.

"I am to be relieved of my duties as Castellan," Prilock replied. "I will be removed to a place of safety for the duration of the inquiry. Removed, of course, for their safety, not for mine."

Christina sighed. "Blame the victim. It figures."

"Is no one to speak up for Prilock?" Shaka asked. "What about doctors from Academy? Ones who spoke for before?"

"Oh, Dr. Fellows will do what he can," Prilock said, "But the Academy is long on prestige and short on real power. It took them years to get me released from the security zone of the lab and years more to get me recognized as an intelligent being entitled to civil rights. And that was when I was just a presumably benign anomaly. How willing are the authorities going to be to listen now that they know I'm from a race of killers? A shadow-slayer." He said it with a sense of miserable doom.

"No," Shaka said adamantly, shaking her head, "Not shadow-slayer. Chimera."

Prilock frowned curiously at her. "That's the name of your ship."

"Is name of ancient gods of Byahail. Only elders ever see Chimera. When stars are right, at time when kalistra blooms, Elders go to Mountains for communion, to renew ancient covenant."

"You never suspected before now?" Christina asked.

"Did not believe in old gods," Shaka said. "When Byahail are killed and driven from land, no great beings come to save. So am thinking Chimera are myth. Only stories told by elders, like gods of humans. But now am hearing of race of great and powerful beings coming down from Mountains to avenge Shaka's people and drive away Kurlu. What else can be but Chimera? Are saying that Prilock is such a being. Then what else can Prilock be?" She smiled at him with admiration. "Is Chimera."

"Chimera," Prilock echoed thoughtfully, sitting down on the edge of a bed. "Not a race of killers. A race of gods."

"I think it suits you much better," Christina said.

He looked up at her. "Thank you," he said. "Madam, I am truly sorry for what I said earlier. I certainly did not mean to include you in my indictment of humans."

"No offense taken," Christina said, dismissing it with a gesture. "And don't worry about the equipment. The U.P. will get us more. Certainly Farport can afford it, thanks to the affluence your efforts as Castellan have brought us." She sobered. "In fact, allowing you to be labeled a spy and hauled off to some fancy prison by a gaggle of braying bureaucrats seems a pretty poor way to repay you for all you've done."

Prilock shrugged. "They make the laws. What alternative is there?"

Christina grinned at him. "I should think a god would have plenty of alternatives. For instance, why don't you simply refuse?"

He cocked his head. "Refuse?"

"Sure. Just walk out. Who's going to stop you?"

Shaka began to grin. "Doctor Christina is right. Chimera does not need to play stupid human games. Has more important destiny."

He toyed with the notion, warming to it. Anything seemed better than facing confinement for who could guess how long. And it was the height of absurd futility to continue trying to obey the rules of a society whose highest ranking members routinely bent or broke those rules to suit their own agenda. "Where would I go?" he mused aloud, but he already had an idea of the answer even as he said it.

"You can at least get away from here," Christina said. "And you'd better hurry. They're going to come looking for you pretty soon, now."

"Will take," Shaka said eagerly. "Come! Shaka knows ways of swamp. Enemies can never find."

Prilock shook his head. "No, I couldn't ask you to do that. If I leave here now I will be a fugitive. If you aid me in my flight they'll come after you, too."

"Will take that chance," Shaka said firmly. "Friend more important."

"Thank you, but you have done quite enough for me already. Besides, you have your own problems. I have no right to burden you with my problems as well."

"Will need help getting out of Farport," she insisted.

"I will manage," he replied stubbornly.

Shaka scowled at him, thinking hard. She said, "Where Prilock go? Perhaps will be seeking other gods, eh?" She grinned triumphantly. "Mountains are very big. Even Kurlu in years of search cannot find city of Chimera. Shaka can tell Prilock where to find path elders take to meet Chimera."

"Hm!" he snorted, "And I suppose you won't tell me unless I let you take me out of here, right?"

She nodded triumphantly.

"All right, all right, you win!" he said, annoyed. "Anyway, I want to find out more about what you remember of the Chimera, and we don't have time for that now." He looked around. "Let's see, how do we get out of here past the guards?"

"They'll let Shaka out," Christina said. "It's you they're on the look-out for. We just have to find a way to smuggle you out of the building unnoticed."

"Ah," he said. "That should be simple. Just find me a window that is overgrown by bushes. It only needs to open a crack. I can ooze out and no one will be the wiser."

Christina thought a minute and then snapped her fingers. "The store room! The jungle presses up against that whole side of the building. Since there's no door on that side, they've given up trying to keep it cut back. We can get to it through here." She pointed to a door at the back of the room.

"Excellent!" Prilock said. "Shaka, I will meet you on the path to your ship."

Shaka walked by the guards without a word, merely an icy glare at them as she went by. Dr. Yoshi and Dr. Fellows were still at it, arguing in hushed tones under the trees. They looked up at her as she walked down the path. "Shaka?" Yoshi called to her.

"Prilock, is he all right?" Fellows asked.

"Is fine," Shaka replied, not slowing down. "All will be well."

"Good, good!" Fellows said with relief, and told Yoshi he must be on his way.

"Damn it, Fellows!" Yoshi exclaimed, "I insist I be given a chance to testify! I won't have them railroading Prilock!"

Fellows turned to protest that it might not be possible and likely would do no good, but Shaka kept walking and didn't hear any more.

She went briskly along the main street, noting that she was being watched with more than the usual puerile curiosity. As she came to the fork that led down to the docks where her ship was moored she paused, checking to see if she were merely being observed, or actually followed. After a moment or two she decided that, because she was alone, her passage was merely being noted. So she continued down the footpath to her ship. At the turn she paused again and cautiously peered through the undergrowth that crowded the path.

Her ship was being guarded.

Prilock found her standing in the path, smoking a ginseng, waiting for him.

"Any trouble?" she asked him, dropping the stub and crushing it out with her boot.

"Not at all," he replied with satisfaction. "No one pays particular attention to a common green snake passing silently through the trees, even if it is an uncommonly long one. And you?"

"No trouble. But am being watched." She nodded down the path. "Also watch ship."

"Not surprising," Prilock said. "Anyone we know?"

Shaka nodded. "Captain Morris. Maybe six, maybe eight others. All Castellan's men."

"Not any more," he said, "At least not officially. But everyone around here has been most flatteringly loyal to me. Let's see if we can brazen it out."

"Is worth trying," Shaka agreed. "If anyone still is loyal to Castellan, would be Morris."

Prilock nodded. He also happened to know the Morris detested Admiral Terat. They walked casually down the path.

"Sir!" Morris exclaimed as soon as he saw them.

"Captain," Prilock replied with a nod of acknowledgment. "Kindly stand aside and let us pass."

Morris looked pained. "I'm afraid I can't, Sir."

Prilock arched an eyebrow. "It's not like you to disobey an order."

"That's just it, Sir," Morris explained unhappily. "I have direct orders from Admiral Terat. And," he added hesitantly, "They tell me you're being relieved, Sir."

Prilock nodded slowly. "What else have they told you?"

Indignation mixed with Morris's pained expression. "I don't believe any of it, Sir! And if I may be so bold, I think it stinks! Sir."

"Thank you, Morris. So you can certainly understand my disinclination to cooperate with the authorities."

"Yes, Sir!" Morris said firmly, but then added awkwardly and apologetically, "But I have my orders."

"Of course you do," Prilock said. "And naturally you will obey them. You have always been an exemplary officer. Carry on, Captain."

"Yes, Sir," Morris said with mixed relief and regret.

Prilock turned and said to Shaka, "You go ahead, Captain Mahdi. I'll meet up with you later."

She hesitated, then comprehended, or at least hoped she did, and nodded. Prilock turned and strode purposefully back up the footpath. Shaka turned and faced the guards.

"Am assuming may go aboard own ship?"

"Yes, Captain," Morris said hastily, motioning to his men to stand aside. "Captain Mahdi," he said as she went by, "I really am sorry."

She looked at him and nodded. "Duty is not easy sometimes," she said, and continued onto her ship.

Morris turned back to resume his position. "Duty stinks sometimes," he muttered.

"You said it," sighed the lieutenant standing next to him. "Sir," the man added respectfully. Morris concealed a smile.

A few moments later there was a subtle splash somewhere near the dock, then more quiet splashing near the Byahail's ship.

"Sir? I thought I heard—"

"You didn't hear a thing, Lieutenant," Morris said.

The man abruptly faced forward again. "No, Sir," he said.

Morris looked sternly down the line. "None of you heard

anything, did you?" He was answered with a chorus of "Not a thing, Sir," and one reply of, "Heard what, Sir?"

A few moments later the ship's engines started up. Again Morris sternly repressed a smile. Captain Mahdi appeared on the deck and went through the routine of casting off. She looked down at the guards. "Am assuming is permitted for ship to leave?"

"It's a free port," Morris called back. "I have no orders to prevent your departure unless the Castellan is aboard."

"Is no castellan on ship," she said.

"Very good, then! Have a safe trip!"

Shaka finished casting off and went back below.

"You realize, of course," Prilock said to her as she took the controls and began guiding the ship away from the dock, "That I am still officially castellan until they formally relieve me, and that wasn't suppose to happen until the conference."

Shaka shrugged. "So Prilock resigned first. Did that, eh?"

"Of course," Prilock agreed with a faint smile. "I wouldn't want to make a liar out of you."

Morris watched the ship depart, and then nodded. "Well, seeing as we don't have anything to guard anymore, let's get back to headquarters, shall we?"

"Yes, Sir," the lieutenant said, then asked hesitantly, "Sir, didn't we have orders to report if the Byahail ship left the dock?"

"That's right, Lieutenant, and report we will, just as soon as we get to headquarters." Morris set off at a leisurely pace. The men fell into step, unquestioningly, behind him.

Things went quite smoothly until they were almost out of the harbor. Then, apparently Prilock's absence was noted, Shaka's departure was reported, and the authorities put two and two together. The port controllers contacted the *Chimera* and ordered Captain Mahdi to return to dock. She ignored the order and shifted the ship into high gear. Thus began the wildest ride that Prilock had ever experienced.

Shaka Mahdi led the U.P. patrol fleet on a frantic chase through the dense tangle of swamp, tearing down weed-choked channels

and abandoned waterways, weaving madly at insane speeds through
the maze of sunken logs, rocks and debris, skimming over mud
bars. Overhanging branches slapped the side of the ship and cracked
against the deck. Prilock watched Shaka with admiration, her
muscles taut, her hands gripping the controls, her eyes fixed in
unblinking concentration on the screen and instruments. Every
time the rear scanners showed a patrol boat gaining on them Shaka
would begin looking for a likely spot—the signs of which would
be invisible to Prilock—and she would abruptly swerve, cutting
the engines and ramming the ship into some densely overgrown
inlet, the heavy branches and vines falling like a curtain behind
them. Then she would shut down everything and go up on deck,
light up a ginseng and wait. The roar of the pursuing patrol boat's
engines would grow closer, pass, and gradually fade. With the
systems shut down the ship was invisible to the patrol's scanners.
To them, their quarry would seem to have just suddenly vanished,
and they would cruise the waterways searching in vain. Shaka, in
the meantime, would finish her smoke, wait another minute or
two until the sound of engines faded into the distance, then go
back down to the control room. With the systems back on and the
engines powered up, she would carefully back the ship out into
the waterway again and resume her breakneck course.

All afternoon they zigzagged down through the maze of the
swamp, heading generally south. When nightfall came she could
no longer use the external screen to navigate. They could still
keep going, navigating by the instruments alone, but not in
the treacherous backwaters. They had to follow an open
waterway. So they moved out into the traffic of a main channel,
mixing with the other freighters, transports and eel boats,
trusting that any passing patrol boat would be at an equal
disadvantage, being unable to pick them out in the dark. The
patrols, on the other hand, were easy to spot and avoid,
identifiable at a distance by their blue running lights. Shaka left
Prilock to pilot the ship while she grabbed a few hours sleep. She
was up again before dawn, and as soon as there was enough light

to use the screen they left the main channel and were off again, weaving through the dense labyrinth.

By late afternoon they reached the southernmost edge of the thick swamp. The vast open marsh spread out before them, flat and grassy, dotted with occasional clumps of awkbush and red willow, stretching as far as the eye could see to the east and south. The thick swamp and jungle curved away to the west. They had seen no sign of pursuit for hours, and once out in the great open marsh the danger was negligible. There was just too much area to patrol and too many thickets to hide in. They had made it. They were free.

It was the first time Prilock had seen the great southern marshland. He stood on the deck, looking out across the undulating expanse of green and gold. The grass traced the passage of the wind with its motions and with an omnipresent rise and fall of shushing pink noise. The dragon flies were coming out to catch their evening meal of gnats, darting swiftly back and forth on broad, iridescent wings. The sun's rays slanted across at an angle that set every feature out in sharp contrast, the fluttering leaves of a distant patch of red willow turned vivid orange on the west-facing side.

"It's beautiful," he murmured.

Shaka nodded, standing beside him. She gestured to their right, towards the setting sun. "In that direction is Reservation. Is on last tip of land before thick swamp and wet jungle. Is one waterway cleared by U.P. that goes there." She turned and gestured broadly to the east. "That way is Kurlu Empire, across marsh. Big trading ports, Heng So and Simpan are that way. Simpan is maybe two weeks, steady travel and good weather. Heng So is three weeks." She gestured to the southeast. "Land of Byahail is that way, great Mountains are just beyond. Can be there in twenty days."

Prilock nodded. "What lies directly south?"

"South is marsh and more marsh. Gets hotter and air gets bad. Gas bubbles come up from marsh mud. Can make very sick. Also, is kind of marsh mustard. Certain times of year makes large patches of bright yellow flowers. Attracts stinging insects. If go through while on deck, can be stung to death. Still further west, come to thick swamp and wet jungle. No waterways. No way to get through. Can go no further."

"And no one knows what lies beyond that," Prilock murmured.

"Maybe Chimera," Shaka said. "Elders say Chimera are old as world and know all of world's secrets."

He nodded, a trace of a smile on his face. Chimera. "Well, Captain, I believe a good torpor is in order. I've been awake for almost two days straight and I wasn't at my best when I started."

"Is good idea," Shaka agreed. "Will secure ship and join in cabin."

When he lay down with her that night he felt a sudden rush of tenderness towards Shaka. It took him by surprise. It was an emotion he was unfamiliar with. Or at least, he had never felt it quite this way, or quite this strongly. I am changed, he thought as he relaxed his substance over her, the familiar feeling of peace and tranquility spreading through him. I have tasted pain and mortality, been brought back to life, and I am changed.

I am Chimera.

CHAPTER 6

The sun blazed down from the starkly azure sky. The hot, humid air moved reluctantly, stirred only by the occasional breath of breeze. The grass was in perpetual motion, shifting in leisurely waves as though by herds of unseen creatures randomly wandering. Insects hummed and buzzed and clicked in an ever-present, irregular staccato. The red willow leaves above them shifted, breaking up the glare of the sun into glittering fragments and casting a stipple of shadow on the deck. The air smelled of wet and muck and heat, and the constant decay and fecund regrowth of the green marsh. Occasionally the breeze wafted to them the fleeting sweetness of blooming things, the purple ironweed, the pale yellow flybalm.

Shaka, sitting on the deck with her long legs stretched out, her tail curved around her, its tip flicking just slightly up and down, leaned back against Prilock who sat behind her, leaning against the railing of the deck. She felt drowsy in the heat of the day despite a good night's sleep. Her eyes half-closed she watched the play of light and motion across the marsh. Prilock was a solid physical presence close to her, and she realized idly how much she had missed that physical closeness. Her people were very affectionate with their off-spring; she had been well-hugged as a child and had been brought up to give and expect lavish and frequent expressions of affection. She had missed that when she left the Reservation to live among humans. She had gotten herself into some very unwise liaisons with humans just because she craved the touch of another creature. It always ended disastrously, and finally she'd hardened herself against the need.

In her friendship with Prilock there had always been the paradoxical formal intimacy of touch. They slept together, him melted over her naked body like a warm, soft blanket, but in their everyday interaction they rarely touched, and never embraced. The only physical contact they ever shared was when he was in his amorphous natural state. The very few times she had touched him in his human form she had almost been startled by how odd he felt, no bone or sinew beneath pliant flesh. He was like hard rubber, sculptured into the form of a being of flesh and bone, a mere statue.

He felt that way now. His cheek was not soft, nor was his chin comparatively hard. No rib cage over a softer give of stomach. But he was warm, and alive, and there was the subtle language of affection in his physical closeness. The hidden scar inside him, and the missing something replaced with the unknown something else, made him need in a way he had never needed before. Shaka felt a little sad, because that need came out of damage done to him. And she knew that ultimately it would bring him pain, as all need did. She was here for him now, and happy to be so. But she would not always be. He was Chimera, an immortal being. His life could last a very, very long time.

At one time in her life she had scorned the notion of wanting such a relationship. But then again, at one time in her life she had scorned the beliefs of her people and called the Chimera a myth.

Prilock spoke quietly, breaking the hypnotic spell of the sun, the heat, the moving grass and the song of the insects. "Tell me more," he said. "What else do you remember?"

Shaka put aside the musing inspired by the heat of the day and the bittersweet pleasure of the moment and cast her mind back to the stories of the elders, memories almost forgotten, buried under years of living in the cynical world of humans.

"In beginning of world, Chimera walked alone. Was no living thing but Chimera. World was very different. Everywhere was like birthing mud of Valley of Byahail. But world began to change. Land rose up. Green things began to grow. Chimera watched and waited. Animals and insects came out of swamp and Chimera said, is good. Will be creatures soon. Company for Chimera. Animals grew and changed, Chimera waited and watched. But was no animal that could be company for Chimera. Gods became lonely. Became tired of waiting. And so, Chimera said, will make from animals beings to be company. Created Byahail. Gave Byahail most beautiful place in world to live. Could not make immortal like Chimera, but made Byahail more clever than any other animal at making children. Taught how to raise children to be good and have noble hearts without evil. Promised that Valley would be for Byahail always, and Chimera would watch over. Chimera said, now will always be company for Chimera. Will always be Byahail."

Prilock indulged a whim to reach up and touch her shaggy mane. He marveled at the texture. Yes, if he were a lonely god he would create a strong, graceful being like the Byahail for companionship. Even scarred and battered by her ordeals, she was still a magnificent creature. And he had recognized and respected the nobility of her soul from the first day he met her. His people had done well with their creation.

She turned to look at him. "Did not believe those stories until now. Am knowing now is all true. Soon Chimera will drive Kurlu from Valley. Byahail will be able to go home. Very few left—were not many when Shaka left Reservation. Will be even less now. But will not matter. When Byahail return to Valley there will be many children. Promise of gods will be fulfilled."

"Will you go with them, Shaka?" he asked.

She cocked her head thoughtfully. "Am planning to go to Reservation when Prilock leaves for Mountains. Must tell Byahail of news, that gods have come down to honor covenant, that Byahail will be going home soon. Then, when time comes, will take people in ship. Maybe stay in Valley, not sure. No place for Shaka in world of humans anymore. Might be good to help rebuild old ways and old life. Will be much work to do. All people will be needed. As for children, am ruined by what Fenrire did. Am not sure if can be future for Shaka. But children need many besides birthers to grow strong. Can teach children of others. Have learned much that would be good for Byahail to know."

He nodded, closing his eyes. He looked inside himself, watching the young god coming awake. So many years in ignorance, confined to the laboratory, his ambitions and knowledge limited by the tiny cage that was the society of humans. How hard he had worked, a performing animal, to received the scraps of reward they allowed him. He had never even taken the time to simply experience things, contemplatively, as he was now. He focused his attention on what each sense was bringing him, each sound, each scent, the broad bands of vibration and radiation, more vastly broad than he could perceive, at least, as yet. A huge, rich world was pressing in on him, fascinatingly complex, and every time he pushed back, his horizons expanded further. His only limitation now was his own inexperience.

Prilock frowned, a thought occurring to him. "Shaka," he asked, "Is there anything in the stories of your elders about where humans came from, and when?"

She thought for a moment and then shook her head. "Do not remember anything. Maybe is story, but Shaka never heard it, or has forgotten. Most of Byahail assume humans are animals, come like other animals, from swamp or jungle. Not created by gods. Gods would not create such things."

Perhaps his people would know. Perhaps, content in the harmony of life in the Mountains and the Valley, they simply overlooked the evolution of humans in the north. Perhaps they simply ignored them as irrelevant, until the creatures had overrun the world and begun wreaking havoc. Prilock smiled. Well, the Chimera had certainly noticed them now. He wondered what his people intended to do about them. He would find out eventually. For now, he didn't want to trouble his contentment with any further thoughts about humans. He wanted to think about his own destiny, and this marvelous being, whose voice, with its melodious accents, was such a pleasure to listen to. "Tell me more of what you do remember, then," he said. He wanted to know, but then, he also simply wanted to listen to her speak.

"Hmm," she murmured, taking herself back to the sound of

an elder Byahail speaking in the way they did when relating something important, something that must be told just right so it would be remembered and repeated with nothing missing or changed. "In early days, Chimera came among Byahail often, to watch over and teach. Teach ways to live. Show how to find food, and how to grow food. How to make shelters. Teach to be noble, strong and just. Teach meaning of honor. Teach peace and wisdom. Teach how to use wisdom carefully. Teach to respect earth and all creatures, not to waste food or life, and to make children only when needed, so always there will be plenty of food and room in Valley for all Byahail. People learn well. Then people begin to learn new things, things not taught by Chimera. Learn how to make clothes, how to make beads and bells, how to make cheese and wine, how to make music and how to dance. When Chimera see this, are very pleased. Say, Byahail have learned most important wisdom of all: how to teach selves.

"And so Chimera go back to great City in far Mountains and leave Byahail to live independent in Valley. Gods say, Byahail must live and think for selves, not like children to be always watched and guided. But Chimera make covenant with Byahail. Always will Chimera come in time of need. And when stars are right and kalistra blooms, gods return to meet with elders in special place, for communion and to renew covenant. Elders speak with gods to seek advice, to speak of news, to renew wisdom so will never be lost. And is said that Chimera look down on people in village on this night. So people put on best clothes, sing and dance, show all that is happy and good, sing to honor gods and show all is well. Elders say that to see this is great delight to Chimera. Gods see creation, and are proud."

Prilock smiled, nodding, thinking to himself, As well they might. Then his smile faded. What had the Chimera thought when they looked down and saw an empty village, the dead bodies of their precious creation, the Kurlu invaders laughing obscenely and spreading their filth in the Valley of the Byahail? I would want to kill them, Prilock thought. I would want to kill every one of them.

Prilock finally exhausted Shaka's memory of every Chimera story she could recall. He decided, having spent the better part of the day in leisure—something he hadn't done in years—that it was time to get something accomplished.

He looked over the edge of the ship down into the whispering grass. He could see the glint and movement of the water. "What might I find down there?" he asked.

"Is snappers and eels and frogs. Probably leeches and burrowers. Turtles and water snakes. Little fishes, some that sting. Is not good to get into water. Can be fatal, is always unpleasant."

"That depends on what sort of creature you are, I expect," Prilock said. "I think I'll try a little experiment." He melted over the side of the railing and down into the grass. Shaka shuddered with revulsion at the very idea of going down into that nasty soup, but she assumed Prilock knew what he was doing.

He decided to try a form approximating an eel, a creature well-adapted to this environment. He experimented with different sensory apparatus, seeking a compromise between what he was used to and what would work best in the murky water, thick with grass and weeds. Then he added a bitter repellent to his skin structure to discourage predators and pests. He was immediately aware of a multitude of tiny creatures trying to burrow into his substance, a behavior he assumed gave them their name. He toughened his external surface until they gave up. It took him a few minutes more to learn how to swim with reasonable efficiency. With practice and a few more bodily modifications he would have no trouble traveling whatever distance was necessary to get from Shaka's ship to land. Once on land he would have to choose a new form, but he'd make that decision when he got there, depending on what he found. Perhaps a dog; they were easy, familiar, and fairly inconspicuous.

Prilock hoisted himself back up onto the deck of the *Chimera*, resuming his human form.

"Who needs ship?" Shaka commented. "Could have done that at Farport and swam down here."

"Yes, but think of the excitement I would have missed," Prilock replied, shaking off slimy water and weeds. "Besides, I probably would have gotten lost in the swamp and ended up in Malowi."

She wrinkled her nose at him in distaste. "Better take shower. Smell is not pleasant."

"Nor is the sensation," Prilock said. The marsh muck clung to him in a way that he disliked. He looked back over the side. "But I think before I do, I'll do a bit more exploring."

"Not Shaka's idea of fun," she said.

"It's not so bad while I'm down there. It's really rather enjoyable. It's only when I return to human form that I mind being covered with smelly muck."

"Is plenty of water in tanks for shower," Shaka said. Which reminded her, she ought to check the filters and give them a good cleaning. Sucking up marsh water was a good deal more of a strain on the system than sucking up the relatively clean water of a harbor. "Take swim. Shaka has work to do."

He melted down over the side. She could follow his movements by the motion of the grass. Gradually those motions got harder to distinguish from the action of the breezes. When she lost track of him, she turned and went down into the ship to check on the filters.

He began threading his way through the swamp, becoming accustomed to his new incarnation. He dodged large, slow-moving creatures with flat shells, and slim, muscular beasts with wide jaws, no doubt the snappers of which Shaka had spoken. He paused here and there to look at his surroundings more closely, to inspect some curious plant or creature. Schools of tiny fish swarmed about him, then vanished in the weeds.

As he got used to the swimming motion he began to pick up speed. He streaked through the water, enjoying the feeling. Abruptly the water became shallow, forcing him up towards the surface. He broke through, and for an exhilarating moment he was flying through the air. Weaving rapidly through the grass, he built up speed and did it again. He discovered that if he flattened himself out a bit as he broke the surface he could stay aloft longer. He kept experimenting, intoxicated by his own powerful versatility. He indulged himself in something he'd never done before: Play.

Skimming along the surface, he kept flattening himself out more, until he was almost a disk. The snaking movement of an eel was useless in this form, but he found that rippling his edges worked as well to keep up his speed. But the grass and brush kept slowing him down. So he searched for a relatively open spot. Real open water didn't exist, but he did manage to find a stretch where it was a bit deeper and the grass was a bit thinner at the surface. He reverted to eel form in order to achieve maximum speed, then immediately converted to the flat, rippling disk when he broke the surface. He managed to stay aloft for several seconds. He enjoyed his success immensely.

Resting in the water, he thought about flying. He remembered a conversation he had overheard once while lurking covertly in the Water Hole. Two Northmen had been talking about the notion of flying machines. They had said something about the weight barrier being insurmountable. Prilock weighed something on the order of two hundred pounds, well beyond that barrier. He might be wasting his time. It's my time to waste, he thought. And I am having fun!

They resumed their course southeast, but leisurely, traveling in the late afternoon and evening. Shaka slept in the mornings. Prilock got up when he felt sufficiently rested, eager for the day ahead. Never before in his life had he felt that sort of enthusiasm. He made use of his newly discovered eel form to inspect the underside of the ship for damage. Their wild ride through the swamp had battered it rather badly. The bottom of the hull was broad and flat, double-plated and sealed, enabling the ship to be able to navigate through extremely shallow water even with a full cargo, and endure minor scrapes without catastrophe. They had been traveling light, the hold empty of cargo, and so the ship rode quite a bit higher in the water. That had helped to avoid damage, but her radical evasive maneuvers, ramming the ship up into boggy, debris-filled side channels, had been asking a bit much from it.

Prilock examined the hull thoroughly and assured her that there were no serious breaches, although the fore had taken some nasty dents. She'd probably want to have it looked at next time she was in port. Whenever—if ever—that was.

That discussion brought up the matter of Shaka's unpaid bills, left behind her in their precipitous flight from Farport. She bemoaned the fact that she had no way to clear them up now, and she disliked leaving that sort of unfinished business behind. It was a matter of honor. So Prilock casually commented that Shaka actually had no unpaid bills. He had been quietly taking care of them.

"Why are doing this?" she exclaimed. "Is not Prilock's problem! Bills are Shaka's business, not Castellan's!"

"You were hardly in any condition to deal with them. After all, you were in recovery, and in no shape to cope with such things," he replied.

"Why did not tell?" she demanded.

"I would have eventually," he answered reasonably. "When you finally were able to resume your affairs, you would have found out the bills were paid, and then we could have discussed the matter."

"Discuss now. How am to pay back?"

"Oh, I hardly think that is necessary," Prilock protested. "It was the least I could do. After all, you wouldn't have run afoul of Fenrire in the first place if it hadn't been for your relationship with me."

"Prilock bring justice on Fenrire!" she cried. "Is enough! Not have to pay bills, too."

"Ah, but my business with Fenrire was personal. What he did to you was actually done to get back at me. Cleaning up that bit of garbage was for my own satisfaction. Besides, you saved my life when that assassin came after me. I owe you for that."

"Am owing for own life first! Would have died if not for little bits of Prilock in Shaka's body. Doctor said so."

They went on like that for several minutes, pursuing a rather silly tally of who owed whom what for which deed, life-saving act, or friendly favor, until the futile absurdity of it was obvious to them both. They finally concluded mutually that the balance sheet was even, simply for the sake of ending the argument.

Shaka puttered about the ship, her preferred recreation. Prilock played in the marsh. He stretched out to eel form and streaked through the water, building up speed. When he broke though and flattened himself, he shot out broad, flat appendages and beat at the air with all his strength. He found he did not merely glide; he actually rose a few feet above the marsh before he splashed down again. Weight barrier, ha! he thought. It's not the weight, it's the form, the distribution of the weight, the energy and speed.

He tried it again, modifying the shape, spreading out the wings, treating the air like water, whose resistance could be used to move oneself. He rose several feet above the marsh and maintained. He did not fall back. He was not gliding, he was flying. He was truly flying. He kept modifying as he flew, concentrating on what was working and why, experimenting with the design of his own body. Suddenly he noticed a clump of red willow directly in front of him. He attempted to rise above it, realized he wasn't going to make it, and attempted to steer around it.

He failed miserably, splashing down gracelessly into the marsh.

Prilock rested there for a few minutes, brooding. He knew he had the right idea. He just hadn't quite hit upon the right form. This business of flying was a hell of a lot more complicated than other modes of locomotion.

Above him, mockingly, dragon flies zipped effortlessly about, emerging in the late afternoon light to seek their dinner. He observed their long, thin bodies and broad, flat wings. True, they only weighed a few grams. But damn it, he had been flying, however clumsily. All he needed now was maneuverability. He watched the dragon flies swooping and darting. He could swear they were laughing at him.

Shaka came up onto the deck holding the two main filters for the water supply and a brush to clean them with. The filters were thick with sludge and probably would have stopped working entirely if she hadn't gotten to them when she did. Filtering marsh water was problematic, but a shower was a necessity after Prilock had been mucking about down there. Only the stupid mind of a human would equate Prilock's clean, smooth, odorless substance with swamp slime. There was certainly an obvious difference, especially when one coated the other.

Leaning over the side of the ship, a ginseng hanging out of the corner of her mouth, she began scrubbing one of the filters. Suddenly, a few hundred yards away, she saw the thing rising out of the grass. It was huge and dark, with great, black wings that beat the air with powerful strokes. She stared, astonished, shading her eyes against the glare of the sinking sun as the thing rose into the sky. Then it dawned on her. "Is Prilock!" she murmured in awe. Such a being! What could he not do?

The answer came as the great, dark form began to falter, losing altitude, and then began to tumble out of the sky. It landed with a loud and undignified splash.

Prilock lay in the muck. He had felt the fatigue growing in his substance when he came out of the water and began climbing. He had lost count of how many times he had transmuted in just a few hours. It had put a terrific strain on his body. Though well-rested at the start of his exploration, he had squandered vast amounts of energy experimenting with form and structure. It was catching up with him quite rapidly.

Changing back into eel form was difficult, and his substance responded sluggishly as he swam back to the ship. He had been so intent on his experiments that he had not noticed how exhausted he was becoming. It was all he could do to haul himself back up onto the deck and resume some approximation of his human form.

"I was flying!" he said excitedly, but his voice was somewhat garbled, his normal humanoid shape only half there. Exhaustion rendered his form quite grotesque.

"Saw," she said. "Must have taken much energy. Are looking like pudding."

"I feel like pudding," he said, partly walking and partly flowing towards the cabin. He paused, and turned. "I don't know if I can manage a shower. I am about to collapse."

"Stay on floor," she said. "Not to get bed all muck."

In the morning when Shaka woke up, Prilock was already up and about. There was a patch of dried mud and bits of weed on the floor where he had been the night before when she had finally gone to bed, falling into her bunk fully clothed. He had risen, quite refreshed, and gotten himself cleaned up, then gone about doing some research while Shaka slept in. He was in front of the computer when she found him. "Good morning," he greeted her.

She yawned. "Are looking better this morning," she said.

"I confess," he said, "that I don't rest as well when I am alone."

She grinned. "Be careful. Are getting dependent. Have eaten yet?"

"Yes, I did. I was quite ravenous when I first awoke. A pity we didn't have a bit more time to prepare for this trip. We're rather low on supplies."

"As long as is still coffee," Shaka said, and went to make herself a cup.

"That we have in abundance." He had noticed that Shaka always took care to keep an ample supply of her favorite vices— coffee, ginseng smokes and opium brandy—on hand at all times. It was one of her few weaknesses.

"Can always fish for eels," Shaka said, watching the coffee brew. "And roots of ironweed are edible. Can Prilock eat these things?"

"Oh, I can survive on just about anything," he said. "What I need is pretty basic." He could metabolize nearly anything, as long as it could be broken down into the simple sugars his substance required for energy. He could produce the enzymes to digest most chemical compounds, extracting what he needed and discarding the rest. The higher the sugar content, the less waste he needed to eliminate, and that simple logistic was why he preferred a pure glucose solution for food. Water was the only other thing he required, plus a minute amount of a few other odd elements, most of which he could absorb directly from the air.

"I'll put this aside for the moment," he said, shutting down the computer. "I don't seem to be getting anywhere anyway." He got up. "Let's see what I can catch you for lunch."

Prilock assumed his underwater form—predatorily modified. He brought back eels, snappers and snakes, the flat-shelled creatures, little fish by the bucketful, and odd creatures with shells and claws which crawled around in the mud. Shaka had never seen these latter things before, nor had she ever tried eating anything other than snappers and eels. But she experimented with whatever he brought her. Snakes proved to be not terribly tasty, the flat-shelled creatures were tough, and the little fish yielded too little meat to be worth the effort of preparation. But the odd creatures with the shells and claws yielded a rich, pinkish-white meat which Shaka pronounced to be delicious. He was also able to harvest a wide variety of roots and sprouts from the marsh bottom which Shaka sorted through, choosing the most edible. Prilock, of course, was pretty much omnivorous and wasn't restricted by taste. So he was quite content to give the choicest morsels to Shaka and eat the rest. It all digested about the same for him.

That evening, when radio reception was at its peak, Shaka tried to see if she could pick up any news. What she was able to tune in was pretty mundane, except that there was to be a major summit between the nations of the United Peoples and the Kurlu Empire. Ostensibly it was to settle long-standing trade disputes and immigration policies, and to take up some sore issues of human rights in the Empire. But Shaka and Prilock had a rather good idea what the summit had actually been called for, and what would be discussed in the back rooms away from the bright lights of the media.

"I'd love to be a fly on the wall!" Prilock said. "It would be most enlightening to know just how desperate the Kurlu are, and just how badly they are losing the war."

The following morning she found him back at his research again. "What are working on?" she asked.

Prilock scowled at the computer screen and then at the small collection of disks on the table. "Do you have any data on animal morphology?"

She looked up from pouring her coffee, puzzled. "Do not have much. Human language is hard to read. Have only books on laws that am needing to know for work. Why are asking?"

"I have been trying to figure out what sort of form to use for flying. If I can perfect a flying form," Prilock said, "I can fly the rest of the way to the Mountains. You don't need to risk taking me any closer. What is the largest thing you know of that flies?"

Taking a sip of the coffee, she closed her eyes, relishing the taste. There were some things she had gotten from humans that she considered to be definitely good. Coffee was one of them. She thought for a moment. "Is chickbird humans keep for meat. But does not fly well. Tellura—what humans call kite—can go very far on wind."

"No, I mean fly, not glide. Able to go anywhere, up or down, without being dependent on air currents."

Shaka opened a cabinet and rummaged about, assembling a breakfast of dried fruit and biscuits. "Did not believe was possible. Everything am reading or hearing says only small creatures can fly."

"So the humans believe. But as marvelous as many of their scientific accomplishments are, I am convinced they are dead wrong on this. My experiments yesterday proved it." He turned off the computer and stood up, strolling thoughtfully across the cabin. "I was actually able to sustain a certain elevation for several minutes, and even gain a small degree of altitude. I was not gliding, I was truly flying. But I don't quite have the details right, and I don't have an animal role model."

"What about dragon fly? Plenty around to watch. Best flyers can think of." She leaned against the cabinets, sipping her coffee and chewing on a biscuit.

"I'm more accustomed to animal morphology. I could learn how to do an insect if necessary, but I'd rather not."

She cocked her head. "Have seen Prilock become chair, floor lamp, and potted plant. Why is insect so difficult?"

"To become a mere object I just have to assume a shape and sit there," he explained. "Becoming a functioning creature is a great deal more complicated. There are limbs that have to be moved and coordinated, and sensory organs, which are extremely complex. Going from a human, for example, to a dog, is simple. It only requires slight modifications. Going down to an eel or a snake is a bit more of a jump, but in some ways is easier. No limbs to have to coordinate. But a dragon fly, for example, has six legs plus a double set of wings, plus a body structure which I am totally unfamiliar with. It would take me weeks of study and practice to acquire and use that form. Now," he murmured, "If I could find an animal form which could be modified for flight, I could learn it in a matter of days." He considered the tellura, or kite, that Shaka had mentioned. Its mode of transportation was not unlike what he had been working on. It had broad, thin flaps of skin connecting its arms and legs, giving it the flat, disk shape Prilock had been using.

"If Prilock can perfect flying form, will not be needing Shaka anymore," she said.

"No," he agreed, preoccupied with kite morphology. "You can do as you please."

She watched him. "Will Shaka ever see Prilock again?" she asked.

He didn't answer at first, then he suddenly looked up. "What?"

She repeated the question. "Am wondering, when Prilock doesn't need Shaka anymore, goes back to Chimera, will Shaka ever be seeing Prilock again?"

The very idea startled him. "Surely you can't think that, after all we've been through together, I could simply fly away and never come back."

"Did not think so," she said, turning to refill her coffee cup, "but wanted to be sure. Did not want to misunderstand."

"I shouldn't think I would have to make it explicit," he said, just the mildest hint of annoyance in his voice.

"Forgive Shaka," she said. "Am foolish sometimes. Been around humans too long."

"Of course," he said, returning to his meditations. "We'll say no more about it." But he felt a secret, guilty sense of comfort. *She would miss me. She needs me.*

"Am remembering peet-peet," Shaka said suddenly.

"Hmm?" Prilock looked up.

"Peet-peet is wild bird; small, not like chickbird. Live in trees above Valley where Shaka grew up. Is size of dragon fly. But can fly. Remember seeing peet-peets in sky above forest sometimes. Byahail sometimes look for feathers to use for decoration for festival of gods. Takes many peet-peet feathers, but can make beautiful things."

"A peet-peet, eh? Like a chickbird, only smaller?" Suddenly Prilock was reminded of the little black sparrows that would sometimes perch on the window sills outside the laboratory building of the Academy. The scientists had dismissed them as common pests that fouled benches and vehicles with their droppings. He tried to remember what they looked like but couldn't. The memory was lost to him. "Could you draw a peet-peet?" he asked her.

Shaka shrugged and nodded. "Will do best." She picked up the pen and a data board. "Look like this. When in sky, look like this."

"Hmmm. Interesting. And its feathers, are they like yours?"

Shaka nodded. "But very small. And many pretty colors."

Feathers could be an ideal way to spread out his body mass into something lightweight. He could model the structure on the feathers of Shaka's mane, only making them longer and sturdier in his wings, better able to endure the pressures of wind and acceleration. She had drawn the peet-peet with a long, flat tail, squared off at the end. He guessed it acted as a rudder. He struggled to remember what black sparrows looked like. The picture of the peet-peet helped.

"The wings," he said, "they simply fold up against the body when the bird is at rest, correct?"

"When peet-peet perch in tree, yes. Wings fold up like this." She made a simple sketch on the data board.

Yes, it would work. It was elegantly simple. He could easily incorporate the senses he was used to using into the new body. It wasn't all that different; two eyes, two legs, two arms became wings—yes! Black sparrows. He remembered. Great flocks of them flying around the building. Flying free. He used to watch them from the window in the laboratory.

"Black sparrows," he murmured, and got up. "Birds."

Shaka settled herself comfortably on the railing of the deck, lit a ginseng and watched. His process of transmuting had always fascinated her. When it was a form he was familiar with it was almost instantaneous, the shift taking a fraction of a second. When he was experimenting, it was slower, more hesitant, as it was now. He focused on one structure at a time, a claw, then a beak. Then he came over to her. "May I see one of your feathers?" he asked.

"Of course," she said, bending her head over towards him. He sorted out a single feather from the mane of feathers and fur, examining it closely in minute detail. He attempted to imitate the structure, changing the fingers on one of his hands to feathers. It was more difficult than he had anticipated, and it took him almost an hour before he was satisfied with the results. There were tiny, almost microscopic details to the feather structure that required painstaking effort to duplicate. But once he had it down, he could repeat the pattern as much as necessary. He began covering his body with feathers.

It took him most of the rest of the day to get the new body right, adjusting details, adjusting proportions, correcting unanticipated difficulties. By the time he finally felt ready for a trial run, he was exhausted. And as eager as he was to test out the new design, there was no point in doing so until he had the energy necessary. Flying was going to take an awful lot of work. So reluctantly he changed back to his more familiar form and waited until morning.

After a good night's torpor and breakfast Prilock was ready. He carefully rebuilt himself into the new bird form. It took him nearly an hour to do. Standing on the deck, he flexed himself hesitantly, feeling somewhat nervous. If it didn't work, after all that thought and effort, he would be furiously frustrated. He tentatively spread out the wings. They caught the air. He flapped them cautiously and found himself lifted off the deck a few inches. The success startled and encouraged him. He might not even need a running start. Prilock tried again, this time putting some real effort into flapping the wings. He rose off the deck several feet, becoming airborne so quickly it took him by surprise. He landed on the railing, gripping it with his clawed feet, rocking back and forth wildly, until he finally got the hang of perching.

"I think it's going to work," he said.

"So, go ahead," Shaka cried. "Do it!"

He looked out across the marsh, dreading another graceless splashdown. He took a deep breath. "All right," he said, "Here goes."

The great, dark bird rose into the air, slowly at first, then picking up speed. He felt stresses on his wings and body, and modified the design accordingly. He rose into the sky, this time easily avoiding obstacles. With his earlier failures still vivid in his memory, he was very careful about trying to maneuver, testing the way his tail worked, observing the effect of various movements until he got a good feel for the aerodynamics involved. Then an irresistible exhilaration began to fill him. It was working marvelously. He had designed the ideal flying body. And he was flying. Flying free.

He soared upwards. He could hear Shaka whooping and cheering below him in unrestrained delight. Prilock reminded himself sternly that he ought to keep this flight short. He shouldn't stray too far from the ship until he was sure he knew what he was doing.

But he couldn't resist flying just a bit further, just to see what he could see.

The marsh rolled rapidly away beneath him. He reveled in the sensation of speed. He found he only needed to beat his wings occasionally to keep up his speed or to climb. Otherwise he could glide, saving energy and letting air currents do the work for him. He was covering an incredible amount of ground very rapidly. He flew higher, seeing how shifting the angle of his wings affected his ability to climb. How high could he go? The only limitation would seem to be the presence of air and his own energy levels. He had to be careful. He ought to turn around soon. But first, just a little higher, just to see what it was like. He soared upwards, then looked down. The rim of the world lay before him. He could see the dark ruffle of land in the distance and then beyond it the jagged edge of the Mountains. It had to be the ancient land of the Byahail, now overrun by Kurlu. That jagged outline would be the mountains of his people. Somewhere among those hazy, bluish peaks was the great, legended City of the Chimera. Soon he would be going there, flying high above the world of humans, high above the stupid, brutal world of humans, a young, stray god returning home.

He lost track of time up there so close to the clouds. The euphoria of flying took him over. The more he did it the better he got at it, forgetting his determination not to go too far from the ship. Suddenly Prilock realized the sun was starting to descend in the sky. He had somehow spent the entire day up there, flying in lazy circles, lost in the realm of clouds and thoughts. Wheeling about in the sky he headed back towards the ship. In the distance, to the north, he could see a bank of clouds approaching. A front of fell weather was headed towards the ship. Or at least, towards him. For a few uneasy moments he wondered if he could remember how to find the ship again. He dropped his altitude, gliding, scanning the swamp for anything familiar. But the swamp was just miles and miles of the same, with very little in the way of landmarks. He began to feel the tell-tale signs of fatigue, and cursed himself for being so foolish. He could very well be lost in the swamp, and might never find the ship again. Rising, he oriented himself to the distinguishing lines of the horizon, the distant mountains. Taking his best guess for direction, he flew. Finally, as exhaustion began to catch up with him, he saw the distant glint of silver and white, tinted orange in the descending sun. He made for it.

Shaka saw the dark shape returning. She stood up, relieved, tossing the butt of a ginseng out into the marsh. There was a nasty storm coming their way. The navigation channel on the radio was warning all ships to make secure. Up north, it had already tossed things around a bit. Farport reported heavy rains and moderate to high winds. Shaka had anchored the ship securely to a sturdy clump of awkbush and red willow, and battened everything down. All that remained was for Prilock to return. He fell, quite gracelessly with a wet plop, on the deck.

"Am wondering when bird would run out of steam," she said with a grin. "Get below, storm is coming."

He obeyed, wordlessly, once again too exhausted for debate or even comment. But he thought to himself, I have seen the Mountains. I have seen the Mountains, and soon I will be going home.

The storm finally expended its violence and passed, and the dawn came clear. Prilock waited until Shaka awoke, staying with her, savoring the peaceful sensation of contact with her. Then they made their breakfast and took it up on deck. In the brilliant morning light the air smelled rich and clean. It would quickly thicken with heat and humidity as the sun rose, but for the moment, all was glitteringly beautiful, droplets of rain sparkling on the red willow leaves that formed a canopy above them. Prilock stood quietly, looking to the southeast with a distant expression on his face. Shaka went over to him and gently put her hand on his shoulder.

"Is time, isn't it?" she said.

He sighed. "I suppose there is no reason to put it off any longer is there?"

She scanned the sky. "Will be a fine day. Good weather for flying," she said.

"Yes," he replied. "Do you have enough food to get you through?"

"Plenty food, thanks to Prilock," Shaka said. "Have full larder with fish."

"You're sure? I could get you a few more shellfish before I go."

"Not to waste energy on changing form. Will be fine. Not to worry."

He nodded again. "You will be careful. The U.P. is probably still looking for you, and there may be pirates—"

"Will be fine," she emphasized. "Prilock be careful. Must travel much farther and to more dangerous places than Shaka."

"Don't worry about me," he replied briskly, "After all, I am a god, remember?"

"God, yes, but not indestructible. Be careful."

He nodded impatiently. "Of course. Shall I look for you at the Reservation when I return?"

"Yes," Shaka said. "Will be there, or will leave word where to find."

"Good."

They stood there in silence for another few minutes. Then Prilock turned towards her and did something he had never done before. He put his arms around her and hugged her. She hugged him tightly in return, determined to remember how it felt. Then she stepped back.

"Is time, Prilock," she prompted him gently.

"Yes, yes, I know," he said irritably. Then he said, "I will return as soon as I can."

"Return when is time to return. Do not worry for Shaka. Can wait as long as must." She took another step away. "Become bird," she said.

It took him only a moment this time. She smiled in deep admiration at the great, dark, sleek creature, feathers iridescent in the sunlight. "Good luck!" she cried as he rose from the deck, stirring the air with his wings.

"Good luck to you!" he called back in his cawing bird-voice, and he circled the ship once before rising into the sky. She watched him, shading her eyes, squinting against the rising sun. She followed the dark form as long as she could, until it disappeared into the southeastern horizon.

Letting him go had been one of the most difficult things she had ever done. Already she felt a deep sense of emptiness, knowing she would be sleeping alone that night. She took a deep breath and took a firm hold on herself. "Is much to do," she told herself sternly. "No time for nonsense." She turned her attention to the business of getting under way.

He covered the miles of marsh quickly. In less than an hour he could see land in the distance, and could pick out the jagged outline of the Mountains. This time he made directly for them. As he grew closer to the land he could see an occasional vessel of some kind, although from his altitude he couldn't tell what they were. To the far south the marsh continued to stretch into the distance as far as he could see. To the east the coast of the Kurlu Empire began to take on a distinct outline. When he had gone there before it had been along standard shipping routes, landing at a major port further north. Most of the area had been developed, the jungle and forests cleared away to make room for cities, roads and factories. But here there was not as much development. Much of the jungle remained intact. Swampland covered the region between open marsh and true land, as yet undredged, with few waterways cutting through it. But there were still unmistakable signs of human activity. Plumes of smoke rose into the sky, and swathes of jungle had been hacked away to accommodate roads and settlements. Canals drained off the waste from large processing plants, emptying sickly-colored liquid into the swamp. At the mouths of these canals the vegetation was stunted, dying, or brown and dead.

Then the land rose up into rolling hills, the jungle becoming less dense and turning into forest. Evidence of Kurlu presence was very noticeable here. Forest was easier to clear than jungle, and easier to develop. The higher ground was a bit drier and better drained, and so was more suited for settlement. The landscape here had been extensively scarred, vast tracts of trees felled and the ground plowed. Settlements and factories had been built, and canals had been dug diverging water from a river through the settlement and then down, eventually rejoining the natural riverway and going on to the marsh.

But something seemed wrong. Prilock risked flying a bit lower to get a closer look. There was no smoke coming from any of the buildings. He could see no activity in the roads, no vehicles coming and going, no ships in the canal. The fields looked untended, and some seemed blackened, as if by fire. Then he noticed more blackening, and realized many of the settlements were in ruins. Large areas were discolored, the foliage withered, as if it had been sprayed by some toxic chemical. The war had evidently taken its toll here, and the Kurlu had gotten the worst of it by far.

At the edge of one settlement he spotted a plume of smoke and flew closer. As soon as he realized what it was he abruptly beat the air hard and got as much altitude as he could as rapidly as he could. It was an army encampment. He estimated some eight hundred or a thousand Kurlu soldiers, although it was difficult to be sure since many were sheltered by the trees. They had a large fleet of vehicles loaded with armaments parked in the clearing around them. A few of the vehicles carried enormous tanks, and Prilock had a very good idea what was in those tanks. He shuddered slightly as a reminiscence of pain passed through him.

Continuing south, the land rose beneath him and then abruptly fell away. The rolling hills gave way to a long valley, cut through at its center by a wide river which glittered in the sun. The valley was beautiful and green, forested in places, and open meadow in others, dotted with patches of color from blooming things. The air was sweet with the smell of some particular flower. Prilock wondered if it was the legended kalistra of which Shaka had spoken. But here, too, were the signs of human invasion. A road cut arrogantly down from the hills into the valley, bridging the river and splitting off on the other side. There were signs of settlements here, but as Prilock flew down closer the evidence of war was even more dramatic. Nothing remained of the Kurlu presence but the foundations of buildings and scattered debris. They had been burned and then violently torn apart. Even the bridge had been sabotaged. There was evidence that an attempt had been made to rebuild it, but the attempt had been frustrated. The middle span was completely gone. He flew along the valley and came to older ruins, and realized it must be an abandoned Byahail village. The shells of modest dwellings remained, scattered about a clearing with a large fire pit at its center and a well off to one side. Everything was overgrown. It would have been what, thirty years? At least that since this place was inhabited. There were other villages like it all through the valley, with faint traces of paths connecting them. He tried to imagine what it might have been like, the valley filled with Shaka's people, living their lives in the rich, traditional patterns that had sustained them happily for generations. The meadows were once fields, used for growing grain for their bread. The forests were a mixture of trees, many of them fruit-bearing, and no doubt the Byahail had learned clever uses for them all, and for the rich variety of plants that grew on the banks of the river and on the sides of the hills. They would have gathered the flowers for their manes and to decorate their homes. What a perfect existence, uncluttered by ambition, deception and greed, without the cheating illusion of what humans called progress.

Prilock reached the far end of the valley and saw where the river came down from the Mountains. There was a faint haze, and a noticeable humidity in the air. The land below him around the water was not green; it was a rich, dark brown. He flew lower, and realized he must be looking at the birthing mud Shaka had spoken of. The cliffs around where the river emerged were riddled with caves. From some, steaming water spilled out. The mud bubbled and sputtered, releasing a mineral smell. Prilock hovered over it, feeling the heat and moisture rising up. How many generations of Byahail children had been nurtured in this mud? Shaka, herself, had, many years ago.

He turned and flew back towards the place where the road cut across. No one lived in the valley now. But soon Shaka's people would be returning. Soon, when it was safe, when the Kurlu had been so badly bludgeoned for their crimes that they would give up and go away forever. Or would they give up? The Kurlu were an insufferably proud race, proud for all the wrong reasons, determined and tenacious with all the wrong goals and all the wrong ideals. They might well fight until the bitter end, just out of principle, defending an unjust cause for the sake of land that wasn't theirs. How far might the Chimera have to go to ensure the security of the Byahail in their rightful place? How far were they willing to go? Did the Chimera themselves have any idea? Were those very doubts the reason why the Chimera had been so slow and reluctant to start this war, hesitating until the very existence of the Byahail was at stake? Prilock circled the blasted remains of the ill-fated Kurlu settlement. He wondered how many had died already, Byahail, Chimera and hapless Kurlu, for the sake of the damned bloody Empire.

After thirty years it would be difficult to find the signs that Shaka remembered that would lead to the path the elders once took into the Mountains. Prilock abandoned the attempt after a few tentative tries, and simply flew low along the southern edge of the valley where the sides rose up quickly to the first low cliffs of the range. Finally he found it, winding leisurely through clefts in the rocks, gradually ascending at a grade that an elderly but agile creature could manage. He followed it to a plateau and was sickened by what he saw. Once there must have been beautiful carvings etched into the living rock. Some still remained, high and noble, intricately designed geometric shapes, some of which bore the features of the Byahail. At one time they must have been inlayed with precious stones and metals, but these had been removed, crudely pried out, the carvings defaced, many of them ruined in what must have been pure malice. Such destruction would not have been necessary simply to remove the wealth of the artwork. Everywhere was garbage, human garbage. The triumphant conquerors had taken malevolent pleasure in despoiling the sacred place of the vanquished.

Trembling with anger, Prilock rose up into the sky so he wouldn't have to look at the obscenity. He tried instead to look beyond the plateau for some sign of a road, a path, any sort of clue as to which way to go from there to find the City. No matter how he searched he could find nothing. The Mountains rapidly grew higher, colder and more desolate, fiercely jagged and forbidding. They stretched rough, icy and immense out to the south and east, and several miles to the west before softening and sinking from sight. Prilock perched on a cliff. The wind was sharp and cold up there. In the small valleys between the peaks were patches of tough grass. He spotted a small herd of shaggy, hoofed beasts grazing on the grass and browsing on the leaves of short, stunted trees that clung to crevasses in the rocks. He'd find precious little to eat here. And few comfortable places for torpor. He glanced towards the sun, trying to estimate how much time he might have before dark. A few hours perhaps, no more. He did not yet feel at all fatigued. He could probably go quite a while before having to stop. The cold didn't bother him much, but the wind might make it more difficult to fly. He could continue his search after dark, modifying his eyesight to adapt to the dim starlight. Or he could rest in the valley a little while, perhaps find some fruit to eat—a good, high-energy form of food. Perhaps even catch an hour or so of torpor, just enough to recharge him fully.

He looked out across the harsh landscape and then back towards the valley. He didn't want to fly back over the hideous spectacle of the defiled plateau. And he didn't want to see the war-ravaged valley of ruins and ghosts again, let alone spend any time in it. No, he had come this far. The City of the Chimera could very well be quite close by, hidden in some secluded ravine out of the wind and cold. The Kurlu, limited as they were to over-land locomotion, could hardly have been able to search far in this hostile terrain. And it seemed unlikely that the Chimera would live too terribly far away from their beloved creatures. Prilock decided firmly that he would keep searching. Facing into the chill wind, he spread his wings and rose up again into the air.

The sun sank lower in the sky, casting the Mountains into sharp relief and plunging the valleys into shadow. The wind fell somewhat, making flying a bit easier. Prilock swept in great circles, studying the jagged peaks for landmarks, trying to make his search as thorough and methodical as possible. The air was growing thinner and colder. The pockets of tough grass were few and far between and the stunted trees disappeared. More of the rough, rocky terrain was covered with snow and ice until the only exposed areas were those which had been swept clean by the wind. Rising up and scanning the horizon, he realized that he could see no end to the mountain range. He wondered, with the slightest stirring of uneasiness, if he had made a serious error in judgement pressing on in his search. He was unsure what he would do if serious fatigue hit him at this point.

When the sun fell below the rim of the world, igniting the sky in vivid orange and purple, the wind began to rise again. He tried to use it to his advantage, coasting on its currents, using the up-drafts to keep him aloft. Icy crystals were beginning to form on his wings. He finally had to land, perching with difficulty on a frozen cliff, and clean his wings off with his beak. He adjusted his eyes to the fading light, looking with a sinking heart at the boundless wasteland of massive peaks and black ravines. No sign of life any-where, only sharp, blasted rocks, the deadly cold and cruel wind. Rising up again, he fought the wind and flew on, straining his sight for any clue. The sky above him turned black, and the stars, glittering like frost, filled the void.

Uneasiness turned to genuine fear as he began to find it more and more difficult to fight the wind, and the first signs of fatigue in his substance began to trouble him. Again he found an uncom-fortable perch and he scanned the horizon. He noticed something. At first he thought it was an illusion of some sort, some failing of his eyesight brought on by exhaustion. But the longer he stared the more certain he was of its reality. There was a faint glow rising from beyond a ridge just to the east of where he clutched the jutting rock. Gathering his strength he rose into the air and made for the light, daring to hope that he may have actually found his goal. As he cleared the ridge he looked down, and nearly forgot to flap his wings he was so startled by what he saw.

Far below him, like a breath-taking, illuminated work of art, was a city. But not a city like anything humans would build. There were no streets, no factories, not even houses in any sense he was used to. It was an indescribably complex, awesomely beautiful collage of structures, delicate spirals, scalloped disks, arches and curves, weaving in and out, melding, soaring, of marble, white, black, delicate pink and veined with gold. It spread out, lining and filling the deep valley, lit from within like some fantastic lantern. What lay below him was only the outer layer; he could see through its intricacies layer upon layer of marble and granite, silver, platinum and gold, arching and twisting in narrow bands, smooth domes and carven, jeweled mosaics, down into some living heart of beauty. He spiraled downwards, finding his way through the delicate, rippled and richly carven shell into the complex labyrinth of the structure. As soon as he entered into it the cold was gone. The air was pleasantly warm and vaguely fragrant with some scent that was unfamiliar to him. All around him the space was filled with artwork, cunningly wrought, infinitely various, using every conceivable material to best advantage, all polished to lustrousness. There was not a single flaw, not a spot of tarnish, not a line out of place nor a curve that wasn't perfect. Illumination came from globes hung carefully to best advantage, but how they produced their soft light was a mystery.

As he descended further he began seeing pots of growing things, flowering vines hanging down into the space below, perfectly cared for, without a single brown leaf or withered stem. Palms swayed upwards, their fronds moving ever so slightly in the breath of rising warm air. There were no stairs, no ramps, just the complex, interwoven architecture. Then he saw something moving, a shape-less, pearl-white and iridescent being winding its way along the spiral of a tall pillar. It stopped moving as he passed, and although it had no face, Prilock was certain it was staring at him. He thought he heard it whistle, loudly, but not shrilly. He began seeing more of these pearly creatures, and excitement overcame exhaustion. They had to be Chimera. He was finally seeing those of his own kind for the first time.

There was a floor of sorts beneath him, or at least a platform of some kind, and a number of the beings were gathering there. The air became filled with strange, articulate music, whistles and trillings and melodious chirps. They rolled back out of the way, moving smoothly and gracefully, allowing him room to land. As proud as he had been of his bird form when he created it, he felt ashamed of it now. It seemed so foolish, so homely and undignified, in these awesome, ethereal circumstances. He let go of it, returning to his natural state but trying to at least imitate the more upright posture, if not the impossibly beautiful color, of those around him. The change triggered an excited trilling and warbling among them. One approached him, speaking to him it seemed, but he had no idea what it was saying or how to answer. When it received no reply, it spoke again, this time in a language he at least recognized as Byahail. But he couldn't understand Byahail, either. He reformed his vocal apparatus enough to greet them in standard human language, but they seemed not to understand that.

Finally the being who had approached him came closer. It moved slowly, as though trying not to alarm him. It trilled in a soft, calming way and extended a pseudopod to him. He hesitated, more out of a kind of humble shyness than out of caution. Again, patiently, the being trilled to him, moving no closer but retracting then extending the arm of its substance to him. Summoning up his courage, he reached out and touched the being. The telepathic contact that resulted did not surprise him; he rather expected it. What surprised him was that he had trouble understanding even this. His long years among humans had gotten him so accustomed to thinking in terms of language that he had difficulty comprehending the true raw material of thought in its pure form. But the being seemed unhurried and unperturbed by his lack of comprehension. It simply kept sending him the same message, over and over. Slowly he began to adjust to what he was receiving and form a picture of it. There was a sense of welcome, an idea of curiosity, a question of some kind. Welcome, then some affectionate recognition of kinship, then an inquiry. Welcome home, something, curiosity, inquiry.

Then it came clear to him; his mind, at the point of comprehension, automatically translated it into terms he was used to.

Welcome home, strange child. Where have you come from?

CHAPTER 7

The old Byahail had been called Nossa Mehika, which meant, "Has much patience." And so it had been, from times of youth until ascension to the status of elder, and all through the terrible days of exile. Thirty years of exile. Thirty years since the last communion with the Chimera, when once again the ancient covenant had been confirmed. But all that time had passed. The People still waited. One by one they grew old and died. One by one the young—and even the old—fell into disillusionment, lost hope, and began to walk through the rituals of daily living like ghosts, dead inside, no light in their eyes, no spirit in their voices. Even Nossa Mehika found it difficult to hold on to faith, to be patient, to cling to hope. The old Byahail had not many days left, and when Nossa Mehika died there would be none left among the People who would remember the old days, the Chimera, and the covenant. Nossa Mehika was the last of those who were elders when the time of exile came.

By the reckoning of the stars, it was the time of communion. But there was no celebration in the village. For the People it was only another day. Few remembered, fewer cared. But with an urgency born of the threat of despair, Nossa Mehika went into the forest to a clearing made for this purpose, to cry a prayer to the silent, absent gods. Lighting a small fire, the old Byahail put on the bells and the beads and took up tenderly a staff still wrapped with dried and crumbling flowers. Nossa Mehika softly breathed an ancient chant and danced as well as old legs could. Then, in a voice quaking with age but still clear, the old one cried out to the dark night.

"Chimera, gods of my people, once more behold me on earth

and lean to hear my feeble voice. You lived first, and you are older than all need, older than all prayer. All things belong to you—the two-leggeds, the four-leggeds, the wings of the air and all green things that live. You have set the powers of the four quarters to cross each other. The good road and the road of difficulties you have made to cross, and where they cross, the place is holy.

"You have said to me, when I was still young and could hope, that in difficulty I should send a voice four times, once for each quarter of the earth . . .

"Today I send a voice for a people in despair. At the center of the sacred place you have said a tree shall bloom.

"With tears running, O Ancient Ones, O Chimera, gods of my people—with running tears I must say that the tree has never bloomed. Old and pitiful you see me here and I have fallen away and nothing has been done. Here, torn from the center of the world, where you placed us when we were young and taught us; here, old, I stand, and the tree is withered.

"Again, and maybe the last time on earth, I recall the great vision you sent me. It may be that some little root of the sacred tree still lives. Nourish it, then, that it may leaf and bloom and there may be singing again. Hear me, not for myself, but for the People; I am old. Hear me that they may once more go back into the sacred place and find the good road, the shielding tree.

"In sorrow I am sending a feeble voice, O ancient powers of the world, O Chimera. Hear me in my sorrow, for I may never call again. O make my people live!"

Four times did Nossa Mehika repeat the prayer, to each of the four quarters. The last echoes of the old one's voice died away among the trees of the forest. The dark sky was mute. Shivering, Nossa Mehika put out the fire and carefully wrapped the sacred things into a bundle. Peering into the gloom with eyes dimmed by age, the old Byahail slowly found the way back to the village. No one was stirring. There had been no one awake to hear the prayer. Nossa Mehika went into the rotting hut that passed for home chilled with the bitter cold of futility.

The old Byahail awakened to the sound of great commotion in the village. Such commotion had not occurred for many years— time in the Reservation had become a long string of days of sameness, nothing new, only creeping despair and the gradual conquest of death. But here was a wild buzz of excited voices, the noise of something new, something startling. Nossa Mehika got up from the sleeping mat with difficulty and went stiffly to the door. "What is happening? Why is this noise?"

One of the youngest of the last generation of Byahail was Lita Shalhi, whose name meant "Dancing Legs." It had been a very long time since the long, lithe legs of Lita Shalhi had danced, but they ran and danced now. "Great news! News like birds and flowers! Eyes Look Far has come back! Has come back with a great ship!"

"What is this?" Nossa Mehika exclaimed. Shaka Mahdi—Eyes Look Far—had been abandoned for lost many years ago. To go and live among humans was as good as walking into the swamp to perish. When that restless child had left, full of doubts and bitterness, it was as if a part of the already dim spirit of the Byahail had departed. There was none so bright, so filled with questions, with promise, with courage, as the one called Eyes Look Far. The elders had pinned their dwindling hopes on the young fighter, as perhaps the leader who could grow and carry the People through these terrible, fearful times. That hope was dashed when Shaka Mahdi abandoned the faith of the People, cursed the name of the Chimera and left with the ship of the humans. Only Nossa Mehika dared to secretly hope that some good might come of it. The humans of the U.P. were not evil, like the terrible race of humans who had slaughtered the People and driven them from the Valley. The humans of the U.P. were merely stupid. They meant well, trying to save the Byahail, bringing them food, trying to teach them new ways. But the humans had no understanding. They did not understand why the Byahail were not happy on this cursed Reservation, why it was impossible to live in these strange lands, why taking food and being kept like pets was a shame and a misery, not a thing to be grateful for. Perhaps Shaka Mahdi could teach them.

Perhaps the great strength and spirit of this brave Byahail could impress them and make them listen. The humans had built great machines and could do many wonderful things. They must not all be hopelessly stupid.

And now here was news that Shaka Mahdi had returned in a great ship. The old Byahail felt vindicated and filled with trembling anticipation. What now would happen?

Much of the elder's excitement was eclipsed by the actual sight of Shaka Mahdi. That straight, strong body had been twisted; that noble face disfigured with terrible scars. So this was what life among humans had done to Shaka Mahdi! What good could possibly be worth such a price?

In the center of the village they all gathered around. Shaka sat beside Nossa Mehika, surveying with dismay the pitiful, sickly remainder of what had once been a great and robust people. It mattered not; all this would change very soon. Shaka brought hope to the Byahail.

"It is good to be home and to be among my people again," said Shaka, glad to be able to speak once again in the fluid, eloquent tongue of the Byahail. "I bring news that will make the hearts of the People sing again. The time of darkness is over. There will soon come a dawning in the Valley of our People which will be greeted by our laughter and songs of praise to the gods of our People. In the world of humans there is rumor of a great war. The humans go in terror of strange monsters, so they say, who have come down from the Mountains to kill them. Foolish humans, they know nothing of what is killing them, and do not see that it is Justice coming down like a hard rain, that their own misery is caused by the misery they brought upon the People, as sure as pulling a plow across the field causes it to be tilled."

"Chimera!" cried Nossa Mehika, feeling tears of incredulous joy overwhelm those old eyes. "The Chimera have come at last to honor the covenant!" The others simply sat and stared in shock, too astonished, the news too enormous, for them to realize what it meant.

"Just so," Shaka nodded. "Many strange things have happened to me in my time among humans. I have learned more than can be told in a span of seed to harvest. But I will tell you this: Humans are not all evil. Some very few even have hearts warm with goodness. But humans suffer a great and crippling weakness. They do not know how to live. They are very clever; they can make amazing devices and build great cities. They know far more of the secrets of the world than the wisest of our elders. Humans have great knowledge, but little wisdom. Even the simplest truths of how to live well and be happy are lost to them. They know less than our tiniest child. Even those whose hearts are warm are still very stupid. But they can be taught. And they respect the wisdom of our People."

The old one nodded slowly. "It is as I supposed, then. So, have you been able to teach them, Shaka Mahdi? Have you brought the humans our wisdom?"

"Some have listened, yes," Shaka replied. "Some good humans have hearts open to the truth. There would be hope in this if it weren't that those good humans are very few. And most of them are powerless. The great and powerful among humans, those who drive their society, are among the most evil, the most stupid, with hearts that know no warmth. And so there is no hope of reasoning with humans, no hope of trusting, no hope of justice without the power of the Chimera."

"The gods will blast the faces of the evil ones and drive them from our lands," said Nossa Mehika. "But if there are warm hearts among the humans, the gods will not kill them all."

"It would be better news to know that all humans were evil, and so could have all their future taken from them and be put into darkness forever," said Lita Shalhi bitterly, and those gathered around grumbled with agreement.

Nossa Mehika raised a hand to silence them. "Shall you kill all slithera because some have a poison bite? Rather, be glad for those who do not. Slithera have their purpose in this world, and it may be that humans will find theirs."

"How can such creatures have a purpose?" cried Lita Shalhi. "They do nothing but eat the world and give nothing back."

"This is not for us to judge. The gods will know what is to be done."

Another one spoke up timidly. "Will the gods come for us now? It has been so long. I know it is wrong to question the wisdom of the gods, but—"

Nossa Mehika nodded patiently. So very many times it had needed to be said, and if it needed to be said again, so be it. The end of the dark times was at hand, and that made the explaining easier. "Time is not the same for the gods as for us. What is a year or thirty to those who have known the age of the world? When the first danger came, we elders chose not to speak of it to the gods at that time of communion, because we did not understand how great the evil would be. We have made the gods proud by our strength and cleverness. When problems come, we use the tools and wisdom given to us by them in the early days, and do not go like children bleating for help. That we did not tell the gods of the humans then was a terrible mistake. But how could we have known? Never in all memory has horror so great struck so quickly and completely. By the time of next communion, already it was too late. Those who were not dead were removed to this place, and there was none to go to the place of communion. What could the gods have thought when they came to the sacred place and heard not our bells and voices? What could the gods have thought when they flew over our villages and saw only ruin and death? What could they have thought, those who loved us and rejoiced in our happiness? Great must have been their sorrow. Great must have been their rage. But would they act in haste? No, haste and passion are not the way of the gods. In such a matter, strange and grave as the sun not rising, the gods would consider and carefully judge what to do. But now they have decided, and have risen up to act. Rejoice! The time of justice has come!"

The rest of the day was spent in celebration. They gathered up all the meager supplies they had to make a feast; the People ate with more appetite than they had in memory. Shaka Mahdi gave away all that was on the ship that could be of use, glad for the surplus of fish Prilock had left her with. Unfortunately, that which was in greatest abundance—coffee, opium brandy and ginseng smokes—were of no use to the Byahail. What Shaka did have in abundance that was most welcome were tales of the world of humans and news of the war of the Chimera. All that day and well into the night Shaka spoke at length of these things. There was no mention of Prilock. Shaka waited until time could be found to speak to Nossa Mehika alone.

"You are the eldest," Shaka said, "And the only one who yet remembers what the Chimera are."

"This is so," Nossa Mehika acknowledged.

"There is a thing of great importance I must tell you. I have many questions which even you may not be able to answer, but I must ask."

"With all the wonders you have spoken of, it is hard to believe there is more still," the old Byahail said. "But speak. I am not too weary to listen."

"I have known a god," Shaka said.

The old one frowned. "Say more. How have you come to know a god?"

Shaka told Nossa Mehika of Prilock, of their meeting and what came to happen between them. All the while the old Byahail listened with an expression that grew more and more grave.

"These are very strange things," the elder said finally when Shaka had finished. "I cannot understand how a god cannot know of being a god, or come to be among humans in the way you describe. It is a mystery beyond all reasoning, incomprehensible to me with what I know of the gods. And yet, what you describe cannot be other than a god. Only Chimera can change their form at will, to take whatever shape pleases them, wondrous or terrible. What you say of this being is like the noble nature of a god, strong and always honorable and just. Most troubling is what you say of this touching and the ease of heart it brings, and how it has changed you. It can be nothing less than the communion, which is only for elders, and only for those times when the stars are right. That you have done this disturbs me greatly."

"Why is that?" Shaka asked.

"The touch of the Chimera is a potent thing. It can ease the pains of aging in an elder and give comfort and strength. Thus our people have their wisest ones around them to teach them and guide them for longer than might otherwise be. When their time of passing comes, it is easier and comes with little pain. Not like it has been for us since the dark days of the Reservation, growing sick and crippled and going into shadows too soon. This blessing of the gods is a great thing, and benefits them as well in ways we do not understand. But this thing that you have done, communing night after night until even death cannot claim a body torn apart beyond all repair—this is not good. It is not in the ways of wisdom. I do not know what will come of this."

Shaka felt a deep sense of unease. They hadn't known what they were doing. It had seemed so natural, such a comfort to them both. And neither of them would be alive at all if they hadn't shared that intimate contact. Yet the gods would not have made such rules if there were not good reasons for them. There were many things which seemed on the surface to be of great benefit, only to prove disastrous when considered over time. Thus was the way of wisdom, to know the truth of these things. That was why rules were made by the wise for those younger, to protect them from the folly of their youth and imperfect judgement.

"Alas," the old one said with a resolute gesture, "What is done is done. You say this strange god has gone to find the City of the Chimera. This is a good thing. Only the gods themselves can know what is to be done about this thing, if indeed anything can be done at all. These are very strange times," Nossa Mehika sighed. "So much that is beyond all that I can understand; so many mysteries which my knowledge cannot solve. Nothing in our history could have prepared us for this. Yet we must cope with all this in the best way we can. To do so, I must now rest. You are welcome to share my house, Shaka Mahdi, such as it is. You are, even without ritual, still well-qualified to be considered an elder."

Shaka would have preferred the comfort of the ship, but it was more important to acknowledge the honor that Nossa Mehika had bestowed. So an extra mat was found and Shaka Mahdi settled down for the night. But sleep did not come for a very long time.

Morris sat in the Water Hole and scowled at his ale. His transport would be leaving in a few hours. There was nothing left for him in Farport.

He had expected a sound chewing-out after the business with the Castellan escaping. Maybe even some sort of official reprimand. But to be busted down to dirt was a bit harsh, he thought. Even the other men on his crew, who couldn't really be held responsible since he was the commanding officer, had been slapped down to latrine duty. It was damned harsh. And Morris was bitter.

His acid reverie was interrupted by someone else sitting down at his table. Morris looked up. It was the one person who could have shaken loose a smile on his face. "Hello, Christina. What's a nice girl like you doing in a den of vice like this?"

"The same as you, I expect," she answered. "Killing time until the transport arrives."

"Are you bailing out, too?"

She shrugged. "It's time to move on. Dr. Yoshi has written me an excellent recommendation. I'm going to try to get into medical school."

"You liked being called 'Doctor Christina,' eh?" Morris said with a grin.

She shrugged. "It sure beats 'Hey you.' Where are you going?"

"I haven't a clue," Morris said, taking a drink of his ale. "I just want out. Too many dickheads in the service. I got spoiled by Prilock and I don't think I can go back to putting up with the chickbird pucky. So I guess I'll head back up to the Northwest and see what I can find."

"This place is going to go to the rats pretty fast, now," Christina said. "They won't be able to keep out the criminal element."

"I hear Haggus is considering selling out while the selling is good," Morris said.

"That's what I heard," Christina said. "How much you want to bet Pousse buys him out?"

Morris chuckled. "She's one tough lady! If anybody can make a go of it when the pirates move in, it's her. She'll own the whole damn port in ten years!"

"She's welcome to it," Christina said. "It's too bad. It's really too bad."

"You're telling me! Damn!" Morris shook his head, impotently furious at the injustice of it all, and the stupid bloody waste. What had been a good thing for so many people was going sour fast, and no good was going to come of it. All because those self-important idiots couldn't leave well enough alone.

"I wonder where they are now," Christina mused softly.

"Hmm?"

"Prilock and Shaka. I wonder where they went."

"Back to where they belong, probably. And they've got to be better off for it. I'll bet you—"

Morris paused. A man came into the Water Hole, looking around nervously. Morris recognized. him. He was the bigwig doctor from the Academy. "What the hell . . . ?" Morris murmured. Christina turned around.

"That's Dr. Fellows. I wonder what he's doing here. I thought they'd all cleared out and gone home," she said, frowning.

Glancing around himself and moving in nervous jerks, Fellows searched the place until his eyes fell on Morris and Christina. Brightening a bit, he came over, looking like he expected to be fired upon at any minute.

"I hoped I'd find you here," the doctor said.

"What do you want?" Morris said inhospitably. "Haven't you great and mighty folk done enough damage?"

"Believe me," Fellows said with hushed urgency, "This travesty wasn't at all what I wanted!"

"Oh, sure," Morris snorted. "You couldn't do a thing about it I suppose."

Christina put a restraining hand on Morris's arm. "Don't mind him," she said to Fellows. "I know you meant well."

"I did, really! You must believe me! This is terrible, terrible!"

"So, why tell us?" Morris asked. "What do you want, sympathy?"

"No, actually, to be honest, I need your help."

Morris arched an eyebrow and he and Christina exchanged glances. "Oh, really? Do tell."

Fellows closed his eyes and shuddered. "They won't listen to me, the fools. Or to anyone else at the Academy. They have their own agenda and they intend to follow it, even though it may mean the destruction of the entire human race!"

"That's pretty dramatic," Morris said. "I mean, even if these so-called shadow slayers take out the whole Kurlu Empire, so what? No big loss. And why should they go after us?"

"Why shouldn't they?" Fellows insisted urgently. "We recognize political boundaries, but there is no reason why these creatures should. They may decide that humans are pernicious pests which need to be eliminated. And believe me, a species as powerful as they are can easily do it. I mean, we theorized that Prilock was a mere child, an untrained, immature creature. And look what he was capable of! If the fools decide to declare war on these beings then we are all doomed!"

"No kidding," Morris agreed grimly. "But what are we supposed to do about it?"

"Perhaps," Christina said, "Prilock can talk to his people and convince them that we are not all evil. He was, after all, the very soul of justice. Not the sort to make a blanket condemnation of the whole human race."

"Oh, I had hoped so!" Fellows moaned. "That was my greatest hope! That Prilock would speak on our behalf! But now, who knows? After the way he was treated—"

"Look, when he left, he was rather embittered towards humans in general, I'll grant you," Christina said. "But he did have sympathies towards some of us. He won't forget that some of us stood up for him."

"But the Byahail! We know now that the attacks on the Kurlu are directly related to what was done to the Byahail race. The Kurlu had suspected it, and what happened here in Farport with Prilock and that Byahail friend of his confirms it. So, what are those idiots up in Malowi going to do? It is the height of lunacy! The ultimate in folly! It was the Kurlu elite's idea, and the damned fools are going for it!"

"What? What in hell can they do to make the Chimera any more mad than they already are?" Morris asked.

"First," Fellows said, again glancing around nervously, "You must understand that I have gotten this information by covert means. There are a number of us in high places that realize the futility of trying to fight these Chimera as you call them. We believe we must, by any means possible, thwart the war effort and make every attempt we can to negotiate with these creatures. Those in the Academy most familiar with the Anomaly, Prilock, know how powerful, but also how advanced and intelligent these beings are. We have faith that beings this intelligent and morally developed can be reasoned with in good faith. But we must act and act quickly!"

"Okay, fine," Morris said impatiently, "So what's your point?"

Fellows spoke in a hushed voice. "The U.P. and the Kurlu are planning a joint mission to the South. They intend to take all the remaining Byahail hostage. They hope that they can then force the Chimera to back down. We must prevent this from happening!"

Morris took a deep breath. "Whew! I can't believe they'd resort to a harebrained scheme like that."

"The war is going very badly. The Kurlu are becoming desperate," Fellows said. "They've managed to infect the U.P. Defense Bureau with their desperation. Because Prilock was so successful passing as human, the Defense Bureau is intensely paranoid about infiltration."

"As if the Defense Bureau needs encouragement to be paranoid," Morris grumbled.

"Listen," Christina interrupted, "I think we'd both agree with you that this is a serious situation, and that the people in charge are trying to solve it in absolutely the wrong way. But I still want to know why you are telling us all this. What can we do about it?"

"As I said, there are a few of us who realize the absolute necessity of preventing further provocation of the Chimera. We have arranged for several ships to go down to the South before the official mission is on its way. We hope to get to the Reservation first and transport the Byahail to someplace safe. Maybe even the Valley, if it's possible. Anything to show the Chimera that we mean well and want to cooperate. But we need people we can rely on to man those ships. I thought perhaps you might be willing. I thought perhaps you might know of others who might be willing as well."

Morris grinned. "You've come to the right place."

Within forty-eight hours they were on their way. Morris found no shortage of volunteers in Farport, mostly among those who had served under Prilock and were disgusted by the way they had been treated. Any expression of loyalty to or support for the former Castellan had been rewarded by instant suspicion. They were blackballed, their careers put in suspension. Ironically, Command had made sure they had nothing to lose by throwing over their loyalties entirely.

Christina went along with them. Her experiences nursing Shaka Mahdi made her an authority of sorts on Byahail physiology. She expected they might need the services of a doctor on the Reservation as well as on the trip afterwards. She had approached Dr. Yoshi, but he wanted no part of the expedition. As much as his sympathies were with them, he was solidly embittered by his experiences with the bureaucracy aligned against them. He doubted the desperate adventure would do any good, and he intended to do nothing to jeopardize his chances of returning to a peaceful and successful practice in a more civilized part of the world. He was done with trying to be a hero.

Strings were quietly pulled to allow passage of the ships out of the port and out into the shipping lanes. They moved quickly, encountering no difficulties. Whoever it was who had made the arrangements higher up had done a good job. Once they reached the open swamp they were met by a small fleet of research vessels manned mostly by students and scientists from the Academy. The Academic fleet was headed up by Dr. Fellows, himself, looking terribly nervous but determined to go through with it. This was to be the unofficial diplomatic delegation, the self-appointed representatives of the human race who hoped they could make the critical difference. They wasted no time. The official ships sent to abduct the Byahail were only a day behind them.

As they made their way up the weed-choked waterway to the Byahail Reservation, Morris wondered what sort of reception they would get. There were a few researchers among them who spoke Byahail. They hoped they could make the creatures understand the seriousness of the situation and agree to come with them willingly. No one had any idea what they could do if the Byahail were not willing. To force them would defeat the whole purpose of the exercise. But to let them fall into the hands of the military would mean the end of any hope to gain the good will of the Chimera. Morris hoped that Shaka Mahdi was already there—it was logical to assume she might have returned to her people—and perhaps she could help persuade the Byahail to come. When they pulled into the harbor and saw Shaka's ship, Morris breathed a silent, grateful prayer.

"Captain Mahdi!" Morris called, waving, when he saw her appear on the shore, surrounded by a rag-tag group of Byahail. As he got closer he felt a wave of pity. Even lame and disfigured, Shaka Mahdi looked a lot healthier than the others around her. They were bent, hollow-eyed and emaciated, a pathetic remnant of a once strong and proud race. Even so, they faced the humans squarely, without timidity, openly curious but neither hostile nor afraid. He could hear Captain Mahdi talking to them in the sing-song language of the Byahail.

"Morris!" Shaka Mahdi greeted him as he jumped off the deck of his ship, splashing and half-sinking in the muck as he slogged his way up onto the shore. There had been a proper dock here at one time, but it had long since fallen into disrepair and been overgrown and partially pulled down by vines and weeds.

"We were hoping we'd find you here," Morris said, shaking the weeds and slime off his boots with distaste.

"Was not expecting visitors," Shaka replied. "Was worried until seeing were friends and not Kurlu."

"Hello, Shaka!" Christina called down, waving.

"Doctor Christina!" the Byahail greeted her with a grin. "Is very good seeing! Am glad have come!"

"Forgive me if I don't come down. I don't have proper boots on."

The Byahail next to Shaka, an ancient specimen with sharp, piercing eyes, spoke up. Shaka translated.

"Elder is Nossa Mehika. Most honored of Byahail. Wishes to know what is human business here."

Morris bowed respectfully to the Byahail elder. The other ships were pulling up to the shore behind him, their crew curious but hesitant to disembark. Fellows hustled up onto the deck. "Greetings! We come in peace!"

Shaka curled her lip in a sneer. "Peace of humans is little better than war."

"Really, Captain," Morris said, "We're here to help."

Shaka turned her attention back to Morris. "So, what is business of humans? Elder is waiting for answer."

"Of course," Morris said, with another deferential bow to the old Byahail. Then he explained as quickly as he could what their mission was, and what they hoped to do. Shaka translated at every break in the conversation to Nossa Mehika, loudly enough so that the other Byahail could hear. When Morris had finished, the two

Byahail conferred briefly. Then Shaka said, "Elder asks where humans intend to take People."

Morris shook his head. "We aren't really sure where would be safe. Out into the swamp initially, anyway. Try to make it as hard as possible for the military ships to find us."

Shaka relayed the answer and the old Byahail considered. Then the elder spoke. Shaka translated, "Elder says People will only go with humans if humans promise to take People back to Valley."

Morris frowned. He looked back at the others on the ship.

"There may still be a war going on in the Byahail Valley," Fellows said. "We don't know with any certainty what's going on over there. At any rate, there would be Kurlu patrols. It wouldn't be safe."

Nossa Mehika's answer was brief and left no room for compromise. Shaka said, "Elder speaks. People will go nowhere but back to Valley. Is no point to go anywhere else."

"But it could be dangerous—" Morris started.

Shaka cut him off, shaking her head. "Death is here, death is there, what matter which death comes? Is still death. Only in Valley can there be hope for life. Must go there. Have faith that gods will protect." Shaka smiled. "Gods have come. Gods are not myth. Morris knows what am meaning. People have no fear. People will go back to Valley if humans will take."

Morris looked back up towards the ships. "What do you think?" he asked them.

"Well," Fellows replied, "They are certainly right that their gods have come. With a vengeance."

"Damn right," one of Morris's men commented. "I'd say we would be in more danger than the Byahail if the Chimera control the Valley."

"That's what we're here for, right?" a student spoke up. "To make contact. To try to show that not all humans are war-mongering paranoids. I say we go. And have faith in the gods."

"I suppose that would be best," Fellows wavered anxiously. "But the Kurlu—"

"For heaven's sake," Christina exclaimed impatiently, "If that's the only condition under which they'll go, we'd best agree, don't you think?"

Morris looked around. It seemed that there was general consensus. He nodded. "Okay," he said. "Tell your people to get their things together. They're going home. But remember, we have to hurry. We've got no time to lose."

When the rescue mission had been hastily thrown together by the pacifist conspirators in Malowi, there hadn't been any reliable figures available on the current size of the Byahail population. They'd made some rough estimates and sent down as many ships as they could get, hoping it would be enough. They needn't have worried. A single transport would have sufficed. Shaka Mahdi had been planning to use her ship. It would have been crowded, but adequate. Dividing the Byahail and their few belongings among three ships assured that no one ship was overloaded, all of them staying light and maneuverable. If the military vessels caught up with them, they agreed they would split up, the better to evade their pursuers, and the small research craft would run interference. Nossa Mehika went with Shaka Mahdi on her ship, bringing along all the most sacred artifacts and relics that remained to the People. The customized freighter had the best chance of getting away in the event of pursuit.

The People left the Reservation without ceremony. Had there been time, they might have wished to exhume the bodies of those who had died and been buried there, so that their bones might be taken to rest in the Valley as they ought to. Nossa Mehika decided that if the People survived, and a future was granted to them, they might someday return and collect those old bones, the gods willing. For now, the hope of life was more important. The dead would rest for as long as the world. A year or two more in cold, strange ground would matter little to them.

Unbeknownst to the others, before leaving the wretched hovel that had been home, Lita Shalhi heaped fuel upon a cooking fire and dragged the sleeping mats up close. Though hate was a thing counseled against by the elders, Lita Shalhi hated the Reservation and hoped it would burn completely, taking the surrounding foul woods of that cursed land with it. The Byahail name for the Reservation was Telika Shih Bo Ley, which meant, "Given to us by our enemy." There was no worse name they could think of.

They made it out into the open swamp again by nightfall. They traveled all night to put as much distance as they could between themselves and the Reservation. Morris theorized that the military ships would probably be baffled when they arrived at their destination and found nobody home. It might take them as much as a day to radio back to headquarters for new orders, and then receive them. Since it was a joint U.P.-Kurlu operation, protocol would have to be followed, there would have to be conferences and consultations and negotiations—hell, it might be days before they decided what to do. In the meantime, the rescue mission would go like blazes towards the Valley. Even at top speed, traveling day and night, it would take at least three weeks. And that was assuming the weather didn't turn foul. Once they got within Kurlu waters, there was no telling what they'd find. In the far Southeast, where the Valley and the Mountains were, there might be no patrols. The Kurlu might have been beaten back. Or they might be swarming and bristling with weapons, ready to fire on anything that moved.

And then there was the ultimate wild card, the Chimera. There was absolutely no way to guess what to expect of them. Even the Byahail did not know.

The students and scientists had hoped to use that three weeks of travel as an opportunity to speak with the Byahail, to try to understand them better, and to find out more about their relationship to the Chimera, and what they knew about their gods. The Byahail were not inclined to talk. They treated their human benefactors politely, but coolly, and made it clear that they wished to have as little to do with them as possible. Shaka Mahdi acted as intermediary, explaining repeatedly that the People did not consider these humans to be benefactors at all, and felt little gratitude and no obligation to them. The scientists pleaded with Shaka Mahdi to try to persuade them to be more communicative, arguing that it was in the Byahail's best interest to help the humans understand them better. The answer was brief and resolute: the Byahail have no need for humans; the Byahail have the Chimera.

Christina met with the same obstinacy when she tried to examine the Byahail to try to treat the worst of their sicknesses. As near as she could tell, most of them were suffering from severe malnutrition, and many had rashes and sores most likely caused by parasites and filthy living conditions. She knew she could treat them and ease their suffering, certainly help them to heal more quickly. But the Byahail would have none of it. They pinned all their hopes on returning to the Valley, convinced that they needed only to return home and they would all be returned to health. They wanted no part of human medicine. Shaka Mahdi explained that the People accepted the offer of transportation home because it was the least of what was owed to them. But beyond that, they wanted nothing from humans. The Byahail sat quietly in the ships, patient and dignified, leaving the humans no alternative but to give up and let them be.

But as the days passed, Shaka Mahdi spoke privately and respectfully with Nossa Mehika. What the elder had so far observed had confirmed their theories about the humans. True, they were motivated at least in part by fear for their lives, but there was also evidence that the silly, stupid creatures truly meant well. The humans wanted to talk. They were curious, seeking knowledge, perhaps open to wisdom. Was it justifiable to refuse them? Shaka Mahdi said they were able to learn; was it not right then to try to teach them? The People wished to have nothing to do with the humans. This was understandable, but was it right?

The gods had taught the People that it was good to learn about the creatures with whom they shared the world. This instruction had led them to study and become well acquainted with all the living things in their Valley and in the forests and Mountains around them. This wisdom was good to possess. It was good and useful to know the habits of creatures, especially the ones that might be dangerous. Therefore, reasoned the elder, it might be better to speak with the humans, become better acquainted with them, teach them if they were willing to learn, in spite of how distasteful it might be. Shaka Mahdi said it was even possible to become friends with certain humans. This was difficult to accept, yet must be true if Shaka Mahdi said it. Yes, Nossa Mehika concluded, there must be a meeting. There must be conversation and exchange. This was the way of wisdom.

They met on Shaka's ship in the late morning. This was the time of day Nossa Mehika felt strongest and most alert. Age weighed heavily on the old Byahail, who had not enjoyed the benefit of communion with the gods for many years. There was now hope that this might soon change. It made the burden of age a bit easier to bear.

Morris felt a sense of awe as he was ushered into the presence of the Byahail along with Fellows and the other scientists. They followed the cues of an elderly Moor anthropologist named Dr. Akashida, whose background made him a bit better equipped to deal with the diplomatic aspects of the meeting. He bowed his head and waited to be told that he was welcome and might sit. The other humans took their places beside him, sitting as the Byahail did, on blankets on the floor, facing the Byahail delegation. Shaka Mahdi and Nossa Mehika sat in front, the others to the sides and behind, spread out so that no one sat directly in back of anyone else. All except Shaka were dressed in brightly colored, intricately woven native clothing, although the cloth was somewhat tattered and worn. Shaka still wore her customary freighter captain's uniform, although she looked less comfortable in it.

"We thank you for this meeting," Akashida said.

"Your gratitude is accepted," said Nossa Mehika through Shaka Mahdi. "It is my hope that we may find ways to share this world with honor and respect."

"That is our hope as well," said Akashida.

"Your ways are very strange," continued the elder. "You are creatures who live in pieces. There is no cloth that unites you. You feel no kinship to each other or to the world. It is a great mystery to us."

"I have no doubt," Akashida replied, "That we must seem quite senseless to you. Believe me, I am often angered and frustrated by the senselessness of humans, despite being one of them. I hope to help you to understand that there are enormous differences among humans. Some of us do feel a kinship to one another and to the world. Some of us do try to rise above the savage, selfish behavior of our fellow humans."

"So it has been told to me by Shaka Mahdi, who has gone out to live among you, and learned much. It might be that there can be peace between the People and some humans. This would be good. But there can be no peace between the People and those humans who have no honor, no respect."

"What," Akashida asked hesitantly, "can we do to solve this problem? How can we who wish peace separate ourselves from those who do not in your eyes?"

"You separate yourselves by your words and your actions. The gods will see this and judge accordingly."

"What do you think the gods will do when they judge?" asked Fellows anxiously.

Nossa Mehika thought for a moment, then answered. "Those who have no respect, forfeit their right to be respected. Those who have no honor forfeit their right to be treated honorably. Those who kill for their own pleasure and gain forfeit their right to life. As one acts, so is one judged."

"We of the United Peoples have always tried to act in the best interest of the Byahail," Fellows persisted, "You know must know that. We acted—"

"Best interest of Byahail?" Shaka interrupted, bristling, this time speaking from the heart and not merely translating. "Took People away from Valley! Were keeping People like chickbirds in pen! Are calling this 'best interest of Byahail'?"

"It was the best we could do!" Fellows pleaded. "The Kurlu were within their rights according to the terms of the Treaty—"

"Treaty among humans is bargain of cowards!" Shaka snorted.

"We had had so many years of war! We wanted peace—"

"What is peace with no honor?" retorted Shaka Mahdi. "Who are humans to seek justice from gods? No justice among humans! What is human justice to People? Humans of U. P. smile with blind eyes at Kurlu evil! Turn deaf ears to cries of Byahail future, dead before born! Offer bitter human peace like thorn knobs to starving People and are not understanding why People cannot eat! What is fate of humans now that gods have come? Is for gods to judge! And justice of gods is not hearing stupid human bleating for pity!"

Fellows started to stand up, crying out, "You've got to understand! You can't condemn—!" but Akashida took his arm and hissed sharply in his ear, "Let it go! Now is not the time!" At the same time, Nossa Mehika spoke to Shaka gently and the two conversed; presumably Shaka explaining to the elder the nature of what had just been said. The elder members of both delegations imposed calm on the proceedings. Finally Shaka spoke to them, relaying Nossa Mehika's response.

"It is for gods to decide. Gods are just, with wisdom greater than can be imagined. Be content to abide by it."

"I believe you," said Akashida, "But we know little of your gods. It is difficult to have faith. Some of us are afraid. What can you tell us about the Chimera?"

"Is well for humans to fear," Shaka muttered, but obediently relayed the question. Nossa Mehika answered, "They are what they are. The gods are as old as the world. Their power is great. It is foolishness to try to fight them, as humans have done."

"We wish no more fighting," Akashida assured them hastily. "How can we make peace with your gods? What would the Chimera have us do?"

"We cannot speak for the gods. Humans have no place known to the People in the great, round cloth of the living world. All beings for all time have woven their place, have ways and meaning in what they do. All is rhythm and cycle and mesh. Humans do not fit. Humans are a great, strange tear in the whole cloth. Chimera must use their power and wisdom to repair the cloth and find a way to weave humans into it, or discard those threads."

"Are you saying that the whole human race might be wiped out if we can't be made to fit into your natural scheme of things?" Fellows asked.

"If such is the judgement of the gods."

He started to protest, but Akashida gripped his arm in a signal to be silent. The anthropologist said, "Let us hope we can find our place then, humbly, and with honor."

This response seemed to please the elder Byahail, who regarded Akashida with renewed interest. "One whose head is bowed sees more of what lies all around than one whose eyes tilt skyward in false pride."

Suddenly the meeting was interrupted by cries of alarm from above. Ships had been spotted on the long-range scanner and they were approaching fast. By the time Morris got up to the deck people were shouting and pointing towards the horizon where dark masses dotted with flashing lights were growing towards them fast. The alarm was sounded and emergency actions were taken. The Byahail were made secure in the holds of the three main vessels which then split up and headed off across the marshes. The small, light research vessels split up to follow them, ready to turn around and, if necessary, ram any military ship that got too close. It was a frantic and valiant effort, but doomed. Within minutes it became clear that they were vastly outnumbered and outgunned. Like wolves herding deer, a broadly spread fleet of Kurlu vessels came down from the north to cut off the escape of those heading that way while ships bearing the colors of the United Peoples came in from the west.

"Damn!" cried Morris, "It's almost like they knew exactly where to find us and what we would do!"

"It is possible that we were betrayed," sighed Fellows. "We had to trust a number of people who had more to lose than to gain by helping us."

"Looks like Captain Mahdi is going to make a race of it," Morris said, pointing to the screen. The *Chimera* was making a direct beeline southeast towards the Valley at top speed. There was almost no chance that the freighter could outrun the military fleet—they were still days away from the Valley.

"Well, I suppose we might as well all make a run for it," Fellows said. "There is a remote possibility that one of us might make it. Perhaps there will be a storm or something—"

"Not likely," Morris grumbled. "We've got damnably clear weather—" He paused. "What the hell—?" He shouted up through the hatch to the deck. "Yo! Any of you up there see something weird on the horizon? Due south, southwest!"

"Looks like storm clouds," came the reply, "But they're the damnedest storm clouds I've ever seen!"

"Morris!" came a voice over the radio, another ship captain in their desperate fleet, "Are you picking up something coming at us—"

"I've got it. Any idea—?"

"Look," Fellows said, pointing to the screen, "She's heading right for it."

Sure enough, the *Chimera* had veered slightly to make for the storm. At first Morris thought Captain Mahdi was hoping to lose the pursuing ships in the confusion of the storm, although it was a risky tactic. The U.P. and Kurlu vessels were converging on them fast, but so was the storm. It was moving at an amazing rate. Morris didn't know what to make of it, although he had had little experience traveling in the southern swamps. Maybe storms were just like that out here. A freighter captain would have had a lot more experience dealing with such things, and maybe knew something the rest of them did not. It seemed the best idea to follow the *Chimera* and hope for the best. Apparently the others thought so, too. Morris saw them all correcting their courses to follow the Shaka Mahdi.

As the storm approached it looked more and more fearsome. The clouds rolled low in the sky, glowing with an eerie iridescence. Spidery flashes of lightning shot through the boiling vapors.

"Captain Mahdi," Morris bellowed into the radio, "I sure hope you know what you're doing, 'cause we're all following you!"

"Am knowing exactly what am doing," came the reply. Far from desperate, the Byahail's voice sounded almost jubilant.

Another captain said, "I hope so, too. I've never seen anything like that storm, and I'll confess, it scares the hell outa me!"

"Is not storm, silly human!" Shaka Mahdi cried, "Is Chimera!"

It took Morris a moment for it to register. He heard Fellows murmur softly, "Well, this is it—Judgement Day."

The freighter cut her engines and cruised to a stop. Milling like nervous sheep, the other ships slowed and settled around her. Everyone came up on deck, their faces reflecting various degrees of curiosity, resignation, and anxiety. Except for the Byahail. They came marching up with slow dignity, their heads raised to the sky. Their time had come.

Apparently oblivious to the enormity of what they were facing, the two fleets of military vessels began maneuvering to surround them. On the deck of the flagship—a tall, sleek Northman battle cruiser flying U.P. colors—an imposing group of dignitaries began to assemble. A voice boomed from a loudspeaker, "Hold your positions and prepare to be boarded!" On the other side of them, the Kurlu fleet massed, bristling with weapons. A voice from their flagship boomed, "It is useless to resist! You will surrender yourselves and the Byahail immediately!"

The clouds moved in over them. The stillness of the air was eerie considering the apparent violence of the clouds above. As one by one the engines in the ships were cut down to an idle, a low, constant rumble could be heard. Morris and Fellows came up on deck. Morris recognized Admiral Terat at the head of the delegation of dignitaries, and apparently, Terat recognized them.

"Well, well, Dr. Fellows," Terat sneered. "So you Academicians just couldn't keep out of it, could you? You'll pay for this absurd conspiracy! You and all the rest who sympathize with the enemy!"

"Think again, Admiral!" Morris shouted. "It's your backside that's in the fire!"

"It's just what I warned you about!" Fellows added with mixed vindication and dread, looking towards the approaching storm. "And believe me, I take no pleasure in saying I told you so!"

The boiling clouds obscured the sky above them, mere yards over their heads. Then a great, dark shape emerged, descending on vast wings to settle on the highest point, the peak of the Northman battle cruiser. It spoke in a deep, sonorous voice that all could hear, but only those who knew the ancient language of the Byahail could understand.

"O, brave People who have suffered so, behold! Your waiting was not in vain! We have come!"

From the deck of Shaka's freighter, the old voice of Nossa Mehika replied, strong and with only the slightest quiver, "We have endured, and greet you with joy. The Covenant is stone, the greatest Mountain, and despite all, the People are here, a great river which still flows in spite of terrible drought. Oh gods of my People! The tree shall bloom again!"

"So shall it be!" the great dark being said in reply, "And we promise to you that the tree shall never cease to bloom, from this day forth!"

From the Kurlu flagship came a defiant challenge. "Whatever monsters you are, don't think we are going to roll over and surrender! We are not children to be terrified by some grand display!" And they fired on the being. But the projectile they fired was dissolved in mid-flight by a bolt of lightning from the cloud. A second bolt struck the ship itself, with devastating effect. Pieces of debris flew into the water and flames shot up into the air. Alarms sounded and the crew of the ship began to shout and race around frantically.

"There will be no more violence!" boomed the voice of the great, dark being, this time in words they all could understand. It towered over them, golden-eyed, with a curved, ebony beak and sleek body; massive, clawed feet gripped the peak of the battle cruiser's upper cabin. Its body was so dark that no features of it could be seen, so it seemed almost like a great silhouette with burning eyes. Several more bolts of lightning sliced through the darkened air, surgically striking other ships. "We know who you are, now," the great, dark being continued, "And we know what we must do. Too long did we Chimera remain in ignorance and indecision. When we found the Valley of our precious Children shrouded in death, we were choked with despair. Too many gentle eons have passed; tragedy paralyzed our reason. But that paralysis is over. Sanity has returned to us. And the time of human arrogance and the suffering of our Children is over!"

"All right, all right!" Admiral Terat called up to the being, perspiring profusely, "What are your terms?"

"Terms?" echoes the Chimera, "Are you proposing to negotiate a treaty?"

"We are always willing to negotiate," Terat assured it. "We are reasonable people."

The being sneered, "Oh, yes, we are well aware of your willingness to make commerce of moral truths!" It reached a great claw down and swiftly, cleanly, swept Admiral Terat off the deck of the battle cruiser. With a splash and a shriek, he landed in the water, thrashing among the weeds. Several crew and dignitaries ran to the railing, looking down in horror and then up at the Chimera in fear. A bolt from the clouds struck the water, and then the only turbulence that remained was that of the creatures which flocked to feed on the corpse.

"My god!" cried Fellows.

The Chimera cocked its head, its expression almost amused. "Did you expect more of beings you considered superior, Doctor? Oh, yes, you are known to us, too. As are your naïve misconceptions. To be sure, we are capable of great gentleness and compassion. We abhor violence. We believe in justice. And we love peace and order. But this thread in time hangs torn from the fabric of being. You humans have shredded your way into our world with your lies, greed and stupidity. We have no use for you, and return to you what you have given us. Is that a surprise, Doctor?"

"I expected superior beings to rise above the worst traits of human beings, not to lower themselves to them," Fellows said in defensive righteousness.

"Did you indeed? The worst among you would have allowed your Admiral Terat to die a slow, agonizing death, gnawed by the small beings of the swamp. We saw no need for his suffering and put an end to it."

"But to kill arbitrarily, brutally—"

"As the Kurlu did in their conquest of the Valley of the People?" thundered the Chimera, rising up and flapping its great, dark wings. "Why should we not do the same? Why do you expect anything else?"

"Because we have faith in your justice!"

It was Christina, speaking up as loudly as she could even though her voice was shaking. The Chimera settled on its perch again, cocking its head and eyeing her. "Indeed?" it inquired, but gently. "And what do you know of the justice of the Chimera?"

"Because of Prilock," she said, looking towards Morris, pleading for support. He didn't disappoint her. He stood next to her and said, "We knew one of your kind, and we learned to respect him."

"That is known to us, too," the Chimera said, "And shall not be forgotten." Then it rose up and proclaimed in a great, booming voice, "A new age dawns this day! The People shall return to their home, and shall begin to reweave the cloth of their lives! The Chimera shall sleep in their city no longer, but shall know the world as they did in ages long ago! But the humans—what shall be done about the humans?" The great being spoke more gently, addressing the Byahail in their own lyrical tongue. "What say you, precious Children? What shall we do about these humans who have sprung up like clusters of poisonous mushrooms to spread through our world?"

There was a low, bitter murmuring among the Byahail, but Nossa Mehika spoke up without hesitation. "It is for the gods to decide. We mortal ones have not the wisdom for a decision such as this."

The Chimera nodded. "Well, humans? What do you say? What is to be done with you?"

The dignitaries murmured feverishly among themselves, unsure what to say. They had seen what response Admiral Terat had received upon offering to negotiate a treaty. But negotiations were all the government officials knew; the military officers knew battle, but that was obviously futile against such an opponent. Fellows wanted to speak up, but lacked the courage in the face of the unknown, for the Chimera were not what he expected. Akashida knew what needed to be said, based on his brief meeting with the Byahail. He spoke for many who were there, and spoke well. The elderly Moor said, "Gods of the People, we humbly ask that you teach us the ways of wisdom, that we may find our place in the cloth of your world."

The Chimera cocked its head, leaning over towards Akashida, who stood on the deck of the freighter with the Byahail around him. "Indeed?" It looked around at the other humans. "What say you others?"

"We're ready to learn!" shouted one student.

"That's what we've come for!" cried another.

"Don't judge us by the others—let us prove ourselves to you!"

"Take us with you back to the Valley," Morris said. "Let us earn our place by helping the Byahail rebuild."

His offer was met with enthusiastic shouts of agreement. The Chimera held up a wing to gesture for silence.

"Noble People," it said to the Byahail, "these humans offer their services to you in rebuilding what was lost if you will tolerate their presence and agree to teach them your ways of wisdom. What say you to this?"

Many were sullenly silent. Some glanced at one another in tentative interest. There was some quiet discussion. Lita Shalhi said, "We do not need the humans. Their presence would be an insult."

Shaka Mahdi retorted, "Who are you to refuse their help? You would refuse an honorable offer to pay a debt that is owed?"

"That debt can never be paid!" Lita Shalhi replied angrily. "And what would a human know about honor, eh?"

"What do you know of humans?" Shaka Mahdi shot back. "I have lived among them!"

"The scars on your body speak of your knowledge of humans! I want nothing from them!"

"Enough!" said Nossa Mehika. "The world is large. We need only our Valley and the land which has always been of the People. What did we care of humans in the world until their evil touched us? If those evil threads are removed and wisdom woven into their place, what might be then? No harm to us. Perhaps even good may come of it."

"What good could come of humans?" said Lita Shalhi. "We have lived through all our ages happily without them! We need nothing from them!"

"How can one appreciate a good one has never seen?" argued Shaka Mahdi. "How could we have known how good might be the taste of cheese before we discovered how to make it? How could we have known the beauty of the bells until we first heard them ringing? Humans are very clever at making things. There are things which they might show us, or be willing to make for us in trade—"

"I want no trade with humans!" Lita Shalhi scowled. It was clear from the cold murmurs of agreement that the other People were of a like mind.

"Gods of our People," said Nossa Mehika to the Chimera, "Forgive the angry words of those whose mouths are full of bitterness from suffering and despair. We have been away from you and away from our home too long, and weakness gnaws at our bones."

"We understand. Our hearts are open to your weakness," the Chimera said. "It will be healed in time, and then we will rejoice again at your strength."

"Until this healing can come," the old one continued, "perhaps it would be best if there were no humans in our Valley. The People are not yet ready for this, so close on the evil that humans once brought to our land."

The Chimera bowed its head in acknowledgement. "So be it. We accept your will, noble People. But it is regrettable. Such a pity that these few good humans, eager for wisdom and seeking with respect and humility to earn honor for themselves with honest labor in your service, must be turned away."

"Then you turn me away as well!" Shaka Mahdi cried, stepping away from the other Byahail towards the humans. "Gods of the People! I speak for the humans! If they are to be kept away from the Valley, how are they to learn? Who will teach them the ways of wisdom? No, I will not speak with the voice of bitterness and anger! I will not condemn those with good hearts because of evils they had no power to control! I will stay among them and teach them! I will help the humans weave their threads into the cloth!"

"Where are your loyalties?" Lita Shalhi cried. "How can you turn your back on us at this time, when there is so much to be done and every one is needed? For humans? Is this what you have learned from them? Bah!"

"Silence!" cried Nossa Mehika, "You shame us in front of our gods! Hear me, and respect what I say!"

They were interrupted by the harsh voice of the Kurlu commander's amplified voice coming from the Kurlu flagship. "Enough of this! We of the Kurlu Empire will not bow down and be enslaved by a race of monsters! We would rather die fighting!" And with that, they began firing on the little fleet and on the battle cruiser where the Chimera was perched. Not a single shot found its mark.

"If it is your desire to die fighting," thundered the Chimera, "then so be it!" It waved a great, dark wing and bolts shot down from the clouds, slicing through the heart of every Kurlu vessel. Within minutes, all but one were sinking into the swamp amid alarms and screams of panic. The solitary ship spared, a small scout ship, bobbed amid the chaos, its crew paralyzed with fear. The Chimera's voice boomed across the water, rising over the din of disaster. "Go! Return to the Empire and tell them what has happened here! Tell them we are coming! Those who wish it will be granted their warrior's death!" The Chimera then rose up into the air, beating its mighty wings. "You go as well!" it commanded the U. P. fleet. "Go back to your union of convenience, your federation of compromise! The time of decision has come! We give you a month, no more! Then we will come! Be ready for us!"

The ships hastily powered up their engines and beat a retreat. The Chimera floated in the air over the small rebel fleet that remained. "Noble People," it said, "it is time to go home. Gather your things and prepare. Tonight you shall sleep among the flowers of the Valley."

Those who had not brought their bundles on deck with them went down and got them. Shaka Mahdi helped Nossa Mehika bring up the bundle containing the precious sacred relics of the People. But then Shaka stepped back.

"I am not going."

"So," said Nossa Mehika, "You are determined to stand with the humans."

"I am needed here."

"You are needed in the Valley," the elder said with mild reproach.

"The People have the ways of wisdom. The People have the gods. What do these foolish humans have?"

Nossa Mehika smiled. "You think as an elder would. Do what you must, Eyes Look Far, but remember, you will always be welcome in the Valley. It is your home."

"I will come when the humans with me are welcome as well," Shaka Mahdi said.

The elder nodded and then looked upwards. "Chimera! Gods of my People! We are ready!"

The clouds rolled low and tenderly gathered up the Byahail, lifting them into the sky. Then, moving as fast as they had come, they were gone, vanishing into the southeast, leaving behind the motley band of students, scientists, idealistic malcontents, and Shaka Mahdi.

They gathered around her, animated and bewildered. Their desperate mission was suddenly over, and they had no idea what to do next.

"What the hell happened?" Morris cried.

"What were you arguing about? Was our offer rejected?"

"What's going to happen? What are we supposed to do now?"

"What do the Chimera expect from us? Did they say?"

Shaka Mahdi sighed and searched her pockets for a ginseng smoke. As she put it to her lips and lit it, she said, "Am needing drink. Come below. Will try to explain."

CHAPTER 8

It had been a very long day.

Shaka Mahdi closed the door of her cabin and sat down on her bunk with a sigh. At last she had the ship to herself. Even the company of her own people wore on her nerves. She had been too long away from the Byahail and had adopted too many ways of her own, some human, some just different. She had grown to like her own company. It was one aspect of being a freighter captain that had suited her well. But that was all over now. The Chimera were abroad in the world, and nothing would ever be quite the same again.

For the last six hours she had endured the consequences of her decision to cast her lot with the humans. Oh, how much easier it would have been to have simply let the gods carry her away to the Valley! Humans were the most insufferable, irrational, contradictory creatures imaginable. They thrashed about like kits fallen into a pool. What are we to do? What do the Chimera expect? Where should we go? Back to Malowi? To Farport? Somewhere else? Stick together or separate? What happens in a month? What will the Chimera do? Why did the Byahail reject the offer of help? What do the Byahail want? And on, and on, and on, each answer debated, each suggestion belabored, each reply to each question spawning twelve more questions. What in the world made her think she could teach these creatures? They were hopeless. Even the ones she knew best drove her to despair.

Shaka fell back onto the bed. Tomorrow was another day. If they were unable to decide for themselves, she would simply have to demand that those who would accept her as a leader go with her, and the rest could go wherever they pleased.

And where would she lead them?

Shaka groped in the drawer next to the bunk for a ginseng smoke. Finding it and lighting it, she inhaled deeply, staring into the darkness. Perhaps she would start a human colony somewhere. Try to teach them how to live according to the ways of wisdom. It would be difficult; there were dynamics in human society that simply did not exist in Byahail society. The sexual element, for instance. There was nothing in the teachings of the gods that would cover that. She'd simply have to improvise. It was not going to be easy. Humans could be headstrong and stubborn, they liked to argue, and even the best of them could not always be trusted. They were forever trying to get away with doing things that they shouldn't. She had little patience for that sort of behavior but the Chimera would have less. Shaka closed her eyes and took a long, deep draw off the smoke. She reminded herself of all the reasons she was doing this, all the humans who had been kind to her, who had tried to help her, who did not deserve to be condemned with the rest.

She heard the shush and click of a door opening and shutting. Shaka sat up, instantly alert. Locking the doors to the ship had seemed to be an unnecessary precaution. Now she wished she'd done it anyway. Even if it was friendly, she was in no mood for company. "Who is there?" she demanded as the door to her quarters opened.

"I should think you'd be more careful than to leave your ship open out here in the swamp," came the reply. "You won't always have a god around to look after you."

"Prilock!" Shaka leaped up joyfully, reaching to turn on the light. He was in his human form, looking as he always had, tall and stern and solid.

"Mind if I sit down? I've had a rather long day."

"Sit! Are welcome! Is very good to see!"

"Please," he said, settling himself comfortably, "Let's use the language of the People. I much prefer it to the chattering of human speech."

"You can speak our language now?" Shaka asked, sitting at the table next to him.

"You heard me today. I take it I made myself sufficiently understood."

Shaka stared in admiration and awe. "That was you? You were the great bird of the Chimera?"

"Who else? I was already fluent in human language. The language of the People came to me quite easily and naturally once I was properly taught. Thus I became the obvious choice as ambassador for the Chimera to the humans."

Shaka leaned against the table, looking at him searchingly. "Why have you come back here? Is this just a visit?"

"I needed to speak to you. No doubt you have a great number of questions that need answering." He smiled at her. "I was very proud of you, standing up for the humans the way you did, insisting on staying behind to teach them."

"I spoke my heart. We both know that the humans would be doomed if they were left to themselves."

"I was rather hoping the People would agree to Morris's proposal. But it's quite understandable that they couldn't. There is too much pain in their hearts. The memory of all they have suffered is too vivid. And they haven't had the benefit of acquaintance with humans as you and I have had. We can see the potential in them; the People can't. Nor, I may add, could the Chimera. There was serious talk of the total extermination of the creatures, and how best to do it with minimal damage to the other creatures of this world. But when I told them of my experiences among humans, they became very interested. Instead of seeing them as a pernicious pest species, they are considering their potential cultivation. If, as Nossa Mehika put it, the evil threads can be pulled out, there may be a way of weaving humans into the cloth."

"I have been thinking about it, my friend," Shaka sighed. "I admit I doubt if the humans can be taught all they must know. Even if they can be taught, I doubt they will live by it. The ways of wisdom are too narrow for humans to walk. They will lose their balance and fall."

Prilock nodded his head in agreement. "I'm afraid you may be right. But over time, it may be possible to bring humans to a higher level of being. The Chimera are a very ancient race. They have watched the evolution of countless species and seen what changes can occur. In fact, the Chimera had been hoping that creatures something like humans would arise naturally, before they gave up waiting and went ahead to create the People. Had we Chimera been paying attention, we would have noted the arrival of humans and guided their evolution. If indeed humans did evolve naturally, and did not arrive some other way, a possibility we have considered, and shall investigate. But regardless of how they came to be here, they are here. And although the Chimera have no need of a second companion creature it might prove interesting and worthwhile to see what can be made of humans."

Shaka reached into the drawer for a ginseng smoke. "And so what will the gods do? How will they begin the cultivation of humans?"

Prilock frowned at Shaka. "Haven't you given up smoking those filthy things yet? You are supposed to provide the influence for the humans, not be influenced by them. And poorly, I might add."

Shaka waved a dismissive hand. "The mountain goat does not change into its winter coat overnight. I cannot give up all the vices I acquired all at once."

"Hmm. I suppose. And you aren't likely to, either, away from the positive influence of your people."

"I cannot live among them anymore," Shaka sighed. "I realized that in the short time I was with them. I've become too different, seen too much. And I am too comfortable with who I have become. The desire to go back is not there. So it is just as well that I have taken on this task. At least among humans I feel a little bit more at home."

Prilock inclined his head. "I must confess," he said quietly, leaning an elbow onto the table, "I know all too well what you mean. I do not fit in easily among my fellow beings. I am an infant among ancients. And what is more, I spent the most critical formative years of my life among humans. There are many basic understandings shared by all the Chimera that are totally unknown to me."

Shaka frowned. "Do you know how this came to be? Can any guess be made about what happened to you?"

"As a matter of fact, yes. It is a very long story which has its beginnings in the first early encounters with the Kurlu. When the Chimera first discovered that the People were gone, it was a terrible shock. It was assumed they had all been killed. The Chimera had dwelled for tens of thousands of years in their city in the mountains, venturing out only to visit the beloved People at the time of communion, lulled into a kind of intellectual torpor by habit and peace and the pleasant rhythms of their lives. The Kurlu invasion threw them into a confusion of horror and indecision. Some reacted in blind rage and grief, killing every human in the Valley. Others were immobilized by depression. All agonized in guilt for allowing the tragedy to happen. There was little rational thinking done for several years. The Kurlu came back, with a vengeance, and a few Chimera attempted to go among them secretly to try to find out what these terrible creatures were. Others still wanted nothing but to kill every human they found. Most simply sank into the city, buried in regret and misery, doing nothing.

"What finally broke this fragmentation and futility was the Kurlu discovery that they could destroy us with acid. That was the second shock that forced the Chimera to their senses. Some twelve Chimera were destroyed in this way. It was the first loss of individuals, the only deaths the Chimera had known, since the end of the First Age of the world, a time only dimly remembered by the Chimera themselves.

"There are one hundred eleven individual Chimera. Each came to be at a slightly different time, and under slightly different conditions, and so are distinct in their own way. But all came to be during the First Age, when the world was a very different place. As the climate changed, the conditions for our creation ceased to exist. Other life forms began to emerge, nothing like us, growing, changing, evolving. But the Chimera remained the Chimera, one hundred eleven beings who grew and changed as individuals and as Chimera, but never died and never gave birth to new creatures. Suddenly, after countless millennia of being one hundred eleven, the Chimera were only ninety-nine. This was intolerable. Much of the way our social organization worked was built around a certain number of individuals. This could not change. But how to replace those lost?

"In one sense, the loss was irreparable. One cannot replace an ancient and sacred tree simply by planting a new one. And the conditions necessary to create one of us no longer existed anywhere in the world. But in the great stores of knowledge available to the Chimera, there existed clues to the answer. A new being could not be created, but might be cloned from tissue donated by an existent individual. It was a tricky process, because the amount of mass needed to create a clone was very close to the amount that would prove fatal to the donor if lost. As you and I know, there are ways around that danger to the donor, but the help of the companion species was needed, and it was believed the People were gone. The second part of the process, also tricky, involved a host. The conditions to encourage the clone to grow into a viable being had to be precise—controlled, stable temperature, a constant supply of easily available nutrients, and a dozen other factors. The simplest solution—and an elegantly ironic one—was to use as a host a human body of approximately the same weight as a fully developed being. With the Kurlu in constant aggressive proximity, such hosts were easily procured.

"Twelve suitable humans were taken captive and the experiment was begun. Because the Chimera were inexperienced with handling humans, there were several deaths and several escapes. Those that died were simply replaced. Of those who escaped, most were recaptured, but a few were never accounted for. It was presumed that they made it back to the Kurlu Empire, and the fetal beings they carried were destroyed. They, too, were replaced. Apparently, one host that got away took an abandoned Kurlu shuttle boat and fled into the swamp. This particular host never made it back to civilization, either because the shuttle became disabled, or he himself became disabled as the being he carried grew and developed. That being grew to the point of viability, ultimately consuming all of the host as if he were a yolk sac. And then there that being sat, awake and alive, but trapped inside the shuttle and completely unaware of what it was and what it should do."

"And then the humans of the U.P. found you," Shaka said softly.

Prilock nodded. "There are twelve others like me, successfully cloned and brought to viability. They are the new generation, and have aroused as much excitement and affection among the older Chimera as did the People when they were first created. This entire disaster has served to awaken the spirit and intellect of the Chimera, stirring them as they have not been stirred in millennia. They look upon the tasks ahead—bringing up and teaching the new generation, helping the People to rebuild, and studying and cultivating the humans—with a great deal of enthusiasm."

"Wait—" Shaka interrupted him. "You said that there were twelve others like you. That means that there are now one hundred-twelve Chimera."

"Yes," Prilock said. "There were too few and now there are too many. They aren't quite sure what to do with me. But more than that, it seems that the clones for the most part turn out to be quite similar to the donors in what would pass in a Chimera for character traits. But I am very different from my donor. I seem to have developed a personality that is—shall I say—uncomfortably human."

Shaka smiled at him in sympathy, reaching out her hand to him. "Once again, my friend, we find ourselves on the same river."

He took her hand and looked at it. "Yes. Have you told anyone among the People about me?"

Shaka nodded. "I told Nossa Mehika."

"Then you know that what we've been doing is against the way."

"Nossa Mehika did not know what would come of it, but found it very disturbing. So it worried me, as well. We didn't know we were doing wrong."

"No, we had no idea. And I'm not sure it was wrong—for us. There are rules that the Chimera and the People have worked out over the centuries, creating a smoothly-working partnership, beneficial to both sides, bringing satisfaction to both sides. The reasons for those rules are good ones, and violating them would only create misery."

"But we are exceptions, eh? We do not fit into the ways of our fellow beings, or the lives they lead. We are loose threads in the cloth."

"We are definitely a part of the cloth, Shaka," Prilock said with affection, "But our design most certainly does not fit the pattern. My donor—my parent, I suppose you could say—said that it is the variations in the pattern that make the cloth more interesting."

Shake grinned. "So perhaps you will not be returning to the Mountains, eh?"

"No, at least not to settle. I must speak with the humans, but that will wait until tomorrow. Tonight I need to rest."

"Do you wish to stay here?" Shaka tried not to sound too eager.

Prilock sighed heavily. "That is what I have been debating." He paused and then looked at the Byahail intently. "There will be consequences. Unpleasant ones, long term. For both of us. Continued contact with me may prolong your life indefinitely, and not in a healthy way. And when you finally do die, it will not be a good or natural death. And as for me, when I finally do lose you . . ." His voice trailed off. Shaka waited. Finally he continued, "The Chimera are beings of very deep intellect, but also very deep feelings. There are those who still grieve for People long dead because the bond forged with them was so strong. Such is the seductive danger of communion. And so they learned to love the People as a whole, delighting in each new generation, never becoming too attached to any one individual. Shaka," he said with quiet intensity, "It is probably already too late for me. It surprised me how much I missed your company when I was away. It disturbed me to realize I couldn't bear the thought of a permanent separation. That is how dependent I have become on regular communion with you. And if I stay here tonight, I know I will not be able to break the habit. I will never be able to leave you again."

"Then, stay," said Shaka. "If the harm is already done, at least allow yourself the pleasures that can be gotten from it. I am not dead yet. And I am here for you as long as I shall live. I promise you that, my friend."

"But there might still be a chance for you!" Prilock said urgently. "If I go away now, busy myself with tasks elsewhere—and there is plenty of work to be done!—you might recover over time. You might yet begin to age normally again. If I must face the pain of losing you I might as well deal with it now, when there is a chance you could be spared."

Shaka raised her head defiantly. "I have no fear of what will happen. No fate could be worse that what I have suffered and endured. All will be worth it if it means an end to loneliness. There is nothing I cannot endure if I know the end of the day will bring peace, comfort, and the sweet sleep of communion."

"You don't know what you're saying," Prilock said softly. "You have no idea the kind of long, lingering twilight you may be condemning yourself to."

"It is my choice. I am not a child for whom you must make decisions. The Chimera long ago granted the People the right to choose their own way and find their own path. I demand that right! Do not choose for me!"

Prilock lowered his eyes as if in regret. But then he looked up and smiled, albeit sadly. "So be it, then," he said.

"Besides," Shaka said lightly, pleased at having won the dispute, "Having you with me will make my task much easier. You can make the humans listen. You always could make them be honest in spite of themselves."

Prilock laughed softly. "That would be ironic, indeed. But these are matters we can put off until the morning. For now, I am tired of humans, and of being a god. I desperately need to rest. And it seems you have accepted me as a somewhat permanent bunkmate. Shall we?"

Shaka got up and went back over to the bunk. She held out her hand. "I have missed the peace your touch brings. I welcome it."

When she lay back on the bed, feeling the wonderful sense of comfort and well-being spread through her body, she opened her eyes and looked down. To her surprise, Shaka saw not the dull, brown mass she had been accustomed to, but a blanket of pearly white opalescence that glowed slightly in the darkness of her cabin. Smiling, Shaka thought, Prilock has become a god. Truly Chimera.

In the morning Shaka Mahdi awoke feeling more fully rested and ready for the day than she had in weeks. She drank her morning coffee more out of habit than out of the need for stimulation, and took pleasure in the flavor. She carried her coffee mug up onto the deck. The day was bright and sunny, and sounds of the swamp buzzing and humming in the background. A light breeze stirred the grasses and the leaves on distant bushy hummocks. Prilock melted down and reformed on the deck next to her.

"Sunning yourself?" she asked, taking pleasure, too, in speaking the musical language of her people.

"The Chimera showed me a way to absorb energy directly from the sunlight," he replied. "It is a most enjoyable way of recharging myself. Much better than eating."

There came a shout from a neighboring ship. "Prilock! Good morning! It's good to see you again!"

"Hello, Christina. I'm glad you came along for the adventure. Are the other humans up yet?"

She shook her head. "Not yet, but they're getting there. I've always been an early riser. So, to what do we owe the honor of a visit from you?"

"I'd expect you could probably guess," he replied.

"Are you going to help Shaka to save our unworthy selves?" Christina asked with a smile.

"Something like that," Prilock replied. "Pass the word along. I'm going to need to speak to everyone, preferably all in one place and all at once, as soon as they can be gathered together."

It took about an hour and a half to do as he asked. They got everyone congregated on the freighter and the research vessel anchored next to it, so all could see and hear. Prilock climbed up to the top of the upper cabin for better visibility. He chose to retain the old familiar human form, the one so many of them recognized. He was startled and surprised when his ascent was greeted with a spontaneous round of applause.

"All right, all right, enough of that!"

"I can't tell you how good it is to see you again, Castellan!" Morris said.

"You may dispense with that ridiculous title, if you can break yourself of the habit," Prilock replied. "After all, it is hardly appropriate."

"Prilock," Fellows said, with an air of forcing himself to a well-rehearsed speech that was nonetheless difficult to deliver. "I do apologize for all that happened. I hope your presence here indicates that we are forgiven, and that your advocacy—"

"Doctor Fellows," Prilock cut him off, "You are one of the saddest excuses for a diplomat that I have ever encountered, and I intend that as a compliment. You do yourself a disservice by trying to be one. Stick to being a scientist. We got along much better."

"Ah, ahem, if you say so, why of course." Fellows reddened, but also looked relieved.

"So, why are you here, Sir? If it's not out of line to ask," Morris said.

"It is not out of line at all. In fact, I will get straight to the point. You all know, or at least have probably guessed, how our three species reached this strange juncture. The Kurlu are mostly to blame for the holocaust to the Byahail, but the rest of the human species is being held responsible for knowing about it and doing nothing to stop it. The Chimera don't recognize the validity of your treaties and international laws. You sat back, wringing your hands and mumbling about what a shame it was, but insisted one can't interfere with a sovereign nation. That, as far as the Chimera are concerned, was as good as stamping your approval on the tragedy. Now, I hear you protesting, but hear me out! You have three things going for you. First, the U.P.'s sadly misguided but basically well-meaning attempt to save the Byahail by relocating them to the Reservation. When the Byahail insisted they could live no where else in the world but the Valley, they were correct. There are physiological reasons for it, the most obvious result of which is that there have been no live births among the Byahail since the relocation."

"We tried to alert the government to that fact," said Akashida, "But they wouldn't listen. They said their hands were tied. They said—they said any number of pin-headed things," the anthropologist finished in disgust.

"Which leads me to the second thing you have in your favor," Prilock continued. "This little conspiracy to try to rescue the last of the Byahail from the futile intrigues of your government. You have made it quite clear that not all of you are willing to go along with the stupidity of your human rulers, and are even willing to break your laws to do it. This indicates that at least some humans have an advanced sense of morality. Make no mistake, we do believe in the rule of law. The first mark of a civilized society is the willingness to form and obey laws. Unfortunately, human society has evolved to the point of the rule of law, but it does not know how to do so intelligently. Consequently, you have an arrogantly ignorant government which passes a great number of bad laws, does not know how to take criticism for it, and its citizens have little respect for law and routinely break the laws for all the wrong reasons, mostly for the sake of personal gain, not moral principle. But the mark of an advanced individual in such a society is the refusal to obey bad laws, the refusal to participate in actions which are clearly wrong, and the willingness to take action against those wrongs at risk to oneself. Your mission of defiance is an excellent example of rebellion against a clear wrong. I could," Prilock added more quietly, looking directly at Morris, "cite other examples personally known to me."

Morris smiled. He never forgets, he thought fondly. Good or bad, he never forgets.

"The way of wisdom is neither clear nor simple," Prilock continued. "And you may find it difficult to understand, and even more difficult to follow. Nevertheless, you must try. It is your only chance of survival. Shaka Mahdi and I will do all we can to help you, which is the third thing you have going for you. The circumstances which brought Shaka Mahdi and myself to be among you were extraordinary, and were an extraordinary stroke of good fortune for you. Had you not had us for advocates, it is doubtful that humans would have even been granted a chance at survival, and the opportunity to find their place in this world."

"We are deeply in your debt," said Akashida with a bow of his head.

"Look," Morris spoke up, "We've all pretty much said we're willing. But since the Byahail rejected our offer to help them, and made it pretty clear we aren't welcome in the Valley, where are we supposed to go?"

"Actually," Prilock said, "the Chimera were quite impressed with your offer and consider it an excellent opportunity to accomplish several things at once. Whether they care to admit it or not, the Byahail are going to need some assistance at first. There is a great deal of rebuilding to be done. And I expect that in a rather short period of time, out of necessity because of their drastically diminished numbers, most of the Byahail who are able to will be carrying children. We hope that they may be persuaded to reconsider their initial refusal. They are a very noble and proud people, but their pride shouldn't blind them to reason. In a few days, after they have had a chance to rest, eat well, and recover some of their health and strength, the Chimera will put the proposal to them again. We have reason to believe that Nossa Mehika is favorably disposed to the idea. The others are expected ultimately, albeit grudgingly, be convinced by the logic of it."

"So, what would be the arrangement?" Morris asked. "Would we be living with them in their village?"

"Certainly that would provide the best learning situation," Akashida commented.

"Would they tolerate that?" Fellows asked doubtfully. "Perhaps it would be better for us to set up housekeeping elsewhere and visit the Byahail village on a daily basis."

"For once, Doctor Fellows, we are in agreement," Prilock said. "Our tentative plan, subject to adjustment as necessity and circumstance dictate, is to settle all of you around the mouth of the river. It is a part of the Valley that the People—the Byahail—have little use for. You will not be intruding on them. Then, when the time is right, and they are ready to accept your help, you will begin going up the river to the village on a daily basis. This will allow you to do the work that is necessary, to be of service to the People, and also to observe them and learn from them.

"Let me make the rules perfectly clear. You must go into this arrangement with a sense of humility and openness. Remember, you have no rights in this world. Your behavior in the past—collectively, as a species—negated what few rights as living intelligent creatures that you might have been entitled to. What the Chimera are granting you is the chance to earn individually what you have lost as a species. Because of the extreme diversity you have demonstrated, we have judged that the effort is worth it. You will not live or die because of the actions of your fellows—you will each be judged on the basis of your actions alone. What is expected of you will be made clear. And ultimately, it may be possible for some of you to earn the right to a place in the world alongside the Byahail and the Chimera."

There was a moment or two of silence, then a voice asked timidly, "What happens to those who don't make the grade?"

"That," Prilock said, "is still being debated among the Chimera."

They glanced at one another uncomfortably. Then one of the students spoke up. "What's going to happen when the month is up and the Chimera go out into the world? What's going to happen to the Kurlu, and everybody in the Northwest?"

Prilock took a deep breath. "That, too, is still being debated. It had been suggested that the most merciful route would be simply to establish the experimental colony at the mouth of the Byahail River and sterilize all other humans everywhere else, allowing the uncontrolled members of the species to die out. But that would be difficult and time-consuming, and we Chimera would much prefer to focus our energy and attention on the Byahail. It would be far simpler to exterminate the rest of the human population and be done with it."

"You mean, they might all be killed?"

"It has not been decided," Prilock said, "But it is a distinct possibility."

"Prilock, for gods' sake," Fellows pleaded, "Isn't there anything you can do? Can't you intervene on our behalf?"

With a fluidity that startled the eye, Prilock grew before them into the great, dark bird of the Chimera. The humans gasped and took a step backwards as the huge, golden-eyed being towered over them. "My intervention on your behalf is why you have any chance of surviving at all!" it thundered, "Do not forget, I am not one of you! I am not your Anomaly Number 35719, an isolated creature dependent on the whims of your government, shackled by your laws! I am Chimera! I will judge you as the others of my kind will judge you, and if you fail, I will have as little patience with you as they! You have no right to this world! You are a chattering race of squirrels who have acquired entirely too much power, and the Chimera shall relieve you of it! You must earn your right to share this world with the Chimera and the Byahail! We do not need you, have no use for you, and would not miss you if you were to vanish from the world tomorrow. It is no benefit to us to help you. So do not count on me to make the way easy for you! I am Chimera, not human! I am not your creature!"

Spreading its great wings the dark bird rose up into the air. "Enough! I must return to the Mountains, to the City of my race. Follow Captain Mahdi and do as she says. Remember! What you do will determine whether even *you* will be permitted to survive!"

Morris swallowed hard, feeling a vague sense of betrayal. "So that is how it is going to be," he murmured.

It was in shaken and stunned silence that the crews of the other ships went through the motions of getting under way, obediently following the freighter through the swamps.

The evening was fragrant. The perfume of innumerable strange and exotic flowers drifted down from the forests of the Valley. The day had been very warm, and very humid so close to the open swamp, but as night came cool air rolled down from the Mountains and brought with it the magic of the Valley. It was no wonder the Kurlu had coveted this land.

They had traveled up the River that morning and spoken with Nossa Mehika. The elder had granted them permission to settle at the mouth of the River, but told them the time was not yet right for humans to come up to the Village. More time was needed for the People to heal, to get past their weakness, and to realize the enormity of the work to be done, and the necessity of accepting help. The Chimera could gently coax and advise, but would never compel the People to do anything that was truly against their wishes.

So they returned to the mouth of the River and found a good place to dock the boats and spend the night. Tomorrow they would scout the area and find the best place to set up camp and begin work on the settlement. There was a lot of debris and shells of buildings left over from the aborted attempt of the Kurlu to colonize the Valley. Part of the agreement that permitted the humans to settle there was the condition that they clean up the garbage and scars on the land. Tomorrow they'd take stock of the task they had ahead of them. Tomorrow would be a busy day. The first of many.

Morris sat on the hull of an old Kurlu shuttle beached on the shoreline like a stranded fish. It was beautiful and peaceful at that place and that moment, with the cool, sweet breeze and strange birds calling in the distance. His mood was pensive. So much had happened so fast, with little time to take stock. He felt a sense of shock at being at the center of it. It was a bit like finding out war had been declared while you were at lunch, and the front line was at your own front door. Welcome home, here's a helmet, duck your head.

"Mind a bit of company?"

Christina smiled up at him. Morris returned her smile and patted the spot next to him.

"Take a seat. My debris is yours."

She climbed up and perched herself. "It's a mess, isn't it?" she commented, looking around at the garbage left behind by the Kurlu.

"Well, there's probably quite a bit we can salvage. We might as well make use of it if we can. Building this settlement is going to require an awful lot of jury-rigging and improvising."

"Hopefully we'll be able to work with the Byahail soon," Christina said. "I'll bet they could teach us a thing or two about how to build a village from scratch."

"I hope so," Morris sighed. "They've sure got their work cut out for them. There isn't much left of their village."

Christina nodded. "Nossa Mehika looked so much better, though. I mean, it's only been a couple of weeks, and the change is amazing."

"I guess that's what the Chimera can do for them. After all, we saw what Prilock could do for Shaka Mahdi."

"It's remarkable," Christina murmured. "The more I learn about the history of the Byahail and the Chimera the more amazed I am. And," she added ruefully, "the less hope I have."

"No kidding," Morris said grimly. "Prilock was our last hope, and he's made it pretty clear where he stands."

"Well, we still don't know for sure what the decision is going to be," Christina said. "Prilock just warned us about the worst case scenario. It might not be as bad as all that."

"Prilock," Morris muttered. "I'll never figure him out."

"Don't try," Christina said. "It's hard enough just trying to understand our fellow humans."

Morris looked up at the sky. Stars were beginning to emerge in the deepening blue. "What if it does happen?" he said. "What if it does end up being just us? Just this colony?"

Christina shrugged. "Then we deal with it. We cope. I've learned that the end of the world usually isn't."

Wordlessly, Morris reached for her hand. He needed to hold onto something solid and stable, and at that moment, Christina seemed to him the most solid and stable thing left in his world.

Christina hesitated, feeling the old habitual aversion. But a newer part of herself said firmly, "Get past it. There's too much at stake, now."

She took his hand. And rather to her surprise—and relief—it felt good.

They heard someone coming towards them through the grass-grown junk. Morris tensed. "Sir. You're back."

"Yes," Prilock replied, standing below them in classic military stance, his feet planted firmly apart and his hands clasped behind his back. "May I have a word with you, Morris?"

"Yes, Sir." He jumped lightly down.

"Any news?" Christina asked, trying to keep the tension out of her voice.

"A decision has been made," Prilock said quietly. "It will be discussed with all of you shortly. But first, would you excuse us please?" He turned to lead the way back down the path along the river. Morris looked up at Christina.

"I'll meet you back at the ship," he said, and hurried to catch up with Prilock.

They walked in silence for awhile, Morris just about bursting with impatience, barely managing to hold his tongue. Considering Prilock's attitude, Morris feared the worst. Finally Prilock spoke, slowly and thoughtfully.

"Morris, I've come to know you fairly well, and I believe I can trust you. I need someone I can trust.

Morris hesitated, not sure whether this was the Prilock he knew, or the Chimera he was learning to fear. He replied carefully, "You can rely on me, Sir."

"Good, because what I am about to discuss with you must be kept in strictest confidence."

Morris nodded, waiting, holding his breath.

"The Chimera don't make snap decisions," Prilock said. "And they dislike taking drastic actions. They prefer moving with what you might call geological deliberateness. So it was not too difficult for me to persuade them to give humanity a bit more time. Now that the People are home safe again, the attention of the Chimera is focused there. They are far more concerned with taking care of them and assuring their future than they are with retaliation for what was done. The Chimera are deeply feeling beings, but they are not naturally vengeful. Violence is distasteful to them, and they don't really understand malice, which is in part why they made such drastically bad tactical errors in first dealing with the Kurlu. No, the Chimera are much more inclined towards compassion and delight, and constructive enterprises. So I was able to convince them finally that humans were worth their compassion and might someday become a source of delight."

"So," Morris interrupted excitedly, "We're going to be given another chance? I mean, everybody? Not just the colony?"

"Don't start the party yet," Prilock replied sternly. "There are some very stiff conditions attached to this reprieve. You humans cannot be permitted to go on doing things the way you have been, acting as if you were the only creatures in the world that mattered and everything was here for you to use as you damn well please. You are going to have to get your house in order. Establish a rational, uniform code of law and morals and stick to it. And you will have to curb your population and learn to live more frugally."

"Well, that's sure better than a death sentence," Morris said softly. "I take it the Chimera are going to oversee this overhaul of human society?"

"No," Prilock sighed heavily, "I am."

Morris raised his eyebrows. "You, Sir?"

"Believe me," Prilock said, "I am not thrilled at the prospect. But it was a part of the package I sold to my fellow Chimera. They weren't too keen on the idea of having a large, uncontrolled population of humans running around in the world. They preferred having a nice, easily managed, experimental colony and just getting rid of the rest. I assured them that I could get the other humans under control. Given a bit of time—which is not a problem; the Chimera are very patient beings—I told them I was sure I could work with human leaders to create an equitable, manageable system. I promised that the human population at large would no longer be a problem. Given that, the Chimera had no real objection to letting them live. As I said, violence is distasteful to them, and the prospect of mass extermination did not appeal to them at all."

Morris closed his eyes and exhaled with relief. "So, what's going to be expected of us?"

"The colony here in the Valley will work with the People and learn the wisdom they need to become a mature, respectable species. This will become a kind of school, preparing certain humans to go back among their fellows and teach them the life skills and moral values they need to have to be accepted by the Chimera and the People."

Morris nodded slowly. "Yes, Sir," he said quietly.

"What the devil is wrong?" Prilock asked sharply. "I should think you'd be a bit more happy about this, considering the alternative."

"Well, Sir, if I may speak candidly . . ."

"Please do. I assure you, I welcome your input."

"I'm not sure exactly how to say it. It's just, well, how much are we going to have to give up? How much of our technology? Our customs? Our traditions? How much of what makes us human are we going to have to sacrifice in order to become acceptable to you? Like, are we not going to be able to have the kind of music we want, or books we want, or play the kind of games we do, because it might encourage the wrong values? Are we going to be told how to dress, and what to eat, and what sort of songs to sing, and—"

"Now, wait a moment! The idea is to teach you creatures a better way to live. I would hope that your culture would evolve as your ideals evolve. Morris, I will have a difficult enough time imposing honesty and order on you. I am not going to be telling you what dance steps you can and cannot do! I don't give a damn what you do in your spare time, so long as it doesn't involve cheating, stealing, or killing. I hardly think that is unreasonable."

"Okay, okay, but that's only part of what I mean," Morris said. "Are we going to be expected to have the same sorts of beliefs, to celebrate the same sorts of festivals, that kind of thing? The Byahail worship the Chimera as gods. Are we going to be expected to worship you? Perform rituals in your honor? Say prayers to you?"

"Of all the nonsense!" Prilock snorted. "The relationship between the Chimera and the People is unique. We would hardly expect you to duplicate it. We did not create you as we created the People. You might say we are adopting you, not as infants, but as savage, willful adolescents. We intend to civilize you and teach you to behave. But, my word, Morris! Why do you think the Chimera are going to the trouble of doing this? It certainly isn't out of pure benevolence! We hope you'll develop into something interesting! Do you realize how incredibly tedious immortality is? The Chimera don't have the rituals of mating and child-rearing that you humans find so engrossing. Our society is stable, peaceful, perfected. We keep busy maintaining our City and periodically looking in on the People, taking pleasure in the happiness and beauty of our creation. But the war with the Kurlu was the only excitement the Chimera have had in eons—and we didn't like it!

Still, it did sharply and unpleasantly bring to our attention how woefully understimulated our intellect has been."

"So," Morris said slowly, "In a way, you need humans. You need the entertainment of bringing us up, so to speak, and seeing what we become."

"That is," Prilock said, "one way of putting it. The point being that you needn't fear the kind of cultural domination you spoke of. What you make sacred and choose to worship is your own business. And within reason, how you entertain yourselves and how you use and develop your technology is strictly up to you. We just expect you to behave. A tall order, I grant you," he added acerbically.

"Even with the help of a god."

Prilock glanced over at Morris. "The Chimera are extremely powerful beings. We can appear godlike, but as the People know, and as you must realize, we are neither omniscient nor omnipotent. And, as we learned, we can die. As I nearly did."

Morris nodded slowly. "I remember," he said. Then he said, "Sir, I also remember what your opinion of humans has always been. Maybe a few of us managed to win you over, and I'm glad for that, but you pretty much held the rest of the breed in contempt. Now, it sounds like you mounted a massive campaign to convince your fellow Chimera to spare our lives, and then you took on the monumental task of reforming us. Not just a select few, but millions of us. That's a bit more of a challenge than cleaning up Farport. And I can't help wondering why. Is it just for the benefit of the Chimera? Or am I detecting evidence of a personal stake in all this?"

Prilock looked sharply at Morris. Then he sighed. "Morris, it is a very long story, which perhaps I will tell you sometime. But at the moment, suffice to say, I may be a member of a race of beings nearly as old as this world, but I am a newborn member. And unlike the other mere handful of new generation Chimera my own age, I was not born among my own kind. They did not even know of my existence until I returned to them a mere month ago. I was literally raised by humans. I even think like a human—a highly unusual human, I'll grant you, but more like a human than a Chimera. And it has made a great deal of difference. Oh, to be sure, I am welcome among the Chimera. They treat me with the same respect and affection they would any other of their kind. But I don't fit in. I don't even have a name among them—at least, not a Chimera name. There are only so many Chimera names, and they are all taken. So I am known by the name you humans gave me. Prilock. Pudding."

Morris felt a wave of sympathy. A god named "Pudding." It didn't inspire a whole lot of awe.

"And so," Prilock continued briskly, "My fate is inextricably tied up with humans. I care about you. I can't help myself. I—" He stopped, glancing at Morris. "You must understand, I can't let the others know this. In order to maintain order and discipline, I must remain aloof, inscrutable, and authoritarian. I must inspire awe and fear. Most humans, to my experience, won't behave themselves unless they are terrorized into it."

"Fear isn't the only thing we respond to," Morris said. "In fact, in the long run, fear alone won't work at all. Fear has a way of turning into hate."

"I know that, Morris. I saw it when I was Castellan of Farport. And yet, there were a surprising number of you who stood by me when Marcus Lars came to assassinate me."

"That's because the fear had turned to respect. You were always fair, never arbitrary or cruel. And, occasionally we got a glimpse of something like a heart deep down inside you." Morris grinned. "Seems like we were right, weren't we?"

"Don't get smug, Morris!" Prilock snapped.

"Yes, Sir," Morris replied, but he was still grinning.

"Anyway," Prilock grumbled, "I don't have the luxury of allowing you humans to get to know me. Just as it was in Farport, it doesn't matter if you hate me, just so long as you behave. I must impose order and peace no matter how terrible a tyrant I have to be to do it. Because, unlike Farport, it is not just my own future that depends on my success. The future of your species depends on it."

"If you try to do it by fear alone, it won't work, I promise you," Morris warned him. "There has to be an element of compassion, something to inspire respect—"

"I know that, too," Prilock interrupted impatiently. "That's where you come in."

"Excuse me?"

"You will be, essentially, my second in command. You will be approachable, compassionate. You will listen to them, explain things to them in ways they can understand, reassure them. And you will then keep me apprised of all the things I need to know. Your power will be absolute, because of me. But unlike me, you will be the leader they can relate to, the leader who can inspire affection and loyalty. Am I making myself clear?"

"Yes, Sir," Morris murmured, awed by the prospect.

"Initially, you will be in charge of the humans here, in the colony, while you are getting trained with the others. I will have my hands full going out there and putting the fear of the Chimera into the general human populace. If I need them, the other Chimera will lend me a hand from time to time. But they are much more concerned about the People right now. I must do most of the work with the humans on my own."

"I understand," Morris said, nodding. "And my role in this will be to tell them, 'Be reasonable. Listen to me. I'm on your side. Let me help you, or else that nasty, inhuman Chimera is going to blast you to bloody atoms.'"

Prilock looked over at Morris, almost smiling. "That's a rather colorful way of illustrating it, but I think you have the general idea."

"And it will be our little secret that you aren't a nasty, inhuman monster at all."

"Yes," Prilock said firmly. "The fewer who know, the better. You know, and that is quite enough." He paused. "Morris, I know that I am going to have to make an example of some of them.

There are going to be those, especially in the Kurlu Empire, whom I will have absolutely no choice but to destroy. I can't permit those incorrigibly bellicose individuals to threaten the chances of the rest. I will be doing a great deal of terrorizing, and killing, and I don't like it one bit. To be frank, it sickens me. But they mustn't know that. They must believe that I am utterly cold-blooded, that I would just as soon kill them as look at them. They must go so much in terror of me that they won't dare even cheat at lots, for fear I'll come crashing down to behead them."

Prilock stopped, looking out over the river. It had gotten quite dark as they walked, the night creatures coming out to send their haunting calls out over the rolling water. The sky above them was full of stars. Morris stood next to him in silence, and noticed with a start that Prilock had begun to glow slightly, just enough to illuminate the path around them. It was easy to forget in conversation that the man beside him was not a man at all. And yet . . . Morris smiled. And yet.

"I don't want to be a monster, Morris," Prilock said softly, "But for the sake of your race, I must make myself one. I can only hope that it will prove worth it. I hope someday you will make it possible for me to cease to play that role."

"I hope so, too, Sir."

Prilock guided them unerringly along the river through the tangle of over-grown paths back to where their ships were anchored. "Good night, Morris," he said. "Feel free to pass along the news of general interest to the others as you see fit."

"Thank you, Sir, I will. And thank you for your confidence in me."

"Hm! Just see to it that you don't get too cocky and make a fool out of yourself, and me for trusting you!"

Morris watched him go up onto the deck and into Shaka Mahdi's ship. There goes the savior of humanity, he thought, a secretly soft-hearted, outwardly ill-tempered, god second-class called Pudding. Not exactly what the old philosophers had in mind.

Morris grinned. We could do a lot worse.